DARK
WYNG

CHRIS D'LACEY

THE ERTH DRAGONS

DARK WYNG

BOOK TWO

Scholastic Inc.

Copyright © 2016 by Chris d'Lacey & Jay d'Lacey
First published in 2016 in the United Kingdom by Orchard Books.
Orchard Books is a division of Hachette Children's Books, a Hachette
Livre UK Company.

This book was originally published in hardcover by Scholastic Press in 2018.

ISBN 978-0-545-90058-4

10 9 8 7 6 5 4 3 2 1   18 19 20 21 22

Printed in the U.S.A.   40
This edition first printing 2018

Book design by Mary Claire Cruz

For Sarah Leonard

Hrrr!

LIST OF CHARACTERS

DRAGONS

GABRIAL • a young dragon, just nine Ki:meran turns old. Referred to as a "blue" because of his overall color pattern. His impulsive nature often frustrates his mentors and superiors, even though he has proved himself in battle. Guardian to Grendel and the two wearlings Gariffred and Gayl.

GALLEN • commander of the feared wyng of fighting dragons known as the Veng. Like all Veng, his coloring is an unmistakable bright green.

GANNET • a good-natured roamer.

GARIFFRED • a precocious blue wearling. His choice of name is controversial because it means "flame of truth," implying he is closer to Godith than other dragons.

GARODOR • a highly intelligent member of the De:allus class, sent to Erth to research and assess the situation after the devastating battles with the goyles.

GARON • Gabrial's father and a member of the Wearle that came to Erth before Gabrial's colony arrived. Believed to have perished in the first goyle conflicts.

GARRET • a talented mapper, thought to be the best in the Wearle.

GAYL • a female wearling and Gariffred's sibling. Gayl is fragile and underdeveloped, but extremely sensitive to the world around her.

GIVNAY • a disgraced Elder, now dead, who almost destroyed the Wearle when seeking to manipulate the dangerous effects of fhosforent.

GOODLE • the only other mature blue (besides Gabrial) in the colony.

GOSSANA • an aging and fearsome queen (and Elder) with an overinflated opinion of herself. Dark green, with eyes that can change color according to her moods.

GRAYMERE • a brilliant dragon of the De:allus class, who tragically lost his life during the goyle conflicts.

GRENDEL • a young, beautiful female with touches of gold in her purple coloring. Along with Gabrial, she has taken on the task of adopting and raising Gariffred and Gayl after their mother, Grystina, was killed.

GRENDISAR • a historical De:allus whose theories about the legend of Graven once caused much controversy among the superior ranks of dragons on Ki:mera.

(PER) GROGAN • once a mentor to Gabrial. A wretched casualty of the goyle attacks, his shocking death has long-lasting reverberations for the Wearle.

GRYMRIC · herbalist, potion maker, and a studious practitioner of the healing arts. His role is to gather up Erth's flora and fauna and assess the benefits of what he finds.

(PRIME) GRYNT · a tough, no-nonsense Elder with a streak of armored silver on his throat and breast, which stands out against his overall light purple colors. Grynt is responsible for the security of the Wearle and is the supreme commander of the Veng.

GRYSTINA · mother of Gariffred and Gayl, who tragically lost her life when those wearlings were barely out of their eggs. Due to her powerful gift of transference, her spirit now resides in and guides the Hom boy, Ren.

GUS · a lumbering, gentle giant of a roamer, blessed with a kind and thoughtful disposition. His one desire is to serve his Wearle faithfully and well.

THE HOM (THE KAAL TRIBE)

REN WHITEHAIR · a young lad of twelve winters with hair lighter than the color of corn. After being bitten by Gariffred, Ren has formed a close association with the wearling and is rapidly learning the ways of dragons, a fact that does not sit well with the men of the Kaal or the dragon high command.

BRYNDLE WOODKNOT · brusque father of Rolan Woodknot. Bryndle takes care of the tribe's whinneys. An injury sustained during childhood prevents him from being involved in any fighting.

COB WHEELER · a loud, brutish man, who only becomes the leader of the Kaal because so many other, worthier, men have died.

EVON TREADER · the widow of Waylen Treader. Evon is deep in mourning for her husband and believes his spirit is around her still.

MELL · Ren's mother. A loving soul, also recently widowed, who is not afraid to speak her mind or stand up for her rights.

MERRILYN WIDEFOOT · wife of the one-eyed Oleg Widefoot.

NED WHITEHAIR · Ren's father. A brave man who, like many of his people, was lost in the fight to regain the Kaal's mountain territories from the dragons.

OAK LONGARM · one of a small party of men who died trying to raise the darkeyes against the dragons.

OLEG WIDEFOOT · so named because his feet, when together, do not point straight. A good bowman.

PINE ONETOOTH • a girl who has just one tooth in the middle of her mouth. Pine "wafts around the settlement like a leaf on the breeze." She is thought to be simple and is generally ignored, until she decides to join Ty in his quest.

ROLAN WOODKNOT • a young man, not much older than Ren, who is considered to be wise beyond his years. He is catapulted into a dangerous quest by virtue of the fact that he is one of the few strong men still alive among the Kaal.

TARGEN THE OLD • the aged, and now dead, spiritual leader of the Kaal.

THE FATHERS • the spirits of the (Kaal) dead.

TY • a stranger who comes to the settlement apparently out of nowhere. His confident manner and magical ways soon win over the Kaal, though his eyes always harbor the threat of darkness.

VARL REDNOSE • a gruff character, who was not dissimilar to Cob Wheeler in attitude. Killed in the skaler battles.

WAYLEN TREADER • a farmer, famed for killing a dragon with an arrow to its eye. Waylen is another casualty of the battles, though his wife, Evon, insists that his spirit has not gone to rest with the Fathers . . .

ALSO

GODITH · a female deity who, according to dragon legend, created the world from a single breath of flame and afterward made all dragons in Her i:mage.

GOYLES (OR DARKEYES) · dark, grotesque creatures with a remorseless taste for killing.

GRAVEN AND G'RESTYN · the two fabled sons of Godith, who allegedly fell out in a spat of jealousy, which ended with G'restyn dying and Graven's third heart being ripped from his chest by his grieving mother. Superstitious dragons have always believed that Graven will rise again one day and take his revenge on all dragonkind.

SHADE · a female whinney with a spiraling horn growing from the center of her forehead. She possesses magical gifts, the most notable being the ability to vanish into thin air. She is ridden by Ty, but seems to have little affinity with him.

THE TREEMEN · a tribe of people that inhabits the Whispering Forest.

TYWYLL · another name for the black dragon that Graven became—just one part of Godith's punishment for killing his brother.

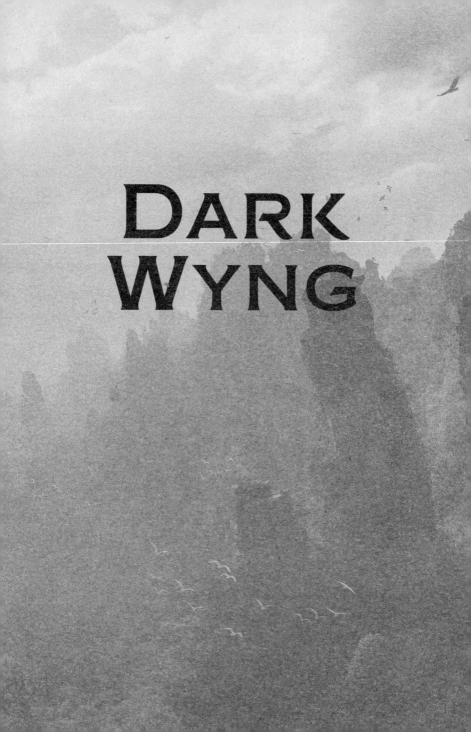

DARK
WYNG

PROLOGUE

In the homing caves of Mount Vidor
On the dragon world, Ki:mera, nine turns ago

"Tada, tell me a story."

Garon snorted softly and rasped his tongue over a run of fine scales around Gabrial's ears. It was late and the pale yellow moon, Cantorus, was throwing its golden light all across the homing caves. *A good night for hunting*, Garon thought, *but equally good for telling stories.* "What kind of story shall it be?" he asked.

"One you *haven't* told before," said Gabrial. "Tell me about . . . the black dragon."

Garon stretched his neck and glanced across the cave at his partner, Gaverne. She was fast asleep, her fine purple head tucked under one wing. Gabrial's sister, Graile, was curled up beside her, snoring softly. "There is no such thing as a black dragon, Gabrial. Whatever you have heard from other wearlings is a myth. We can have black markings—you have some on your wing tips and tail—but no dragon can be completely black."

"Why not?"

"Godith forbids it."

"Doesn't She like black dragons?"

"No."

"Why?"

That word again, Garon thought, the one that Gabrial used like a hook to draw all worldly truths out of him. Was *he* this inquisitive when he was a wearling? Possibly so. He licked Gabrial's ears again. Sooner or later, the drake would come to hear this story, so why not now? It was the right of every dragon to understand their beginnings, to know what was—and what might have been. "Very well, but don't expect to sleep tonight."

"Mama says I sleep too much."

"Hmm. And Mama will growl if she hears me telling you a tale like this. So this is for your blue ears only, yes?"

"Yes, Tada."

"Good. Then this is how it begins—at the very beginning. You know that Godith created Ki:mera and all the worlds beyond from Her fire?"

"Yes. *Hrrr!*"

"Shh! Don't wake your sister." Garon glanced at the females again. Gaverne would roast his stigs to points if the wearmyss was woken for no good reason. Quietly he said, "You know, as well, that Godith created dragons in Her i:mage?"

"Like me?" Gabrial gave a swish of his tail.

His father immediately trapped it under his.

"Like you and Graile, like the Veng and the De:allus and the Elders and the Prime. Like every class of dragon you can think of. We are all one in the eyes of Godith. But there was once a dragon who defied Her will. His name was Graven. He was Godith's firstborn."

"And he was black?"

"Not in the beginning, no. When he was created his scales shined gold."

A little breath of wonder seeped out of Gabrial's spiracles.

"Brighter and deeper than Cantorus, they shined. So pleased was Godith that She said to Her son, 'I give this moon, Cantorus, to you. There you shall build your eyries and make more dragons in *your* i:mage.'"

Gabrial's mouth fell open in awe. His primary teeth, perfect and white, glinted in the moonlight like a row of small mountains. "Graven made gold wearlings?"

"No. Keep listening. As you can imagine, Graven was pleased with his gift. Here he was, the first son of Godith, and he had a whole *moon* to himself. He bowed to Godith and pledged his love to Her always."

"Hrrr!" went Gabrial.

Garon opened his foreclaws and used them to gently close

his son's mouth. "Quite. And so Graven flew to Cantorus, there to explore his new surroundings. He was pleased with what he found. One day you and I will fly to Cantorus and you will see its giant mountain ranges, and the rivers and fire beds that flow through them. But for now, just listen, don't hurr, yes?"

Gabrial nodded.

Garon eased his claws. "Now, if you've been watching the night skies, you will know that another moon rises in front of Cantorus sometimes."

"Crune," said Gabrial, eager to show his knowledge.

"Yes. Well done. I can see you've listened well to the teachings of per Grogan."

Gabrial twisted his snout.

"What was that for?"

"What, Tada?"

"I didn't miss that snouty twitch. What's the matter? Don't you like per Grogan?"

"He's mean, Tada. Every time he roars at me he says it makes another wrinkle in his eye ridges. He said his body was as green as the Marad Valley once and that it's wearlings like me who turned his head scales gray. He says he bit off his third claw because a drake he was teaching couldn't tell the difference between a rock and a hard place!"

Garon snorted a smoke ring from his nostrils.

"He *did*, Tada!"

"He did not," said Garon. "He lost his claw in a battle. He's teasing you, Gabrial. Per Grogan cares for your welfare. He is a good and wise mentor who will always stand by you. You must listen to him. He can teach you the history of your family line and more. Now, where were we with our story?"

"On Crune."

"Oh, yes. Now, Crune glows blue, like you of course. Godith gave this moon to Her second son, G'restyn."

"She had two sons?"

"Hmm. What do you think about that?"

"Per Grogan says a mama can only have a myss and a drake."

"That's right. She can."

"But you said Godith had two *sons*, Tada."

"Patience, Gabrial. We're not finished yet." He blew smoke into Gabrial's ear, making the wearling snort and wiggle. "Graven was happy with this arrangement because Cantorus was bigger than Crune and as the firstborn son he felt it was his right to be . . . better than his brother. But of course there came a time when Crune rose up and cast its shadow over Cantorus. Not only that, it blocked Graven's view of the center of Ki:mera, where Godith had Her settle.

"Graven was furious. His fire sacs ignited and his claws

extended as far as they would go. He flew to Crune and demanded that G'restyn hurr on his moon and move it to a different orbit. Both dragons were very large. They could move planets with a single breath. But G'restyn refused to do it. He said the orbits were made by Godith and no dragon had the right to change Her plan.

"Well, they roared at each other until they both grew tired and grumpy. Graven flew back to Cantorus, and G'restyn stayed on Crune. But Graven could not rest and his anger would not settle. And so he came up with a plan. The next day, when Crune had risen to its peak and was casting even bigger shadows over Cantorus, Graven focused his optical triggers on his brother and waited and watched. Eventually, he saw G'restyn lift away from the surface and disappear around the far side of the moon. When G'restyn did not reappear, Graven flew down to Crune and positioned himself to one side of it, the side that his brother had left abandoned."

"He's going to hurr on it himself," said Gabrial. "Tada, this isn't very scary."

"It will be," said Garon. "Graven took a breath so huge and blew a wind so strong it could have made the mountains bend. Crune began to move. But it did not change orbit as Graven had intended. Instead, it began to spin. And spin. And spin. And spin.

"Graven was annoyed. He tried hitting the moon with his tail, but that nearly broke off his isoscele."

Gabrial twitched his tail. He checked his own isoscele, just in case.

His father went on. "So, instead he did something very foolish: He tried to move the moon with his fire."

"Did it burn?"

"Yes; that's why to this day you'll see dark craters on Crune. Those are the scorch marks Graven created. But it wasn't just the moon that burned. G'restyn was asleep on the surface. He was big, but he was blue, just like you and me, and Graven didn't see him. Only when G'restyn took to the air in a blaze of wings did Graven realize what he'd done. He had flamed his only brother."

Hhh!

"Poor G'restyn fell back to the surface, dead."

A flutter ran down Gabrial's wings. The fine scales on his neck began to clink.

His father rested an arm to calm him. "I told you it was scary. Perhaps that's enough."

"No," said Gabrial. "What about Godith? What did She *do*, Tada?"

Garon sighed, but hid the sound well enough. He remembered pausing like this when he was young and had first heard the tale. How the icicles of terror had crept under his scales and made gritty bobbles of the flesh underneath. He looked out at Cantorus and offered Godith a silent prayer before he continued. "Godith heard G'restyn's squeals as he burned, and came to see what had happened. She found his body and wept so freely that storms blew up all over Her universe. She saw the scorch marks on Crune and knew what had happened. She flew to Cantorus, there to punish Graven for his wild act of jealousy. Some say She planned to kill him, to tear off his wings and burn him as he had burned G'restyn. She found Graven quaking, weeping at his foolishness. He begged Her to be merciful. And in some small way She was. She decreed three laws: First, no dragon could ever give birth to two sons; second, gold could never be a dominant color; and lastly, and most mysteriously, no dragon would ever be able to flame any dragon it was related to."

"So I can't flame Graile?"

"Definitely not. The pers will tell you these are good laws, but you must know they rose from a moment of sadness. For Graven, the sadness did not end there. Godith used a cold flame on his scales to suck the color out of them. That beautiful shining gold She'd created was reduced to nothing, to black. Her flame was so strong it opened Graven's chest and exposed his three hearts. Godith reached in and tore out the smallest, the one that keeps us closest to Her."

Gabrial shuddered from his nostrils to his isoscele. He crossed his forearms over his breast, where his primary heart was thumping like thunder.

His father went on, "You might hear it said that Graven was born without a third heart and that this is what led to his vanity and foolishness. But that will come from the mouths of those who want to believe Godith has no fury. Understand me when I tell you, Gabrial: Godith is a loving but vengeful Creator. She punished Graven severely. In Her claws, his third heart turned to stone. She crushed it into a thousand pieces and scattered the fragments in a hiding place known only to Her. It's said that his blood poured out of the heart like scalding rain and killed every living thing it landed upon. Graven was never seen again. Yet the legends insist his auma survives because his grieving mama could not bear to destroy it. This has led some Elders to teach that Graven will rise again one day. They say that even now the fragments of his auma reach out into the universe in search of the evil that will help him restore his heart and his power."

Gabrial gulped back a smoke plug. "Will he come here?"

"No, Gabrial. He won't come here. Shall I tell you where he is?"

The drake's soft blue eyes grew large and round, losing their slanted aspect for a moment.

"Look again at Cantorus," his father whispered.

Gabrial turned his head and peered at the still, imperious moon.

"Some pers say that if you look hard enough, the blackness around Cantorus will form itself into the shape of Graven. They call him by another name then: Tywyll, a word from the old tongue meaning 'the darkness.' So there he is, Gabrial. There's your black dragon. Flying close to his moon—where he'll stay. And that, my brave son, is the end of your story. Rest your weary head now, and know that in the morning the darkness will be gone."

And with that Garon curled his tail around the drake and hugged him into a deep and dreamless sleep.

PART ONE

TY

1

The Kaal settlement, out beyond the scorch line, present day

"I hail from a distant land," said the stranger, "too far from these mountains to warrant description. I look as you do but I am not of Kaal blood, and the sound of my name will fall harsh on your tongue. I will say it once—Tywyll—so you have heard it true, but you may call me 'Ty' and this will do me no dishonor."

"'Ty' what?" asked a young man, Rolan Woodknot. Nearly half the Kaal tribe had gathered around a fire to greet this wanderer in their midst. The women, in particular, were curious about him, for Ty was a handsome, dark-haired man and he dressed unlike any man of the tribe. The Kaal wore single robes to the knee, made of roughly woven thread. The stranger was dressed in a shorter robe and full leg coverings, all of it fashioned from a finer cloth than anyone from the mountains had ever seen.

Rolan picked up a twig and flicked it at the embers of a dying fire. "Each of us here is described by our work or our father's work, or some mark we carry." He opened the neck of his robe to show a bloodred stain on the skin that had grown with him since the day of his birth.

"My name describes my . . . bearing," said Ty, taking a strand of his hair between his fingers and twisting it as if it were new to him. "It needs no attachment. But if it pleases you to raise one, I do not object."

"It would please me, stranger, to know about *that*." A voice laden with the juice of many berries rose loudly above the rest. Cob Wheeler scratched his coarse gray beard and pointed to a pure white whinney tied to a post behind the stone on which the stranger sat. "What manner of magicks saw the beast so abused that a horn was left growing from its head?"

Ty pressed his fingertips together. "It appears to you unsightly?"

"It appears to me unnatural. A mutt would not piss near it, and nor will I."

A few around the fire chose to laugh at this remark. Cob was pleased to hear it. He was one of only a handful of men who had survived a clash with the fire-breathing skalers, a horror that had left the wisest Kaal dead and the youngest ones visited by night terrors. With Oleg Widefoot half blinded by skaler fire and Rolan too young to assume command, the Kaal had looked to Cob to lead the tribe. The arrival of this man who dressed in dark clothing and rode a strange whinney and spoke in words melodious to women was shaking Cob's authority with every breath.

The stranger's hand came up slowly.

The laughter stopped.

"Where I come from, such a beast would be prized."

Cob burped and wiped an arm across his mouth. "For what? Their ability to poke at scratchers?"

More laughter. Someone clapped Cob's shoulder, spilling his drink. He broke wind loudly and called for more juice. Rolan was pleased to see some merriment after so much recent pain. But not everyone was joining in. One of the quieter women had noticed Ty's eyes. They had turned the color of a pale red sunset and lay sharp on Cob Wheeler's loud, bowed mouth. Wanting no more woe among the tribe, she threw back her head and spoke up loudly. "I like the beast. I find it pleasing. What name do you give it?"

"I call it Shade," said Ty after a moment's thought. He moved a tress of hair off the woman's shoulder. The redness had faded and his eyes were now brown. "You may ride it, if you wish." He clicked his tongue. The beast whinnied, and shook its thick, white mane.

"Mell Whitehair mourns for her man," said Cob, with just enough chill in his rugged voice to turn a droplet of rain to ice. He tightened a burly fist that had been charred by a burst of skaler fire—his own souvenir of the battles. Mell was a prize he had set himself on winning. Her man, Ned, had lost his life in the conflicts. Likewise, her only son, Ren, was missing beyond the scorch line in skaler territory. Cob had promised himself that after a suitable period of grieving, there would be no challenge on his right to court Mell—not least from anyone new in their midst.

"I would ride the whinney," a young voice said.

The laughter now came sprinkled with scorn.

Rolan said, in a manner not unkindly, "That would be a reckless venture, Pine. The whinney has feet more nimble than the wind. Look at it. It dances on clouds. I fear it would throw you before three steps."

"Aye," said Cob, "and what man would ever love you, girl, if you broke that fine tooth in your head?"

The girl—Pine Onetooth was her name—stood fast and soaked up their cruel humor. She was a strange young thing: a carefree orphan who floated through her days like a restless feather. Her mother lay dead in the ground from a fever, her father crushed by a falling skaler. Washing was a thing unknown to her. Her face was dirty and her hands the same. Her hair hung down in twisted spikes like fat set hard on a cooking pot. Despite this, her spirits were always lively. She swung her hips and smiled at the stranger (as best her single tooth would allow). In return for this small kindness, he said, "Shade will not throw you, girl—not unless I command it. You may untie her."

Pine tossed aside the flower she'd been plucking and ran to the post where the whinney was tethered.

"Why do you call it Shade," asked Mell, "when it more resembles a fall of snow?"

Ty smiled. He clicked his tongue again. Shade walked toward the fire with Pine on her back. "Girl, turn a circle," he said.

Pine kicked gently. The whinney turned.

Immediately, rider and beast disappeared.

A clamor of fear took hold of the gathering. Cob Wheeler, who'd been near to the whinney when it faded, jumped to his feet and staggered backward. Panting, he snatched up a half-burned log. He wielded it close to Ty without seeming to know what he wished to do with it. "Bring her back . . . or you die!"

Ty seemed not to feel the heat. Nor was he disposed to count the beats of his life. He simply said, "Girl, turn the other way."

And back came Pine and the whinney, met by gasps of disbelief.

"What are you?" growled Cob. "How caused you this?"

Ty closed his hand around the glowing log, quenching it. Again, Cob Wheeler staggered back. Many looking on clasped their robes in fear. "I have learned many tricks on my journeys," said Ty. He turned his face and looked at the mountains, which rose like a silent menace in the distance. "I have come among the Kaal to hunt down skalers. I will give you back your lands and more if you are with me. Any who agree, I bid you say 'Aye.'"

"Aye!" said Pine, as cheery as a shiny seed fresh from its pod.

And she was just the first. The voices came slowly, but come they did.

Aye. Aye. Aye.

Until Cob Wheeler sat down once more and accepted the course he knew he must take. He threw the log back into the fire. "I know not what manner of man you are, but I will fight skalers till my dying breath." He laid a fist across his heart. "I too say 'aye.'"

2

But how are we to do this? they asked of Ty. *How will we win back what is ours when we cannot defend ourselves against their fire?*

Ty said, "I will show you how to tame them and take their powers. But it may not be this day or the next day or the next. We must wait for a moment most apt to strike. First, I must find a companion who is prepared to ride with me deep into their territory."

"On what manner of quest?" asked Rolan.

Ty stroked his chin. He looked keenly at Rolan, as if here was a man well suited to his needs. "We go among them to steal the heart of a skaler."

The people of the Kaal poured scorn on these words. Many quickly lost faith in Ty and drifted away to continue the work of rebuilding their shelters, damaged or burned in the skaler conflicts. Oleg turned his one good eye on the stranger and said Ty must think himself asleep and dreaming. Cob Wheeler, likewise, had anger in his spit. He put aside his jar of juice and made ready to revoke his pact there and then. Rolan stayed Cob's departure, saying, "Ty, this is surely a jest? Only a fool would ride among the beasts. Fortune once laid a dying skaler in our path, but in all other aspects we are help-less against them."

"How so?" Mell Whitehair spoke up bravely. She pointed to a woman called Evon Treader, widow of the farmer Waylen Treader. "The husband of this fair woman put an arrow through a skaler's eye before he died."

"That is a feat indeed," said Ty. He looked carefully at Evon. She was clamping her knees and hiding behind the fall of her hair. She had been rocking gently since the meeting began, all the while talking quietly to herself or whatever spirits surrounded her.

"A feat unproven," Cob Wheeler sneered.

This did him no favors with Mell. "My Ned was a man of plain words. He would not speak false on the fate of friends." She turned to Ty. "My husband, Ned, who now rests with the Fathers, led two men to a distant cave hoping to raise a dark-eyed fiend against the skalers. He returned alone, but with a grim tale of vengeance. He told how Waylen had struck a blow against a skaler they drew down from the skies, before that skaler in turn struck Waylen and left him rotting in the cave."

"A hunter's babble," Cob Wheeler argued, juice spilling down the front of his robe. "This came from the mouth of a man who claimed his son spoke in the skaler tongue!"

That caused much muttering among those present. Ty made no comment, but he looked around the circle at all who spoke.

Rolan raised a hand to quiet the voices. "We know there was truth in Ned's words, Cob."

"Pah!" went Cob. He broke wind again, an act that drove away all but those in the conversation. But Evon Treader also stayed by the fire.

Rolan wafted the odor aside. "Many witnessed the magicks the boy performed."

"Magicks?" said Ty. His eyes began to glimmer with interest.

"Aye," said Rolan. "A trick to rival your whinney's, I fancy."

"What shape did this trickery take?"

So Rolan told how Mell's boy, Ren, could not only disappear in the blink of an eye, but could also make fire from a skaler horn held strong in his fist.

Ty picked up a twig and began to scratch a shape in the dirt between his feet. "Where is the boy now?"

Mell hugged herself against the cold. She shook the first spots of rain from her hair. "Truly, I do not know. But not a day passes that I don't pray to the Fathers to let me see him again." She kissed her hands in hope.

Cob Wheeler held a different opinion. "Why do you float in your dreams, woman? We all know where the boy has gone." He jutted his chin at the mountains. "He plots against us among his skaler masters."

"That rumor is as foul as your odor," Mell snapped.

"If it is nought but rumor," Cob growled, "why does he not return to us?"

Mell rose and threw a handful of dirt his way. "Why do *you* sit slaking your belly with juice when you could be out riding, looking for him?" She turned to the others, her pale hair flying. "I say as I've said before: Ren was false accused of all wrongdoing. If he is in skaler territory, how do we know he is not held by them against his will? And I would say this to you, Cob Wheeler: If the loss of my boy cannot entice you onto your whinney, why do you tarry over Evon's suffering? If there was grit in your soul, you would go to this cave and bring home Waylen's broken body, so that Evon might send him to the Fathers in glory."

Evon, on hearing this, hurried away, her face as pale as a winter's moon.

"Forgive me, I must go to her," Mell said to Ty. "She is grieving, and I have made her sorrow worse." She spat at Cob Wheeler's feet as she went.

Cob growled and wafted a hand of good riddance.

"A passionate speech," Ty said, when Mell was gone. He scratched again at the dirt by his feet. He was drawing a slanted eye, Rolan noticed, its center made up of many parts.

"Mell too is grieving," Rolan said. He was about to add more when Cob thundered by his ear: "Girl, stop your pitiful whining!"

Pine was off Shade's back by now, stroking the whinney and singing to it.

"Girl, retie her," Ty said quietly.

While she did, Rolan picked up the thread of Ty's challenge. In all the bluster and argument, the business of hunting down skalers seemed to have been forgotten. Rolan asked, "This quest you speak of. I see no aim in it. What use is a skaler heart to us?"

Ty paused with the twig. "When a skaler dies, its spark of life passes from its heart to its eye, where it is shed in the form of a tear. But if the death should be unnatural or sudden . . ." He stabbed the twig into the eye and twisted it. A chill wind blew across the site. ". . . the heart hardens around the fire and the skaler's spirit cannot be freed. The skalers fear this. They see it as a slight against their Creator. They will not break the heart, even if they could, for fear it will raise a demon against them. Sometimes they will bury it deep in the ground. Most often, they hide it away and protect it."

"And you would have us steal such a thing?"

"I would."

"And then?"

"We break it open and . . . drink the tear."

Rolan exchanged a glance with Cob. The older man was growing weary-eyed, but not too tired to snort in disbelief. "Drink a tear of fire?" He thought back to those moments just passed when Ty had put his hand around a glowing log. "Answer me this, magician: How is it any man can play with fire and not see skin peeling off his bones?" He looked at his raw-knuckled hand. There were welts on his face and neck as well, still healing from exposure to that accursed skaler heat.

Ty showed his palms. "Riding grease. Not all things are achieved by magick."

Rolan laughed and clapped his hands together. "I counsel you, Cob. Do not stake wagers against this man. He is as clever as a caarker and twice as dark." He glanced at a small company of caarkers who were squabbling over a discarded bone and generally keeping the mutts at bay. He looked Ty full in the face. "Your tongue is as sharp as the first wind of winter, but you leave many snowflakes scattered on the ground. Even if your enchanted whinney could veil us from the eyes of the skalers, why would we risk a journey to the mountains when we do not know if such a heart exists?"

"I know," said Ty. "I have eyes in the mountains." And by way of explanation he let out a rasping cry that brought one of the caarkers to land close by.

Rolan narrowed his eyes. The wind left its cold mark on his neck as he watched the caarker strut back and forth, seemingly awaiting its next instruction.

"Girl, put out your arm," said Ty.

Pine stepped forward and did as she was bidden.

Ty rasped again.

The caarker extended its lazy wings and flapped to Pine's arm, where it settled.

Cob spat halfheartedly, leaving dribble on the front of his robe.

Rolan could find no words to say.

"There is a heart and it will be ours," said Ty. And as the rain began to fall in sudden earnest, he called the caarker to his own strong hand. He stroked its glistening feathers, saying, "Go again. Watch. Return. Bring me news of any boy you see." He raised his hand high. In a few short wingbeats the caarker had disappeared under the mask of brooding cloud. "If the boy lives, we will soon enough know it."

Rolan nodded in silence, still not sure what to make of what he'd witnessed. "The shelters," he muttered, drawing up the hood of his robe. "No talk was ever aided by a head of wet hair." He helped Cob to his feet. The older man was lurching toward a deep sleep, the juice beginning to wear at his joints.

Ty, however, did not move. "I find the rain refreshing. I will sit awhile longer."

"As you please," said Rolan, sweeping a strand of hair from his eyes. He put his strength behind Cob and helped him away.

The moment they were gone, Pine skipped across the puddles and sat on the nearest stone to Ty. She bathed her face in the rain, but said nought.

Ty stroked his fingers one by one. "I need an ally, girl. Someone who can be my ears and eyes when I am elsewhere and the caarkers are about their skaler business. Will you be that thing? I can reward you well."

"What will you give?" asked Pine. She picked a flower to hold against her heart.

"What would you like?" said he.

Pine looked at the drawing of the eye in the dirt, slowly beginning to dissolve in the rain. She quickly fell to her knees and redrew it, making the eye resemble a mouth. Into the mouth she drew that which she most desired in the world.

"So be it," said Ty. "One tooth for every deed or message you bring me."

"Where shall I listen first?" Pine asked.

Ty cast his gaze toward the shelters. "The home of Evon Treader," he said.

3

And there Pine went, despite the rain. Waylen Treader had built his shelter close to the fields he had farmed while alive. It was one of the few that had not been blazed or pounded to dust when skalers and darkeyes had warred above the settlement. Pine leaned against a mudstone wall at the rear and let her ears be party to the conversation drifting out of the window. This is what she heard first: the sound of Evon weeping. And then Mell Whitehair saying, "Evon, speak your woes to me. Whatever ails you is better shared."

"I cannot," replied Evon, sobbing so. "I am deep in fear of Waylen's spirit."

"Why?" said Mell, her voice, as always, rich with kindness. "Waylen loved you more than any man could. In turn, you gave him two strong sons, who even now go out and sow his fields. He would not harm you in life; why then in death?"

Pine turned and looked across the fields. Seeing no sons of Waylen about, she stood on tiptoe and put her eye to the gap between the window ledge and the hide that covered it. She saw Evon kneeling on a straw-dusted floor, clasping her hands in her tear-soaked lap. Mell was kneeling beside her, an arm laid loose across Evon's shoulder. A mutt lay asleep nearby.

After a silence, Evon said, "I am not certain that Waylen's spirit rests with the Fathers."

Mell put a hand on her friend's pale cheek. "You think him alive? How so?"

Evon shuddered. Her teeth were chattering so much it was enough to shake the scratchers out of their holes. "Because of this stranger who calls himself Ty. When I look at him, all I see is Waylen."

Mell attempted a laugh, but her breath fell short and she cast her gaze to one side instead. Evon saw something in that expression, for she gripped Mell's shoulders and said, with some vigor, "You see it too, don't you? Your eyes speak loud. Tell me, Mell, that this is no mere folly."

Mell fed a wisp of hair behind her ear. "I met Ty by the river on the day he arrived. I jested then that he had the eyes of someone I knew. He told me he had no kin. Evon, how can we believe aught other than that? Men are men. They share a look sometimes. If your hair had the sun like mine, we might be hailed as sisters."

"No," said Evon. "When you stared into the eyes of Ned, you saw more than a man made of hair and bone; you knew his nature. When I chance to look at this stranger, I see my

Waylen bound inside him. I see the phantom of my husband in the eyes of a man who is wily and dark, a man who talks bold about skaler hearts and rides an enchanted whinney. How do we know he is not a demon? What if he has stolen Waylen's spirit?"

Mell kneaded her fists together. "For a moment, by the river, I did ask myself the same."

"Then—?"

"No, Evon. It was nought but a fleeting fancy then, and I find it so now. We have heard Ned's story of Waylen's end. There was no talk of Ty being present."

But Evon would not have it. Pushing her hands through her hair, she said, "I see what I see. I tell you true, my heart does not deceive me."

"Then the remedy is clear," said Mell. "Tomorrow, when Cob has slept off the juice, we will bother him to go to the darkeye cave and bring poor Waylen's body home. We will send your husband to the Fathers on our love. And should we fear there are demons watching, we will call them out with fire and—"

"What was that?" Evon looked anxiously toward the window.

Mell shook her head and shrugged.

"I thought I heard a sound."

The mutt stretched its legs and yawned.

Mell stood up and pulled aside the flap. "Nothing," she said. "Just the rain, making puddles."

And a flower head, which she did not see, lying plucked on the ground.

Later, when the rain had grayed to mizzle and darkness was ready to close the day, Evon made her way alone to the river. She knelt and rested her hand in the flow, there to gather water in a pot. As she did this, a voice said, "Woman, look upon me."

And there, floating up through the clear gray water, she saw the rippling face of her husband.

"Waylen?" she gasped.

A man's booted foot trod soft behind her, but Evon could not take her eyes off the river.

"Reach out to me," the face in the water said. Hands appeared beside it. Hands that had warmed her often in the night.

"Waylen?" she said a second time, her voice aquiver with sorrow and need.

The pot tumbled out of her hand.

"Come to me," he said. "I would be with you again."

"And I with you," poor Evon whispered.

And she stepped into the water, deeper and deeper, until she would never step out again.

❦

A short while later, Pine Onetooth came to the water's edge, there to take her place beside Ty.

"You listen well, girl," he said. He handed her a small black pouch, tied at the neck in a pretty bow.

Inside the pouch, Pine found a tooth.

She took it out and held it against her gum, trying it in different places while she admired her reflection in the river. "Master, how will I fix it?" she asked.

But Ty was gone and night had descended.

And the rain had begun to fall once more.

4

Evon's sons were the ones who found her. They pulled her cold from the reedy shallows at a place where the trees bowed into the river. While the elder son wept and stroked his mother's head upon his knees, the younger one ran to Cob Wheeler's shelter. It was not long into the night and Cob was still weighted down with sleep, but the rumpus woke up Rolan and Mell, and they came into the clearing to hear the news. Rolan immediately woke more men, then leapt on his whinney and rode to the river. While Mell was comforting the sobbing boy, Ty approached them, carrying a fire stick.

"I heard a clamor."

Mell felt her eyebrows pinch. Here was the man who Evon and she had spoken about this very night, who Evon had accused of being a demon. She clamped the boy tighter to hide her shudder. "Evon was found in the river, drowned. The men are heading there now."

Ty cast his gaze at the gaggle of folk. Oleg came hopping out of his shelter, trying too hastily to put on a boot and slipping in the wet dirt because of it. "Then I must join them."

"Aye, go swiftly," Mell said, though the words felt shy on her tongue.

And Ty did go, but it was Rolan who in time staggered into the settlement with Evon draped across his arms. He set her down and stepped back from her body, so all might see her and wail if they would.

By now, Cob Wheeler was awake and growling. Snatching a fire stick off one of the young, he bullied his way through the stupefied crowd. "Make way! Make way!" The fire stick flared with every puff of his voice. Red embers skittered into the night. He paused, hot and giddy, over Evon's body. When he saw her, his harsh expression softened. A heartbeat passed before he said, "What foul deed has been done to this woman?"

Rolan answered when no one else would. "She was found in the river where the trees touch the water. She has no wound or mark."

Cob held the fire stick over her face. A water trail was running from the corner of Evon's pretty blue mouth. Her long, dark hair lay slick to her skin, matted here and there with dying weed.

"I spoke with Evon tonight," Mell said, still hugging the younger son. "She was confused and much distressed about Waylen."

Some of those gathered around touched their hearts.

Rolan said, "Are you saying Waylen's spirit called her to the river?"

"I . . . I do not know," Mell stuttered, fearful of Ty. He had just walked into the clearing, the light of the fire sticks glowing in his eyes. He sat on a nearby rock and said nothing.

A mutt ranged up and sniffed at the body. It received, for its pleasure, Cob Wheeler's boot in its shaggy brown belly. As it ran, yelping, Cob threw down his fire stick and fell to one knee. He picked up Evon's cold, wet hand. Her fingers were as slim as feather shafts across his huge and crusted palm. "This is my burden," he muttered. "Forgive me, woman. If I had acted sooner, your sorrow would not have lain you here." He squeezed the hand and put it back at her side. "Men of the Kaal! On the morrow, we ride!"

"Where to?" asked Oleg, crossing himself.

Cob pushed up. He breathed through his long nose, skaler fashion. "To the cave where this woman's husband lies. We will bring him home and lay him on a bed of fine branches beside her. Their spirits will dance together once more." He thumped his chest and looked at Mell. She gave a tearful nod. This was Cob's finest moment, she thought.

"Ty?" said Rolan, to the man on the rock. "Will you and your whinney join this quest?"

Ty looked on as the girl, Pine Onetooth, laid a flower on Evon's breast. "Aye, I would see this cave you speak of. And if a ride will settle this matter, I will join you."

"Prepare her," barked Cob. "Tend her kindly. Lay a wreath at her door. Take care of her kin." He lingered a moment to say a swift prayer, then walked away.

Rolan nodded at some of the women and together they moved Evon into a shelter, there to do the work of cleaning the body and dressing her in a plain white robe, ready for her final journey to the Fathers.

The moon had moved halfway through the sky before he stepped into the night again. He found Mell Whitehair waiting for him. "Rolan, I would speak with you." She drew him hurriedly into the shadows.

"This is a sorry business," he said, his mind still much on Evon's death. "I can make no easy sense of this, Mell. Evon has been laden with grief for days. Why would she give up her spirit now?"

Mell put her fingers to his lips. "Hush. What's done with Evon is done. I come to warn you to be wary on your journey tomorrow."

Rolan lifted his youthful shoulders. "Your worry is kindly heard, Mell, but the ride is not harsh. And it will not take us through skaler territory. Do not concern yourself. We—"

"It's not skalers that stir my fears," she said. She gripped his arm to prevent him from leaving. "I caution you to be wary of Ty."

"T—?"

Again she put a hand to his mouth. "Harken close and say nought in return. Earlier this night, Evon spoke to me in dreadful terror. She feared Waylen's spirit had been stolen by Ty."

Rolan's mouth tried to form a question that Mell's hand would not allow him to ask. She said, "Do not speak to Cob about this, for he will take Ty's head off and want no proof. I set this troubling tale on you because I see more wisdom in you than your years. If evil has been done to Waylen and Evon, I worry the source of it lies in that cave."

Rolan thought for a moment, then nodded. "Ty did seem pleased to be going there, as if it suited his purpose well."

Mell cupped her hands around his and warmed them. "Aye. I saw that sly look too. I confess I found Ty pleasing at first, but now I begin to see an unkind light in his devious eye. I fear his magicks. But I fear his command of the caarkers even more. They are spiteful creatures that would take a man's finger for food if they could."

"And lately I see more of them about," Rolan muttered.

"Then do as I ask and be wary," Mell said. "The Kaal need you, Rolan. Ride with care. May the Fathers bless you and bring you home safely."

And she kissed his hands and parted from him, leaving him standing alone in the night, wondering on all she had said. When at last he turned to go back to his shelter, he found his way blocked by Pine Onetooth.

"Girl, be about your bed," he said, striding past and giving no heed to what she might or might not have heard.

"I would ride with the men on the morrow," she called.

"You will not," Rolan said bluntly. He wafted her words away into the darkness.

Pine smiled and raised her arm. A large black shape quickly settled upon it. "They know," she said.

Ark! the caarker replied. It leaned forward, making a retching sound. And out of its throat it brought up a tooth, which it dropped, along with a trail of black dribble, into Pine's open hand.

5

Despite Rolan's protest, Pine did journey with them on the morrow. As the men were assembling, Ty trotted Shade forward. Pine was sitting in front of him, singing a tune so sweet the whinney was almost dancing to it.

"Ty, what game is this?" A dark look sullied Rolan's face. He pulled his mount around to halt their progress.

"No game," said Ty. "If skalers are about, you may see the girl's worth."

"The cave is not in skaler territory," said Oleg.

"Nor was it last time," Ty pointed out. "Yet one of your tribesmen slew a beast there."

A fair point, which Rolan acknowledged. "That cave is no place for a child, even so. How do we know what evil awaits us?" As he looked into Ty's mysterious eyes, he heard his heart beating out Mell's dire warning. The Kaal knew nothing about this stranger, yet here he was, about to ride with them to bring home the body of a man whose spirit he might have *stolen*? Rolan forced himself not to shudder. "I see no worth in taking Pine on this quest."

Cob Wheeler agreed with him. "What's the brat doing mounted?" he rumbled, striding manfully out of his shelter. A long sword hung from his belt. He jutted his chin at Pine.

"Ty wants her along," said Rolan.

"For what? Has he not spit enough to polish his own boots?" Cob swung onto his nut-brown whinney and signaled Oleg to do the same. "We four are enough. Put the girl on the ground and let's be on."

But Ty would not. He waited till he had Cob's eye and said, "Tell me something. How many times did the men of the Kaal attempt to cross the scorch line?"

Cob mused on this a moment. Leaning sideways, he spat at a scrawny mutt that was looking to raise a leg against his whinney. He lifted a bandaged hand, spreading his fingers as far as his scalds would allow. "Too many."

Rolan said, "The beasts patrol the line. Sometimes we would steal across it, but they would always find our scent and drive us back. Cob's burns are evidence of our endeavor. What has this to do with Pine?"

"I say she would fare better on their land than you."

"She?" roared Cob, as if a buzzer had stung his pride.

Mell was standing close by now, a shawl around her shoulders, listening keenly.

"Men are fueled by pride and foolishness," said Ty. "But women, especially the young of your kind, have a greater edge where skalers are concerned."

"Our 'kind'?" said Rolan, thinking this was an odd choice of word, but it was Mell whose voice was heard the loudest.

"Are you saying Pine can enchant the beasts?"

Ty hushed the girl. "I am saying her sweet songs might."

"Sweet songs," sneered Cob, tugging a rein. His whinney snorted. "The sweetest song I will hear will be the screech when I slit a skaler's throat. Bring your songstress if you will, but lay no blame on me if she wets your whinney at the first stroke of danger."

And he kicked his heels and the ride began.

They traveled long, in single file, at a pace considerate to their mounts. Under a sky blown clear of rain, they moved north with the mountains at their back, aiming to cross the vast swaths of moorland that would lead them to the fells where the cave was known to be. Many times Rolan looked back. Always he saw Ty trailing, though the stranger and Pine were never out of touch with the rest of the party. Pine sang all the way, though her melodies did not reach Cob's aging ears. More disturbingly, caarkers were often in the air. Some came to Ty's arm, bringing messages Rolan could only guess at. And only once, at a place where the sun had baked the green-ness out of the erth and the yellow grass cracked like stubble under hoof, did they encounter a skaler. The beast sailed high overhead, its giant wings making the sun twice blink. "Should I sing to it?" Rolan heard Pine say. Ty replied with a quiet no. He shook the reins and let Shade walk on, paying no heed to the beast. Rolan, for all his doubts about Ty, found himself admiring the stranger's boldness. For although the men were well clear of the scorch line, there would be nothing to stop the skaler attacking if the fancy took it. *Was it patrolling the region?* he wondered. Did it know that one of its kind lay dead in a cave just a day's ride away from here? Was it looking for those who had slain its kin? Its spiked head tilted suddenly, the eyes rippling like a stone breaking water. For one terrifying moment, they seemed to focus on Rolan alone. It was like the worst chill of winter, that look. But the beast turned away and was swallowed up by cloud. Slowly, its wingbeats diminished. With it Rolan's fear began to thaw.

❧

At a bend in the river where the men made camp that night, there was much grim chatter around the fire. Some of it to do with the skalers, and some with the darkeye creatures that had twice appeared from nowhere to battle the beasts.

"I have been thinking on a thing," said Rolan, stirring a pot of congealing stew that he no longer fancied he would put into his gut. "It bothers me that Ned came home from his quest, speaking his yarn of a skaler slain, but saying nought about the darkeyes he and the others planned to raise against them. Does that not seem to you strange?"

Oleg warmed his hands by the fire. "There would be no tale to tell if the darkeyes had already flown. We all saw them in the sky a second time, doing battle."

"Aye, mebbe," Rolan sighed. Oleg's deduction was reasonable enough, but only half an answer, he thought. He was thinking about Mell Whitehair's warning that some kind of evil might be present in the cave. But if that were true, why had Ned not spoken of it? He tipped the gristle from his stew pot onto the fire, preferring to chew on his musings instead.

"It seems to me," said Ty, who was idly whittling a stick to a point, "that our quest would be thwarted by the presence of these creatures. Perhaps we should be thankful that your friend reported no sign of them."

"Ned Whitehair was no friend to the Kaal," muttered Cob, digging a stone from the heel of his boot. "He and his boy have brought nought but death upon the tribe. I'll hear no talk of them."

Rolan knocked his fists together. "And I cannot sit here and slight the dead. I will be at peace when this deed is done and we are riding away from that cave with Waylen."

"Or what's left of him," Oleg said.

Cob and Rolan looked his way.

"It has been many days," Oleg said plainly. "The scratchers and the buzzers may have done some ugly work."

"Then we will send you in first to find out," growled Cob, "while you still have one good eye to see with."

Oleg saw the humor in this, but Rolan guessed Cob meant what he said. And now that he thought about the prospect himself, he could understand Cob's reluctance. Oleg was right: Retrieving Waylen's body was not going to be a pleasant business. "We should draw lots to decide who enters first."

"Aye," Cob grunted. "Let the fates decide who will carry the mulch of death on his shoulders. Break the twigs. One for each man—and a fifth for the girl."

He met Ty's gaze.

"No," said Rolan, sensing a storm about to blow between them. "Pine cannot be involved in this." He glanced at the girl, who lay asleep beneath a blanket.

"She rides, she draws," Cob said bluntly.

But Rolan would not have it. "Break five," he said to Oleg, "and I will draw twice. The girl can scarce lift the flowers she plucks. How could we send her to heave a dead man out of a cave? I will take her place."

"I say two should go in," said Ty, not looking up from his whittling. "One to bear torches, the other to wield a free hand."

"Against what?" sniffed Cob.

Ty twisted his knife. "Who knows what lurks in the darkness? I know more about skalers than any of you. I put myself forward. I will enter first, without fear. Draw your lots if you would light the way for me."

"Wait," said Rolan, as Oleg looked for a twig to break. "I also put myself forward. I will go into the cave with Ty."

Cob spread his hands. "Has the stew made heroes of us all? This was *my* burden, pledged to Evon. If it's to be this way, without twigs, I will lead us in and Ty will bear the torch. And there's an end to it."

"So be it," said Ty, when no more was being said. "I go with Cob and light his way." He tossed the twig aside and pushed his knife into his belt. "Sleep beckons me. Rest well, friends."

"Aye," they muttered, with some hesitation. Who was he yet, to call them friends?

That night, a shadow visited Rolan's sleep. It had no face or erthly form. Again and again it spoke Ty's words, but in the tenor of Waylen's voice: *Who knows what lurks in the darkness? Who knows?* In the morning, Rolan was pale with sweat. The first thing he saw in the misty half-light was Oleg standing by a tree, passing water.

Rolan approached him and made in like manner. "Oleg, I must speak a worry to you. Do not look around until my words are out."

Oleg trickled more water on the ground. "Speak. What ails you?"

Rolan glanced over his shoulder. Ty was tending Shade, the white whinney. Pine was nowhere to be seen. "Before we left, Mell Whitehair told me a tale. She came to me saying that Evon believed that Ty had stolen Waylen's spirit. *Do not look around! Face the tree. He may be watching.* I fear you may be right about Waylen's body. Some ugliness has surely been done to him, but in a manner no good Kaal could predict. I think this stranger who calls himself Ty is not a man possessed by Waylen's spirit—I believe it to be Waylen, possessed by a demon that lurked in that cave. *Listen to me, Oleg, this is not the berries talking.* When Ty and Cob go into that hole they will leave us outside to watch the skies. I say we follow, with knives and arrows ready and sharp. Ty is planning something, I know it. I would take my side with a host of skalers before I would trust this stranger in our midst."

"I agree he is sly," Oleg whispered, "but where is the proof of what you say?"

Rolan lowered his robe. "I have no proof. But the terrors were in my sleep last night and I swear they were trying to show me something. My gut is sour with grave foreboding. Say you are with me in this."

"Aye, I am with you," Oleg replied. He bent down and picked up the stick that Ty had been whittling the night before. "If the terrors speak true, let this become the arrow that pierces the demon's fiendish heart."

"Aye," said Rolan, gulping at the thought.

And with that he made his way back to the camp.

6

Rolan's dark imaginings were to trouble him for the rest of the ride, but he spoke no more to Oleg about it and instead took counsel within himself. How could men protect themselves, he wondered, against that which they could not see or understand?

He had still not settled on any kind of answer by the time they arrived at a branch of the river that trickled around the foot of a common green hill. Over this sleepy rise, Cob said, the darkeye cave would be found.

Oleg slid off his mount. He picked some hairs off a dried-out thornbush. "These came from a whinney's tail." He let the hairs float on the wind, then knelt to the ground and ran his fingers over a trace of hoof marks invisible to all but a hunter's eye. He looked east of the way they had come, then turned to squint at a chin of rock that jutted out of the hill about three-quarters of the way up. "The others were here, for certain. They tied their mounts and climbed the rest on foot. The whinneys left at speed. Mebbe the skaler frightened them off."

Cob dismounted and cupped one hand in the stream to

drink. "Well, I see no skalers now. Tie the whinneys and let's be on. We climb the hill together."

"Not Pine," said Rolan. "I say we leave her to tend the mounts."

Cob dried his hand on his beard. "You would bring her this far and deny us the amusement of her skaler songs?"

"You said yourself, there are no skalers."

Cob grunted. "What does Ty have to say?"

Ty slid off Shade's back and handed Pine the reins. "I see pretty flowers growing all about. Let the girl gather them if she will."

"Aye," said Pine, who liked the prospect.

"And if a skaler should happen upon us?" said Oleg.

"Then we call her to us and she sings."

"Or dies with flowers in her hand," Cob snorted. "Let's be on, before my legs forget their use."

Rolan counseled Pine as he dismounted. "When we are over the rise, hail if you see a beast in the sky, for it is possible we may not."

Pine looked at Ty, who raised no objection.

She nodded, her one tooth glinting.

So, leaving the whinneys with Pine, they began their steep ascent of the hill. Though the ground trod heavy with the rain it had gathered, the grass was well grown and thickly tufted. An easy climb for mountain men. Cob posted Oleg wide with his bow, while he led himself and the others on a straight path up to the jutting rock. At the brow of the hill, all three pressed themselves low to the ground and peered at an area of barren gray scree on the other side. Straightway Rolan touched his heart, for any grass that had clung to that side of the hill had been deadened by fire, leaving a black streak on the erth. Oak Longarm had lost his life there, he guessed; those were his arrows scattered about.

"And so we come to it," Cob said grimly, his gaze, like Rolan's, resting on the scorch marks. "Curse every skaler from here to the sea."

"This is an unforeseen prospect," said Ty.

He nodded at an area of rockier ground. Not far below their position, the land cut away like a yawning mouth. Great cracks had appeared in the rock face above it and some generous hunks of stone had fallen, blocking the entrance to the cave with rubble.

"That will not be easy to get through," said Rolan. "A slitherer would struggle to find any passage."

"Yet we must look for one," Cob said heavily. "Evon's spirit will haunt us to our end if we abandon this quest too soon."

With one eye on the sky he climbed over the ridge and scrambled down to the edge of the rockfall. He found Oleg, who had come at the cave from a different route, there already.

Oleg shook his head in disbelief. "If this were a tomb, my spirit would sleep most snug in it." The task had looked bad enough from above, but at this level the plugs of stone were impossibly huge, too heavy for a group of four men to clear.

Cob clambered up them nonetheless, looking for any gap he might squeeze through. He leaned against a wedge with all his might, but managed to move nought but the sweat on his brow. He slapped the rock in anger. "Skalers," he said. "Skalers have done this. Buried their kin, and Waylen too."

"I find that unlikely," said Ty. He had set himself down on an isolated rock, a role that by now seemed customary for him.

"How so?" asked Rolan, feeling no less easy in the stranger's presence. This tumble of stone had dismantled any plans Ty might have had, but the look in his eyes suggested the pursuit was far from over. Rolan felt his hand creeping nearer to his knife.

"Aye, amuse us, say your piece," Cob grunted, sitting down on top of the rock pile. "Maybe your clever words can charm the rocks aside."

Ty studied the sky for a moment, as if he was looking to the clouds for inspiration. After a moment's thought, he said, "Skalers flame their dead or let them fade into the dirt when their tear is shed. They do not bury them away in caves. Most likely the skaler that entered here disturbed the hollow during the fight and in time a collapse occurred—but it does not have to be an inconvenience." He leveled his sinister gaze at the men. "I cannot charm the rocks aside, Cob Wheeler—but I can call upon something with the strength to move them."

"Sweet mercy of our Fathers," Cob said suddenly. He leapt up and tried to draw his sword. Almost at once his ankle gave way and one foot became lodged in a gap between the rocks. He roared in pain and called for assistance. But Oleg and Rolan had followed Cob's gaze and were staring in terrified wonder at the sky, where a strange formation of clouds was brewing. "W-what's this?" Oleg jabbered, fumbling for an arrow.

"A lure," said Ty. He had not moved.

Now Rolan did draw his knife, though he seemed uncertain of what to attack: the sitting man or the changing cloud. A familiar shape was forming above them, casting its shadow over the hill. A monster in puffs of grays and blacks. A *darkeye* full with horns and teeth.

"A lure for *what*?" Rolan demanded.

Beyond the brow of the hill, Pine's voice rose shrill. "Skaler!"

She had seen the cloud too. And more.

"Curses! Help me!" Cob was all the while crying.

Oleg lowered his bow and ran to Cob's aid.

Meanwhile, Rolan chose his target. "What foul deed are

you about, magician?" He aimed his knife at the flesh of Ty's throat even though he was more than an arm's length away.

Ty gave the blade nought but a cursory glance. "You would be wise to take cover, boy. Or better still, let Shade hide you. The girl sees a dragon coming. The beast is going to attack this apparition, then land and claim this hill. When it moves these rocks aside and finds what lies inside that cave, it will kill every Kaal it sees."

Rolan's gaze jumped feverishly into the sky. He could see no sign of a skaler yet, but he had no reason to doubt Pine's call. A furious drumming started up in his heart. His teeth were so tight they could have trapped water, but he managed to force one word off his tongue. "Dragon?"

Ty pressed his fingertips together. "That is how skalers name themselves."

Rolan shook his head in disbelief. "How do you know this? How can any man claim such knowledge of the beasts?"

Ty stretched his arms, as casual as if he'd been around the fire, whittling sticks. He seemed to care nothing for the threat of the knife or the approaching danger from the sky. "I know, because I was one of them once. What you see before you is a darkeye in the form of a man."

A droplet of sweat fell off Rolan's brow. It seemed to take an age to meet the ground. Impossible as it was to make sense of Ty's claim, the dread of thinking it might be true had frozen the young man where he stood. He risked a glance behind him. Oleg was calling for help, desperately trying to free Cob's foot. Pine was riding up the hill on Shade, singing, but taming nothing yet. In the sky, the dark shape was almost complete. The knife shook in Rolan's hand, cutting tiny slivers of air. He stepped closer, at last more menace in his shape. "What do you want with us, demon? Why did you come among the Kaal?"

"To draw one of you here," Ty said, standing up. "The timing of this quest has been most . . . convenient. Lower your knife, Rolan. A dragon is about to swoop. I can *scent* it. Only one of this party can survive and join me. My choice would be you."

But with that, the balance tipped against Ty. Rolan lunged at him, crying devilry and murder. Yet Ty had time enough to spin a finger and call some magick out of the sky.

A flash of light shot out of the cloud apparition and danced along Rolan's blade. The force of it catapulted Rolan backward. His head struck a rock at the side of the pile and he was knocked half-senseless. An arrow winged through the air, fired fast from Oleg's bow. Ty's heart was its target and its aim was true. But at the moment the arrow struck, Ty's body turned to dust and regathered into the form of a caarker. It flew fast at Oleg, driving its talons deep into his face. Oleg screamed as his flesh churned loose. He raised a hand to

43

protect his one good eye. Cob, still fighting to free himself, roared at the heavens and lifted his sword. He swung wildly. It was not a kind outcome. The blow missed Ty and instead half severed Oleg's arm. Oleg screamed loud enough to burst a lung. Cob cursed and struggled to free the blade. But by now a worse fate was upon the men. Their blood ran cold as a screech split the sky.

Just as Ty had predicted, a skaler, a real one, had entered the fray.

7

It was bright, bright green, the kind with the terrifying slanted eyes. Ty fled as it plunged on the cloud from above, blazing at the shape without calling out any challenge or warning. The cloud burst in a veil of steam, but the skaler's fire continued to travel, laying its ferocious heat across the rocks. Oleg and Cob were burned where they stood. Long after the blistering wave had subsided, their scalding residue was still floating down to coat the stones.

Incredibly, Rolan survived the flare. Ty's blow had sent him to the rear of the rubble, where there was one small nook the fire hadn't found. Rolan had curled tight into it, though he feared he must be only counting the moments until the skaler poked around and scraped him out. He found himself praying that the scent of two incinerated men might be pungent enough to cloak the living sweat of another. A shameful thought, but no worse than Oleg or Cob would have begged for, had they been in his position.

With a thump, the skaler landed. Rolan tried not to breathe or make a sound. The ground beside him darkened into shadow. The skaler clumped forward, three, four paces. It pressed itself right up against the rubble, its weight making even the largest stones grate. It grizzled and pawed at the wreckage, all the while clicking and growling in confusion. It seemed unsure of what it had flamed. A few stones tumbled clear of the pile, landing close to Rolan's hiding place, blocking him slightly from view. He tensed as the beast made a graarking sound, its muggy breath finding the nicks between the stones. The heat coming through them tickled one side of Rolan's face, making all the sweat trails sizzle. Such a horrible sensation that was, as if the skaler were giving him an early warning of what its abominable fire could do. With a *whup*, the giant lifted its tail and raked the rocks. Another large boulder hit the dirt. With it fell what was left of Cob: a blackened corpse, missing one leg. Small fires were flickering on patches of skin not fully burned. Rolan retched but managed to contain it. The skaler graarked again. This time its voice rang clear with surprise. After that there was no more raking of rock. With a scrabble, it took off in a plume of dust, shrieking loudly across the moorlands as it took a turn back toward the mountains. Rolan's heart thumped with a greater fear than ever. He felt sure the beast had seen into the cave (or scented the air drifting out of it). That could mean only one thing: It had discovered its dead companion and gone to seek help.

But where was Ty in all this? And Pine, for that matter? Through the faintest of cracks, Rolan saw the girl appear out of nowhere, repeating the vanishing trick with the whinney.

"Master," she called. "Master, where are you?"

Master. The taste of her deceit fouled Rolan's throat, a tang far worse than the food he'd tried to vomit.

A caarker, the one that Ty had become, landed on the whinney's head.

Ark?! it cried.

Rolan saw Pine nod, wide-eyed. Somehow, the bird had mesmerized her and made her understand it. "Aye, master. The fire blew harsh. It covered every rock. Nought could escape it."

A tear ran from Rolan's eye, forced out by his churning anger. For there was nothing in the tone of Pine's wispy voice to suggest she knew that he had survived. Her words were not a deliberate pretense intended to save him from any more harm. She assumed him dead and now basked in it, despite his previous kindnesses to her. *Let me live through this,* Rolan begged the Fathers, *for now there are many more scores to settle.* Pine would pay dearly for her betrayal one day.

The caarker took off and landed with a scrabble on the rocks, not far above Rolan's head. He couldn't see what the skaler had achieved with its poking, but if it *had* dug a hole, there was every chance that Ty could fly through it, into the cave. A sudden flurry of wings confirmed this.

Five heartbeats passed. From deep within the hill came faint echoes of caarker cries, as if Ty was calling something to wake. Rolan considered his choices. If he sprang out of hiding now, he could try to block Ty's exit and seal him within the cave forever. But that would be a risky venture, for his body was raging with pain and he could not be certain of stopping up the hole, especially if Pine called out to her "master." So he chose the safer alternative, which was to wait and see what came out of the cave and to judge what might be done about it.

From out between the stones there came a pink mist.

Rolan watched in confusion and dread as it swirled around Pine like a slitherer preparing to crush its prey. In the same breath, Ty flew out of the cave and turned into a man without losing momentum in his stride.

"Girl, do not be afraid," he said.

Pine was ducking away from the mist as she would to avoid an angry buzzer.

Ty reached slowly behind him, to the long knife sheathed in his belt. "When this is done, you will be more alive than you could ever imagine."

In one swift move he drew the knife.

And plunged it into Pine's unsuspecting heart.

8

Rolan bit one side of his tongue, tasting his blood, the shock was so great. Despite his growing dislike of Pine, it was all he could do not to cry out, "MURDER!" Somehow he stayed his torment yet again, reducing his pain to the quietest of whimpers and swallowing the bile still rising in his throat. He watched Ty catch the girl's body as she fell in a loose heap from Shade's back.

The villain laid her flat to the ground, withdrew the knife, and cleaned it.

Pine's head lolled to one side, the life fast ebbing out of her.

Her faraway eyes drifted shut.

As if it knew it must be swift, the pink mist gathered itself into an arrow shape and went into her through the wound that Ty had made.

And then came the greatest horror of all.

Pine's body went through a series of spasms. Five, maybe six strong tremors, one of which lifted her feet off the ground. Her fingers clawed at the ground with such strength they made furrows of mud from the hardened erth. A fountain of spit shot out of her mouth. And then her eyes reopened.

Bigger.

Rounder.

Black.

A few silent moments passed.

Then, to Rolan's astonishment, Ty pulled the girl to her feet.

She swayed, but did not otherwise falter.

"No," Rolan breathed, hardly able to believe what he was seeing. Pine slain and now standing? What manner of evil was this? He watched her stretch her limbs as though she'd done nothing more than put on a robe. She put a finger to the blood and tasted it. "Am I Hom?" It was her voice still, but wrapped around a note of something darker.

"No more than I," said Ty.

Pine shuddered again. "I feel the girl's memories. Her pleasures. Her desires." She bent down and snapped a flower off its stalk.

"Search deeper," said Ty. "The Hom know more about dragons than they think, but this is not the moment to discuss it."

"Are they mindful of Graven?"

"I can find no trace to suggest it—other than their fascination for the birds."

These words intrigued Rolan greatly. For it seemed that Ty was speaking of some knowledge long suppressed in the

Kaal. But how was that possible when the beasts had been on Erth for barely two seasons? And who or what was Graven? He looked again at Pine and saw her examining her fingers, a look of deep repugnance clouding her face.

Ty noticed it also and said, "We need these bodies for now. The Hom form is weak and imperfect, but it has adapted favorably to parts of this world. Further transformation will be possible in time. I changed the appearance of the man they called Waylen so I might move freely among the Kaal. It will serve us well if you continue as the child they call Pine. The girl's voice and manner will come to you."

"And what do *you* continue as, 'Tywyll'?"

Rolan's eyebrows twitched when he heard this. There was more than a grain of disapproval in Pine, as if Ty had committed a treacherous sin. Rolan listened intently as she went on.

"You dare to call yourself 'the darkness'? Some might say you take the name of our master in vain."

Master. Again.

Ty replied, "I mean no slight against Graven. When I changed my appearance, the name seemed fitting. And if the dragons should ever learn of it, it will cause fear and confusion among them."

"If they do not slay you first," Pine said. She spread her arms as though she wished for wings. "I do not feel whole."

"That is because your auma is divided."

"*Divided?* How?"

Now Rolan detected a growl in her voice. Here were seeds of hope, he thought. Where there was animosity, there could also be a rift.

Ty explained, "When the Hom first found us, your stasis was interrupted. I had completed my regeneration and was wakened by the call of a dragon that entered the cave. But you were a day behind me. A rock was thrown at your outer husk. The husk was damaged and a small amount of your auma escaped. I saved it in the only way I could." He gestured at Shade. "I found the horse beaten, its spirit clinging to a grain of life. A leg was broken, its skull part crushed. I transformed it using your auma loss. It was lying on a dragon stig, which fused with the injury to its head. The beast regenerated strongly. It has zest and unexpected gifts."

"I am split between forms and you talk of *gifts?*"

"There is a dragon heart in these mountains," growled Ty. "When we have it, and Graven is restored, we will both regenerate fully."

He turned to see a caarker flutter down onto a stone.

Arrar-arrk! it reported.

Ty peered at the skies. "The Wearle is coming. We must leave." He strode toward the horse.

"What news of the boy?"

The starkness of the question stayed Ty's mounting. "It matters to you?"

Pine stroked Shade's mane. "It matters to the horse."

Ty frowned and spoke with the bird again. "They have moved the boy to an isolated place. The bird is unsure why. The *horse* asked of him?"

"I feel a strong connection to its rider, Ned Whitehair."

"Then drive it out," said Ty. He tapped his chest. "This is a vessel, nothing more. The host influence must be crushed. The Hom and their ways are inferior to us. Interference from their memories is damaging."

And he climbed onto Shade's back with Pine, and together they rode away over the hill.

❧

Pursuit was Rolan's immediate thought. But that, he knew, was a hopeless ambition from the moment he squeezed his body out of hiding. A bone was unhinged, somewhere by his hip. That whole leg raged with pain. He would be lucky to hobble, let alone ride. Yet hobble he did, back to a point where he could look down the other side of the hill. The whinneys were gone. From the pattern of their tracks it looked like Ty had seized one whinney and set the others loose. There was no way back to the settlement for Rolan, and nowhere to hide from imminent doom. It would surely not be long before the skaler came back, bringing at least one other with it.

No escape.

And so he sat on the hill and awaited his fate, enjoying the glowing sun on his face for what he assumed would be the last time.

Soon, the skalers did appear. Not a pair, but a host of them. A starburst of greens and purples, snorting their smoke and sweat. One had shining yellow eyes that almost burned him with their glare. The beasts surrounded Rolan, baring their glistening, stench-heavy fangs, all the while growling in what appeared to be urgent conversation. Quaking, he raised his hands in surrender, only to have them almost snapped off by a swipe from a pointed tail.

The largest skalers set to work on the stones, tossing them aside as if they were no heavier than the cones that fell from the spiker trees in the Whispering Forest. Within a few beats they had opened a passage into the cave. One of the bright green monsters poked its slender head inside. *Now comes the test of the tale*, thought Rolan. For if a skaler lay dead in there, slain through the eye by a Kaal arrow, the beasts would turn on the tribe as Ty had said and burn every man, woman, and child they could find, beginning with him.

The skaler withdrew its head. Its savage eyes tightened. *It has seen what it has seen*, thought Rolan. *My time is done.* He began to mutter another prayer. The skaler duly lunged at him, roaring so loudly that he felt as if his chest had been plugged with sand. Rolan covered his eyes and gave a cry of despair, but his spirit did not go up in flames. An unlikely savior came to his rescue. The peculiar yellow-eyed skaler stepped across the green one's path and began an angry exchange with it. For several ear-throbbing moments their argument raged, a quarrel the yellow-eye eventually won. The green beast swept away, angrily calling others to follow. The yellow-eye puffed with relief and nodded at a purple skaler beside it. The purple one ranged up to Rolan and spread its enormous claws. Rolan lowered his head, fearing he would end his days as pulp. Instead, the beast clamped him with just enough force to lift him off the hill. It took him high into the air and made no sign of dropping him. It turned smoothly away from the cave, setting a course for the distant mountains. Whatever had been said, Rolan's life had been spared. They would not burn him this day.

He was their prisoner instead.

PART TWO

THE NAMING

9

Prime Grynt's eyrie, earlier that day

The rain had begun to fall again. Yet the wind that often swept in tireless eddies around the mountains was mercifully absent on the morning of the Naming, and the interior of Prime Grynt's eyrie was dry.

Gabrial landed on the wide, shallow ledge, remembering not to shake the water off his wings. To shower the Prime dragon at the outset of a summoning would not have been the most appropriate of greetings. Lifting his bright blue scales a little, he allowed some body warmth to escape. The raindrops quickly turned to steam. His partner, Grendel, landed beside him, adopting the same approach. She was a gloriously beautiful dragon. As the steam pearled and fizzed around her neck, the golden braids that ran along her snout lit up as sweetly as a cluster of stars. Although they had not been together long, Gabrial still felt proud (and a little amazed) to be her mate.

"You're late," said Grynt, inhaling deeply. His silver breast scales clattered as his chest expanded.

Grendel bowed. "Forgive us, Prime. The wearlings were restless."

"Who tends them?" said a dragon to Gabrial's right. This was Gossana, the only other adult female in the colony. She was considerably older than Grendel and had twice given birth to wearlings, earning her the right to the title "matrial." She jutted her ferocious dark green head, fanning the sawfin scales around her neck. Her eyes, famously capable of changing color, slanted back to their narrowest position.

"Ren has care of them," Gabrial said.

"Ren? You mean the *boy*?" Gossana's lips rolled back. Saliva glinted on a broken fang. "You left a Hom guarding our precious young?"

"They don't need to be guarded," Grendel said dismissively. "The wearlings are happy and relaxed in Ren's company. And you know as well as we do that since the war with the goyles, one cry would bring a flurry of roamers to our cave. They were playing seek when we left; I believe Ren was winning."

"I don't approve of this," Gossana said, turning to Grynt. "This closeness with the Hom boy is disgusting and unnatural. It should not be encouraged."

Prime Grynt raised a claw. He turned to a male dragon standing at his right. He was plain green, as many adult males were, with some lighter flurries sweeping out across his shoulders making bleached and staggered patterns on his wings. What made this dragon stand out, however, were his huge yellow eyes. They sat like colored stones well back on his snout. Even half-lidded, they lit the area around the ledge in a pool of light the Erth sun would have envied. "This is De:allus Garodor," said the Prime. "He arrived through the fire star last night, from Ki:mera. He is here to assess the situation with the boy."

"What situation?" The short stigs around Gabrial's ears began to bristle. "Ren is our friend and ally. There is no situation. He's—"

"Be quiet," said Grynt, stopping him with a growl. "In my presence, you speak when I ask you to, or order you to— particularly if you have an *opinion* on anything."

De:allus Garodor said quietly, "This 'Ren' is the Hom you spoke to me about?"

"Yes," said Grynt. "A recent trail of events brought the boy into our midst. He was bitten by the male wearling he rescued, but the wound did not kill him. Instead, the drake's blood appears to have infused the boy with our auma. There is also a suggestion that the drake's mother, Grystina, invested the boy with some of her knowledge before she died. He claims he has a link to her spirit and that she aids him in times of need."

"Faah," said Gossana.

"As a result the boy now has certain . . . abilities, one of which is the power to speak a weak form of dragontongue."

"He speaks it well," Gabrial cut in. "He learns more of our words every day."

Grendel brought her tail around and stroked his back with her isoscele. *Shush*, she said, with just a blink of her eyes.

Grynt continued, "This is how Gabrial learned the boy's Erth name. The Hom has bonded with the wearlings, notably the drake. I notified the Elders on Ki:mera because nothing like this has ever happened before. I sought their wisdom on how to proceed."

"And they sent us a head-scratcher," Gossana snorted, "when what we need is greater security! More fighting dragons! More Veng!"

Her outburst made Gabrial flinch. *Head-scratcher* was a derogatory term for the De:allus class, whose primary interest was to understand the workings of the universe and its Creator, Godith. And while he too was surprised that more Veng hadn't been sent to Erth, the arrival of Garodor was no great surprise. Every Wearle had at least one De:allus. But until this talk about Ren had begun, Gabrial had supposed that Garodor had simply been posted here because both his predecessors had died in the struggle against the goyles. Now he wasn't so sure.

"Bite your tongue, Matrial," Prime Grynt warned her. "I raised you to Elder status believing it would instill in you a little more tolerance, an advancement I can easily retract.

De:allus Garodor is the most senior dragon of his class. You will treat him with all the respect he deserves. The Elders have decreed that the boy will be given into his care, whence we will decide what is to be done with him."

"*Done* with him?"

"Gabrial, be calm," Grendel advised. She used her tail to prevent him from stepping forward. She had seen Grynt's brawny eye ridges narrow, a sign that his patience was wearing thin. Gabrial was young and had proved himself more than once in battle, but Grynt was the supreme commander of the Veng, the most ferocious of all dragon classes; he did not have armored breast scales for nothing.

But Gabrial would not be contained. "Fewer than seven days ago," he blustered, steam blowing out of the lines of tiny spiracles that stabilized the air pressure in his throat, "Ren exposed a traitor among us and saved the life of one of our young. The Elders acknowledged his worth to the Wearle. He can be of help to us. If the Hom are made to understand we mean them no harm, we can live in harmony with them and roam the planet without interference."

Gossana gave another halfhearted snort.

Gabrial ignored her, saying, "I pledged my life to the boy for all he did. With respect to De:allus Garodor, I cannot stand aside and see Ren turned over for . . . examination."

"You will 'stand' where I order you to stand," Grynt said, twisting his lean snout forward. He held Gabrial's troubled gaze for a moment. "I understand why your loyalties are divided. This course of action does not run easily with me, either. The boy showed courage during our conflict with the goyles, but you are deluded if you think he is not a threat to us."

"But why would he attack us?"

"Him, probably not," the De:allus broke in, "but if he breeds, whatever dragon auma he possesses will be passed on through his generations. As I understand it, the Hom are exceedingly cunning creatures. Surely you can see the dangers they would pose if we gave them more resources? Imagine a whole host of Hom with the ability to i:mage or phase through time. Do you want to be the dragon who brings that menace upon us?"

Gabrial sank back on his haunches. He looked for support from Grendel, who said, "Will De:allus Garodor guarantee that Ren will not be harmed?"

"You need to remember your place," Gossana snapped, her amber eye darkening more toward red. "Your role is to rear the young in your keeping, not to poke about in matters that concern your superiors."

"How suddenly inflated you've become," Grendel hissed, "if indeed you *could* rise any higher."

"Enough!" Grynt thundered, before either dragon could bare their teeth. "Elder Gossana speaks well on this matter. After the misfortune that befell Grystina, her wearlings were entrusted to you, Grendel. A decision that was not without its measure of controversy. You swore to nurture and protect your cousin's young. Anything less would dishonor her memory. Is that what you would wish?"

Grendel bowed her head, the scales around her neck flushing green for a moment. "No, of course not. But—"

"But nothing," Grynt said. "We came to this planet to explore it with a view to colonization. Very soon we will push out beyond these mountains to expand our domayne. If, as we suspect, the terrain is suitable, more dragons will come to Erth. To achieve these ends, we must subjugate all other life-forms—that includes the Hom. Are we clear about this?"

He looked hard at Gabrial, who tightened his claws.

"I said, are we *clear* about this?"

Gabrial forced himself to nod.

"Good," Grynt said, making sure he had Gabrial's eye. "Forget about the boy. There will be greater challenges for you this day."

Gabrial looked up, his blue eyes blinking. "I don't understand."

"He's talking about the Naming," said Grendel. "Today

65

the whole Wearle comes to learn that we intend to call the wearmyss 'Gayl' and her brother 'Gariffred.'"

"Gariffred?" The cave light dulled as Garodor's eyelids shuttered down. He turned to Prime Grynt. "Did I hear that correctly?"

Grynt's solemn expression suggested he had. He said to Grendel, "You will not reconsider? You know it is your right as the wearlings' adoptive mother to give them any name of your choosing?"

Grendel raised her snout. "According to Ren, Grystina chose the name 'Gariffred' just before she died. I cannot dishonor her or the drake."

"Once the Wearle hears *that* name," Gossana said scathingly, opening her throat and treating everyone to the stench of her latest kill, "you might not live long enough to swallow a smoke ring, let alone dishonor anyone."

"The matrial speaks wisely," De:allus Garodor said. "To call a young dragon 'flame of truth' could incite those who remember the lineage wars. Some are sure to see it as a slight against Godith."

"The past is the past," Grendel said bravely. "I have pledged my auma to Godith, and the wearlings will do the same. Should anyone try to speak ill of them, we have Gabrial to protect us."

"Then they're doomed," Gossana said, her cynicism ringing out around the walls.

"May we leave now?" said Gabrial, his manner taut. He had had enough scorn for one day.

"In a moment. I have more to say." Grynt raised his head. "The Naming will take place at the great ice lake. Shortly, I will call the Wearle to gather at Skytouch to see you formally present these young. Let us pray to Godith they are accepted and welcomed. Now you may leave. Oh, and Gabrial?"

The blue dragon turned.

"Ren will not be with the wearlings; I ordered him taken from them while you were away."

"What?" Gabrial flashed his tail, destroying a spiderweb strung between a cluster of low-hanging rocks.

"Taken?" said Grendel, rearing in shock. "You brought us here under a deception?"

"I brought you here to tell you what you need to know," said Grynt, "and to do what had to be done. If I'd dealt with the boy any other way, you would have resisted."

"And you think we won't now?" Gabrial spread his wings. "Where is he?"

"Nowhere you would want to look," snarled Grynt, "unless you want a quick passage back to Ki:mera."

Gabrial snorted angrily, gouging the cave floor with his claws. He growled and took off in a cloud of smoke.

"Skytouch," the Prime dragon said to Grendel. "Make sure he's there. If the wearlings are not Named, they will grow up as savages."

"This is wrong," said Grendel, glaring at them all. "It won't only be Gabrial who opposes this action, it will be Ren, and Gariffred as well—when he grows. I hope none of you lives to regret it." And she backed out of the cave and took to the sky.

Almost immediately, her place was taken by a bright green dragon with a serpentlike body.

"Trouble?" he said as he landed. "That idiot blue was leaving in a hurry."

Grynt nodded. "I just told him we've taken the boy. Keep an eye on him, Gallen. His second heart is ruling his head at the moment. When he's calmed down, give him a task to do. Something that will stop him thinking up foolish ideas of rescue. Where have you put the Hom?"

"In a pit on the far side of the mountains. He can't get out and nothing could scent him. We'll hold him there until you're ready."

"And the other business? Where are you with the search for the Veng that went missing?"

"Still nothing. We're extending the hunt north, beyond the scorch line."

"Missing?" De:allus Garodor tilted his head inquisitively.

Grynt looked at the sky. "During the rise of the goyle mutants, one of Gallen's Veng disappeared. It is still unaccounted for. It's possible it was brought down by the goyles, but that seems unlikely, given we've failed to find its remains."

"Could the Hom have killed it?"

"Impossible," snarled Gallen.

Garodor reared back a little. Although he was in no danger, a mere hiss from a Veng was deeply unnerving. "Then there are only two alternatives. I understand it was dragons of the Veng class that were primarily affected by the mutation?"

Gallen flicked out his claws. "Four of my wyng were unchanged; I was one of them."

Garodor bowed to him slightly. "It was not my intent to disrespect you, Commander."

"Then get to the point," Gossana sighed, "before Gallen plucks those yellow eyes out of your head and uses them to light his settle tonight."

De:allus Garodor took a moment. "Either the missing Veng has mutated and deserted the domayne because the odds are against it, or it is dead and its remains have been consumed—or hidden."

"Consumed?" said Gossana. "By what?" Her red eye flickered to green for a moment.

"That I do not know," said Garodor.

"Then the way ahead is plain," said the Prime. He glared at Gallen, gesturing for calm. "We keep on searching—until we learn the truth. Do you wish to see the boy now, De:allus? There will be time before the Naming."

Garodor shook his head. "No, I have a more pressing matter. I believe there is a mapper called Garret in the Wearle. I'd like him to accompany me on a short mission. I understand from your report that the goyle mutations were caused by the ingestion of a reddish-pink ore you named fhosforent. I'd like to see the area where the fhosforent was mined."

"Entry to the mines is forbidden," said Gallen.

A wisp of gray smoke issued from the corner of Garodor's mouth. "I was sent to this planet by the will of the Higher. Nothing is forbidden to me, Commander."

"The ore was discovered by the Wearle that came before us," Grynt interjected. "After the battles, all caches were destroyed."

"But there is ore in the ground? The seams are still visible?"

"Only a fool would mine it," said Gossana.

"I'll need a scratch, no more, for analysis," said Garodor. "In all the history of dragonkind there has never been a story of transmutation quite like the one seen here, on Erth. If I'm to make sense of these goyles, I need to know everything about that process. I'm sure the spirits of Gallen's dead Veng would agree."

Gallen's eye ridges twitched. For once, he looked slightly uncomfortable.

"The mapper?" said Garodor, floating the question before them all.

Grynt nodded his assent. "Summon him," he said to Gallen. "Now."

🎨 10 🎨

The removal of Ren was a clever, two-stage operation.

The cave in which the wearlings nested (and where Ren slept most nights) lay in a ripple of green and rocky hills not far from the mountain in which they'd been born. Every day, Ren played with the youngsters. He even shared their food as long as Gabrial flamed the rawness off it first. In truth, there was little else for Ren to do. Although he was allowed outside the cave, he had been ordered, by Grynt, not to roam far. A not entirely comfortable situation, but one that Ren was happy to exploit. Every day he spent with the dragons, his knowledge of them grew. And there was still much joy to be had in the strengthening bond between himself and Gariffred.

All that was to change on the day of the Naming.

Halfway through their game of seek, a young dragon called Goodle approached the cave. He was a handsome blue, like Gabrial, but with no aggressive instincts or inclination toward fighting. He arrived soon after Gabrial and Grendel had departed for Prime Grynt's eyrie. Strictly speaking, only Elders, healers, or Veng-class dragons were allowed to approach another's territory uninvited, though in a colony this small, most dragons came and went at will. Goodle landed on a smooth bald rock well back from the cave entrance. He was preparing to announce himself when he caught sight of Ren stuck at a peculiar angle among the branches of a nearby shrub.

That was something you didn't see every day.

Ren immediately worked himself free. Despite their overwhelming difference in size and power, he stood up and boldly challenged the blue.

"Who are you? Why are you here?"

Goodle tilted his head. It was still a wonder to most of the dragons that this pale Hom boy with even paler hair could speak their tongue. He glanced at the arm that was said to grow a layer of scales sometimes. There was nothing but Hom flesh there at the moment, but on Ren's hand was the star-shaped scar where Gariffred, the drake, had bitten him—allegedly the source of the boy's dragon powers. Goodle swapped his gaze to Ren's face. "I was ordered to attend you while the wearling guardians are with Prime Grynt. My name is Goodle. If it's not too impertinent a question, why were you in the shrub?"

Graaarrk! went a young dragon voice.

Gariffred had just toddled to the front of the cave. He barked excitedly and pointed the end of his tail at Ren. A purple isoscele was developing there, not yet fully scaled.

"We're playing seek," said Ren. "At least, we were until

you interrupted us." He climbed over a small spill of rocks and came to stand by Gariffred. He ran his thumb along the drake's neck, making the emerging scales rise. "We don't need a dragon to attend us, thanks."

Goodle twizzled a stig, unsure of what to do. "But those were my orders. They came directly from Veng Commander Gallen. I can't disobey him. Isn't this cave too small for seek? Surely there aren't enough hiding places?"

Ren wriggled his nose. "There are if I phase before I'm spotted."

"Phase?" Goodle folded his ear stigs back. "But that's cheating. You're not allowed to *phase* during seek."

"You are in my game," said Ren. *Phasing* was the term for the dragons' ability to move, in an instant, through a small space of time, effectively allowing them to leap from one location to another.

Goodle made a humphing sound, as if he'd suddenly worked out why he'd never won a game of seek in his life. "You can do it, then, phasing?"

Ren shrugged. "Still practicing." Things hadn't gone quite to plan with the shrub. He spat a rogue leaf from the side of his mouth.

All these expressive movements, thought Goodle. *The Hom are so interesting to watch. So . . . supple.* "Well, if it won't disturb your game too much, I could just sit out here and wait for

Gabrial to return? Or I could drive those crows away?" He nodded at a cluster that was pecking at the remains of a kill. A small bony carcass had slipped down the hillside, discarded by Gabrial after the wearlings had finished picking at it.

"Ca-rows?" said Ren. To the Hom, the black creatures were known as caarkers, because of the angry noises they made.

"Crows," Goodle repeated carefully. "They're rather interesting, and surprisingly bold. Most birds stay away from us, fearing we'll eat them, but—"

"Burrds?"

Goodle flapped the tips of his wings to demonstrate. The stalks of the yellow flowers that grew on the hill bent back under the pressure of air. "A word we use to describe the different varieties of small flying creatures."

Ren nodded, beginning to understand. The dragons had many more words than the Hom, though not all dragons used them as well as this one did. Goodle reminded Ren of the healing dragon, Grymric, who had tended Ren's wounds after the battle with the goyles. Grymric also liked to talk about the world around him, especially the widespread plant life and its seemingly endless "varieties."

"Shall I chase them off for you?" Goodle asked. He snorted at the birds, making them hop. They returned a few squawking complaints, but descended as a flock on the carcass again. All except one, Ren noticed. It was sitting on a jut of bare rock, a little way separate from the others. It was huddled up and staring at the cave as though it wished it could be out of the damp gray air.

"Leave the caar—crows where they are," said Ren. "He likes to chase them if they come too close." He closed a hand around a stig on Gariffred's head and waggled it. "Gabrial says it's good training for him, for when he'll need to hunt for himself. You can come out of the rain, if you like."

And so Goodle entered the cave and for a while all was well. Gayl, the female wearling, soon joined them. Goodle relaxed onto his haunches and made i:mages of twinkling stars for the wearlings, encouraging Ren's attempts to do the same.

Then a second visitor arrived.

This was a tall and gangly green roamer, probably some ten years older than Goodle. He announced himself as Gannet. He came with what he said was an urgent message: Ren was needed at the Prime dragon's eyrie. When Ren asked why, Gannet said he didn't know, except he was to pass on the message that Gabrial had requested Ren's presence.

Ren looked across the hills. Somewhere beyond them were his mother and the rest of the Kaal tribe, broken by grief and war and bitterness. Twice Ren had asked to be allowed to leave the mountains, even once suggesting that Gabrial fly him back to the settlement to demonstrate the trust between the two species. Both times Prime Grynt had refused. Perhaps, at last, the moment had come: the chance to go home and heal so many scars.

"You should go—quickly," Goodle advised him. "Prime Grynt is not the most patient of dragons. I will amuse the wearlings until you return."

Gannet knelt and spread a wing low to the ground. Ren was immediately persuaded. A flight on a dragon's back was exhilarating. He hugged both wearlings and told them he would not be away for long. To Goodle, he said, "Guard them with your life." He glanced at Gariffred one last time, then climbed onto Gannet and was lifted away.

They had barely crested the hills when Ren knew it was a trap.

Two Veng closed in, one on either side of the startled roamer.

"Set the boy down," one ordered.

Gannet bravely flew on. "My orders were to deliver the boy to Prime Grynt's eyrie."

"Your orders have changed," said the Veng.

"Gannet, take me back to the cave!" Ren screamed.

But the words had barely left his mouth when he felt himself snatched off Gannet's back.

The Veng banked swiftly to the right and was gone.

As the ground sped by beneath them, Ren could do

nothing but tend his anger. But as the Veng pitched sideways again, Ren felt an awareness in his mind that pressed him to look down and not be afraid. *Watch. Remember*, a voice seemed to say. Her voice. The mother of the wearlings. Grystina. She was often in his mind at moments of danger, trying to encourage him to use his gifts and *think* like a dragon. He felt the aching strain behind his eyes as they tried to move like her eyes would, to flick back and forth, push and retract, to focus on the detail flashing by: the position of the trees, their size, their number; any glints of water, no matter how small; unusual deflections in the mountainsides or significant shading changes in the rock; where the snow lay, where it didn't. All of this she encouraged him to store. Especially so when the Veng changed course and started its swift descent to the ground. They came down over what looked like a quarry, a place dug and burned and scraped and worked, where stones as big as Ren's head and bigger had been tossed aside in giant heaps. A dark spot loomed up. A hole among the rocks with no visible floor. Into this pit the Veng dropped Ren.

He landed with a crunching thud. A trickle of wetness spread across his face and he feared, wrongly, that his head had split open. With a sigh of pain, he rolled onto his back and looked at the portal of light above. The Veng poked its slender nose in, a snarling silhouette against a grim backdrop of overcast sky. There must have been half a spiker's height

between them. Though it pained him to the edge of scream-
ing, Ren raised an arm and pointed a finger. "You're dead," he
said dizzily, careful to speak in Hom, not dragontongue.

The Veng snorted and pulled its head back.

The hole that defined the prison walls blurred. The sky
thickened to a darkening ball. "Dead," Ren muttered again.

And passed out.

11

Gabrial flew home at full battle speed. Normally, he approached his cave directly, calling across the deep green valley so the wearlings might see him from some distance away. Sometimes he performed a roll to excite the youngsters and show them what they would be capable of one day. On this occasion, there was no such exhibition. He swept in over the ridge of the hills, keeping tight to the sharp, precipitous slopes as he arrowed his wings and thundered down. He closed in on the cave at considerable velocity, planning to surprise any guards that Gallen might have posted. Sure enough, the heat of an adult dragon was spilling out over the patchy grass as Gabrial approached with his thermal sensors engaged. He raised his stigs and checked his fire sacs. Full. Ready for battle. Then he swooped. He let out a warning cry and created a rolling canopy of fire over the topmost edge of the cave. The burst would alarm the wearlings, but it would also disturb the adult dragon and make it take to the sky—which it did (along with a group of startled crows). Much to Gabrial's surprise, however, the color of the dragon that flapped into the daylight was not bright green but his own color: blue. His roar of anger was immediately commuted to a muddled hurr as he realized the dragon he'd disturbed was Goodle.

Goodle paddled the air, landing awkwardly on a jag of stone a few wingbeats away. In the cave, both wearlings were squealing in terror. Gayl was turning frightened circles with her wings outstretched, clouting her brother on every circuit. Gariffred was hissing at the sudden intrusion and had not yet recognized the aggressor as his father. A quick *hrrr!* from Gabrial settled both youngsters, though Gayl continued to mew quietly.

"Gabrial? What are you *doing*?" said Goodle, scrabbling for a foothold and a wisp of understanding. They knew each other reasonably well. There had never been a cross word between them before.

"I could ask the same of you," Gabrial hissed, emptying the last of the air in his throat. The resulting snort sent a ball of fire flying Goodle's way. He ducked to avoid it, tenting his wings to maintain balance.

"I'm following orders," Goodle said, his ear stigs bristling. "I was sent here by Gallen and told to sit with the wearlings until you or Grendel returned. I was making i:mages for them. Why are you flaming me? What have I done?"

"Where's Ren?"

Goodle's foot slipped again on the rock, which fractured

as he tried to adjust his position. He sighed and jumped off it, landing with a splat on the rain-sodden hillside. From a combat point of view, a terrible maneuver. But combat was never in Goodle's mind. At least down here he could fold his wings and get a better purchase. "With you, I thought. Not long after I arrived, one of the roamers came and said the boy was needed at Prime Grynt's settle. Ren climbed onto his back and they left. That's all I know."

"Which roamer?"

"Gannet. Why? What's going on?"

Grendel swept in and landed effortlessly at Gabrial's side. She scented the fire in the air and was relieved to see that the two weren't tearing into each other. She called the wearlings, who came scrambling to her.

"I'm going to leave now," Goodle said, though it was more a hopeful request than a statement. He nodded at Grendel and backed away warily.

Gabrial let him fly.

"What's happening?" asked Grendel. "What was Goodle doing here?"

Gabrial retracted his claws. "He was a decoy, to keep Ren calm before they took him. Grynt was clever. He didn't use the Veng to seize Ren from the cave, though they must be involved if Grynt's holding Ren somewhere. They sent a roamer called Gannet with a false message. Do you know him?"

She shook her head.

Gabrial muscled his shoulders. "Look after these two. I have to go."

"Where?"

"To hunt down Gannet and find Ren, of course."

"Gabrial, no." She put herself in front of him.

"Tada," pined Gayl, wrapping her tail around one of his legs, a favorite trick to gain his attention.

"You can't leave," said Grendel, using her isoscele to stroke Gayl gently. "For one thing, you don't know where to look. And if you start asking questions or flaming innocent roamers, there's going to be trouble. Serious trouble. The kind we could do without before the Naming."

"But—?"

"You're right: Grynt *was* clever. If he'd done this any other way, the hills would be running green with blood." She funneled two wisps of smoke from her nostrils. "We could have been renegades by sunset."

"Grendel—"

"Listen to me," she said, speaking over him again. "I feel for Ren just as much as you do. But our duty is to rear these two and see them Named. We are dragon, Gabrial, before all else. Don't ever forget that."

As if to make Gabrial's tension worse, just then none other than Veng Commander Gallen landed outside the cave.

Gabrial's stigs, which were still half upright, immediately flicked into their full position. His claws zinged out of their protective sockets.

"Gabrial?" Grendel hissed in alarm. She ushered both wearlings into the shadows.

But Gabrial was pushing forward already. "You," he snarled. "How do you dare to show yourself here when—?"

"Freeze your fire," Gallen snorted tiredly, making no attempt to defend himself or give off any sign of impending conflict. "I haven't come to make further orphans of your wearlings. Trust me, it would be a short battle if I had." He flicked out the rows of sharpened spikes common only to a Veng tail.

Gabrial allowed himself a glance at them. Gallen had been badly injured in the fighting and had almost lost his isoscele. But that hardened triangular scale, which the Veng kept honed with their blistering fire, had repaired itself remarkably quickly. Gallen twisted it to make the point.

"I am the bearer of good news," he said. "How do you fare in this poky little hole?"

"Not well," Grendel said truthfully. The cave was small for five of them. Gabrial usually slept outside, with Ren curled up to him on the coldest nights.

"Then you'll be pleased to know that your thoughtful Prime has asked me to assign a new home to you."

"Where?" said Gabrial, deeply suspicious of Gallen's motives. Nothing came from the Veng without a price.

"A natural opening on the slopes of Mount Vargos. It was offered first to Elder Gossana, but she prefers the sun on her wings in the evening; this eyrie faces the wrong way for that."

"Eyrie?" asked Grendel. A large cave, then. Her eye ridges lifted.

"No," said Gabrial right away.

"No? What do you mean 'no'?" argued Grendel.

"There's only one vacant eyrie on Vargos and we're not going there. Gossana didn't refuse it because of the sun. He's talking about Givnay's settle."

"Oh," said Grendel. Now she appreciated Gabrial's hesitation. Givnay was a disgraced Elder who had died in the conflict with the goyles. The unnerving nature of his death, coupled with his treacherous actions while alive, had left an air of superstition hanging over the colony. His cave had been avoided ever since.

"Hear me out," said Gallen, casually drumming his claws on a rock. "I'm sure Gabrial remembers his mentor, per Grogan."

"Of course I do," said Gabrial. "What's your point?" Per Grogan was another casualty of the battles. He had taught Gabrial much about the history of dragons and stood beside him when he'd fought to be a father to the wearlings.

"We have his heart."

"What?" said Grendel, tilting her head. She wondered if she'd heard the Veng commander correctly.

"You sound surprised," he said, as if she shouldn't be. "You witnessed Grogan's end. You know what happens when a dragon dies the way he did. His primary heart turned to stone."

"But it happened at the mines," she murmured, reliving that awful moment when she'd seen per Grogan destroyed in Veng flames. "There was a heavy rockfall. Surely the heart was buried?"

"It was recovered on Givnay's orders. It was in his keeping before he died."

Gabrial's head came up. "You mean it's in the cave? Grogan's heart is *in* that eyrie?"

"It is," said Gallen, casually examining his secondary claws. "And Prime Grynt wants it guarded. What better candidate could there be than you? You won't be assigned any roaming duties until the wearlings are independent, and given your natural affinity for Grogan—"

"No," said Grendel, shuffling back a little. "You can't expect us to put *wearlings* close to something like that."

To her surprise, Gabrial thought otherwise. "We'll do it," he said quietly.

"*What?* Gabrial, no."

"This is Grogan," he said. "He was my father's friend and ally. He's almost kin to me, Grendel."

"Then it's settled," said Gallen, before Grendel could interject again. "I'm sure you'll find the eyrie very comfortable. Now, if you'd like to pick up the wearlings and follow me, I'll escort you there myself . . ."

12

"All the slopes you can see," said Garret, "from that pale gray crag to the point where the snow trails wind down into the valley floor, that's where we found the fhosforent. A few areas were mapped to either side, but the main body of the ore is concentrated here."

De:allus Garodor breathed in through his nostrils, rocking with the wind as it curled in blustery arcs around him. He was sitting, wings folded, alongside the mapping dragon, on a peak directly opposite the mining area. He had asked to see the general layout of the mine, but even to his extraordinary eyes there was nothing remarkable about these hills. A run of dull bluffs that barely qualified as mountains. Rocky expanses like this existed all over the southern pole of Ki:mera. "How do you think the first Wearle found it?"

"Under moonlight you can sometimes see a seam twinkling, but I think it more likely they chanced on it. The lower slopes are strewn with a lot of loose chippings. They would have been looking for an easy supply of grit."

"And the quarry area?"

"Just over that peak." Garret nodded at a blunted spike. "It's not a natural pit. We flamed out what we thought was a good location according to the i:mages I mapped. I can take you to it, but I warn you, there is a strange auma about it. A dragon called Grogan died there. Grogan was sent mad by the fhosforent. Some of the roamers believe his spirit haunts the place because his heart . . . well, I'm sure you know about the heart. Most dragons were reluctant to go near the quarry even before the Prime closed the mine. I haven't been there since. Shall we go?"

"No, that won't be necessary," Garodor said, glancing into the sky where a crow was circling. "But I do need a sample of the ore. Can you show me a likely seam?"

"Yes, of course." Garret folded down his wings. "I mapped all the seams from this side of the range into a single i:mage. You may find it helpful to study it."

As Garret closed his eyes to concentrate his thoughts, a floating i:mage began to form in the space between himself and De:allus Garodor. It showed the profile of the mountains in single green lines, with every silhouetted slant drawn exactly to scale. Between the lines were pale pink patches, all of them annotated in dragon numerals.

Garodor nodded in admiration. Garret was good at his job. "The pink represents the fhosforent caches?"

"Yes. As you can see, most are quite small. We took samples of ore from every part of this range, but concentrated our efforts on seams seven and fifteen."

"Is it possible to see how deep they go?"

"Certainly." Garret rotated the i:mage slightly, bringing an extra dimension to it. He rocked it back and forth so that Garodor could get a general impression of how much body there was to each seam.

"They're quite shallow," he said. "That surprises me."

"Initially, the pick of the seams ran deeper," said Garret, lifting one foot to stretch his claws. "The ore seemed almost to pool below the surface, as if hiding itself from the glare of the sun. It took time to dig those out, and we realized in doing so how fragile the fhosforent is—it degenerates quickly, almost as soon as it's exposed to air. So we concentrated latterly on shallower seams that were easier to find and quicker to work. Your predecessor, De:allus Graymere, used to say the ore was alive, it bedded so strangely into the rock. A jest, of course. He was a fine dragon with a brilliant mind. One of the cleverest I ever met. With due respect to you, his death was such a blow to the Wearle."

"I can i:magine," said Garodor. He dipped his eyes for a moment, as if to catch sight of some passing thought. A quiet *ark!* brought him slowly out of his reverie. The circling crow had been joined by another. "What else did Graymere say about the seams?"

"That they looked like some kind of spill."

"Spill?" Garodor glanced at the i:mage again. It was fading as Garret's concentration weakened.

"I know. It sounds ludicrous," the mapper sighed. "But I understand why he would describe it so. The seams are at their richest near the tops of the mountains. They trail down and peter out into random spots as you drop. In Graymere's own words, it looks like the fhosforent was splashed on the mountainsides from above and trickled down them. And there's another interesting anomaly: the terrain you see here, the basic composition of the rock bed, is no different from many other regions we've mapped, yet this is the only place we've found the fhosforent. Strange."

Strange indeed, thought Garodor. "All right, take me to it."

"This way," said Garret. He banked left as he launched, soaring across the valley in a minimum of wingbeats.

They landed together on a small area of scree about a third of the way up from the valley floor. There was a curious air of abandonment about the place. Snow had gathered in pockets between the stones and all the tufts of vegetation looked twisted and unnatural, as though they had been poisoned or neglected of nutrients. Garodor could see lengthy furrows in the underlying bedrock where claws had earnestly gouged through the surface. He looked at his own near-perfect talons and wondered how much physical damage the fhosforent had caused before it got into any dragon's nervous system.

"My apologies for the looseness of the ground," said Garret, sending chippings shooting down the slope as he scrambled for a better hold. "Be careful, De:allus. Some of the stones are sharp. Healer Grymric spent much of his time mending the soles of feet as well as aiding the repair of claws. I've brought you here because the fhosforent lies nearer the surface in places that have suffered the most thermal stress. Where water runs through joints in the rock it freezes and expands, creating fresh cracks that are easier to work. Try scraping there." He nodded at a likely-looking rut.

Garodor stepped sideways until his right foot was over the crack. He extended a talon and carefully dug into the grit at the base of the hole. Before long, something pink glinted back. He immediately withdrew his foot, instinctively closing the claws into a fist.

"You've found some?"

"A few particles, yes."

Garodor went in again, slowly exposing a larger scratch, a line wide enough to scan with his yellow eyes.

Garret looked on in admiration. De:allus dragons possessed the ability to analyze organic substances just by looking at or tasting them. The most powerful of their class were even rumored to be able to evaluate the fine structure of compounds by setting their optical triggers to *burn*. Garret had watched De:allus Graymere attempt it soon after fhosforent had been discovered. He remembered that Graymere had been puzzled by the crystals, and how curious (and mildly suspicious) the young De:allus had been about the ore's capacity to increase the strength of a dragon's flame.

Garodor, at this point, seemed no wiser. He pulled away, tightening his eye ridges until they creaked. He then hooked his smallest talon under the fhosforent and scraped a small amount of it out of the erth. He extended his tongue and tasted it. At the same time, Garret looked up, distracted by the circling crows. There were four now, flying dangerously close, as if they wanted to share in the discovery.

Without warning, Garodor flashed his tail upward and dug his isoscele into one of the birds, skewering it straight through the chest. The other three screeched and flapped away in terror. Even Garret jumped. It was rare to see a De:allus dragon carry out such an act of violence. Garodor brought his tail down slowly, his prey still on the end of it. The crow twitched and fell limp, its eyes open, its wings flapping loose.

"You're hungry?" asked Garret.

Garodor turned the bird as if he was considering which way to best put it into his mouth. "No. It was an experiment of sorts. What do you know about the properties of fhosforent?"

Garret lifted his wings at the shoulder. He winced as Garodor thumped the crow's body against a rock to make the bird bleed. "That it increases the strength and durability of our flame—and if taken in excess, turns us into goyles." *Is that about to happen to Garodor?* he wondered. The De:allus had been acting a little strangely since he'd sampled the pink.

"I think it's more than that," said Garodor. He lifted the crow again, squeezing it into a curl of his tail. Blood spouted freely from its wound. "In the report I received from Prime Grynt, the Hom boy, Ren, claimed he'd been told by Elder Givnay that the fhosforent could be used to enhance all of a dragon's natural skills—that would include the ability to strike at speed. I'm too old and too slow to spear anything as agile as a crow. The fhosforent did that."

"And this?" said Garret, stretching his neck to get a better look as Garodor dripped the crow's blood into the seam. The pink ore fizzed and a small white wisp rose out of the rocks.

"Another experiment. I've analyzed the seam as best I can. I've reached a conclusion about it, but the results are stretching the boundaries of my intelligence."

The white wisp suddenly combusted into flame. "What happened?" said Garodor. "What have you discovered?"

"That fhosforent is not a naturally occurring compound. It's a crystalline form of a substance that runs through the veins of us all. For some reason I don't fully comprehend, it reacts powerfully when it engages the same substance from another host."

"So it's blood?" said Garret.

"Dried blood," the De:allus corrected him, "desiccated for centuries."

"In this amount? Where from?"

"I don't know," said Garodor. "But you will say nothing of what you've seen today, Garret. Do you understand?"

Garret nodded. "You can trust me, De:allus."

Garodor bent down and blew out the flame. "I know," he said. "Now, let's get out of here."

13

The eyrie *was* comfortable. Grendel couldn't deny that. The main cavern, despite the cluster of ice spikes hanging from its roof, was four times the size of their previous cave and had a scopey chamber off to one side. The chamber was dark and ran with moisture. A sheen of mosses coated its walls. Bats trilled and shuffled in its niches. Not ideal conditions for growing dragons, but in its favor, the chamber was out of the wind and offered better shelter than the wearlings had been used to. Looking farther around, Grendel was also pleased to see a number of natural steps and ledges, perfect for the wearlings to fly between and perch upon. What pleased her less was a fleeting thought about Ren and where he would be sleeping tonight. She told herself she must put such worries behind her. Ren was in the custody of the Elders. From now on this would be . . . a normal dragon family. It was going to be difficult explaining it to Gariffred, but for the moment, at least, the drake was happy. Grendel looked up to see him squabbling with his sister over who should have the highest ledge, even though neither had the wingpower to reach it. She quashed the tiff with a motherly *hrrr!* then led them away to explore an assortment of warrens and tunnels that wormed back into the body of the mountain, leaving Gabrial to speak alone with the Veng commander, Gallen.

"What exactly am I supposed to do with it, Gallen?"

Grogan's heart was resting on a stone pillar, nearer the front of the cave than Gabrial would have liked, within plain sight of anything that flew by. It was larger than he'd expected, almost the size of his foot when closed. The only scent coming off it was the flat spoor of stone. No hint of the devastating burning that had destroyed Grogan and caused the heart to harden. It made Gabrial uneasy just to look at the thing, for those muscular convolutions, now set rigid, had once flexed and pumped and kept alive one of the most dependable dragons he'd ever known. A mentor, as Gallen had put it. A true friend to Gabrial, and his father before him.

"You guard it—with your life, if necessary," Gallen said.

"Guard it from what?"

"From anything that tries to steal it, of course."

Gabrial squinted at the bright blue sky. The sweeping profiles of the scarred gray mountains stretched back in layer upon layer of rock, blurring into the pale horizon. The snow-draped gradients were beautiful to look at, but Elder Givnay hadn't chosen this place for its view. The cave was part of a vast, impenetrable stronghold. It had to be one of the most secure eyries in the domayne. *Who could steal a dragon's heart from here?* "The cave is too high for the Hom to climb," he said. "And if they were foolish enough to try, we'd see them long before they reached this ridge."

Gallen twisted his snout. "We thought the Hom couldn't take a wearling from under the wings of a queen, but they did. Don't leave this . . . relic unattended. That's an order."

"Gallen, wait."

The Veng grizzled in annoyance. "What?"

"I have to—leave it unattended. I have to be at the Naming later today. You too. The whole Wearle has to be there."

Gallen shook his head. "I will be in official attendance, but the Veng are exempt from ceremonial tedium if there are possible security risks elsewhere. And we can co-opt others if the need is great enough. A capable roamer has been watching this place ever since it's been empty. I'll reassign it to that duty while you're away making your pretty speech."

Oh, yes. Gabrial had forgotten about that. At the Naming, he would be expected to spread his wings and talk of noble deeds and his merit as a parent, a prospect that left him numb with nerves. He turned his thoughts back to the heart. "Can't we bury it? Here, in the eyrie? I could push it deep into one of the tunnels?"

"No."

"But what if the wearlings knock it off and break it?"

Gallen growled impatiently. "They could kick it down the mountain and it wouldn't crack. You know as well as I do that opening a dragon heart is impossible. Didn't Grogan teach you that? There are five just like it on Ki:mera. Not even that puffed-up De:allus has been able to find his way into one."

"So why guard it?"

"Because it stops the superstitious types panicking."

"And if it were to be opened? If Grogan's auma was freed?"

Gallen backed up toward the cave mouth. "You think too much. Just guard it."

And he flew.

Barely moments later, Grendel shuffled up to Gabrial's side. "So this is it," she said, sniffing at the heart. She ran the tip of her isoscele down it, tracing the path of the largest vein. "I suppose there could be worse vocations. You have to admit, it's a small price to pay for such a wonderful settle." She moved to the very lip of the cave, stretching her neck to feel the breeze.

"Grendel?"

"Hmm?"

"Do you believe in the legend of the black dragon?"

"No," she said. "Come and stand with me." She filled her lungs and let the air trickle sweetly through her spiracles. "It's so fresh up here."

"When I was a wearling, my father used to tell me scary stories about how Graven would return one day, looking for a heart just like—"

"Gabrial." She cut him dead. "Do I need to remind you why we're here? These wearlings you're supposed to be parenting both had traumatic starts to their lives. I don't want you making things worse by muttering to me about Graven, the Tywyll, a black dragon, the fallen son of Godith, or whatever else you want to call it. Gayl and Gariffred are not to hear talk like that in this eyrie, or ever have cause to believe that a black dragon could exist. Are we clear about that?"

"But?"

"*Gabrial . . . ?*" A tiny growl left her throat.

"All right. If you say so."

"I do. Now, come and stand with me and look at this amazing sky."

Gabrial blew a short puff of smoke. He had often heard it said that brooding females lost any trace of meekness at the first sound of an egg hatching, but he hadn't quite expected such bossiness from Grendel. She was only fostering these young, after all. All the same, he bowed to her wishes and came to the cave mouth.

"We'll need to be careful here." He looked at the drop to the next level down. In the old cave, the wearlings had been allowed to roam freely onto the hillside. One slip here and they could fall to their deaths. Both were learning the benefit of wings, but a drop of this height could make a young dragon panic and put it into a challenging spin. He looked over his shoulder for the wearlings. "Where are they?"

"Playing in the tunnels. Don't worry, I've sounded every shaft; they don't go terribly deep. The worst Gariffred can do is get stuck. These mountains are incredible. We could settle here, Gabrial. Have more wearlings—of our own."

Gabrial looked out across the peaks, remembering his many flights patrolling the scorch line. "The Hom might have something to say about that. When do you think we should tell Gariffred—about Ren?"

"Visitor," Grendel said suddenly, spotting the arc of a gliding dragon.

Gabrial raised himself to full alertness, but relaxed when he recognized who the caller was.

"Grymric," Grendel called out warmly, as the healing dragon of the Wearle set down.

"Grendel. Gabrial." He nodded at them both. "Wonderful morning, isn't it?"

Grymric's glowing appreciation of the Erth weather seemed a slight contradiction to Gabrial. An anxious look was always resident in the healing dragon's eyes, despite the herbs he took to improve his well-being. He folded down a pair of light green wings that were prematurely weathered on their undersides.

"Yes, very pleasing," Grendel said. "I'll call the wearlings. Grymric's here to check them, Gabrial."

"A small tradition, before their proud moment," said the healer. "Are you looking forward to the Naming?"

"I'm not sure," said Gabrial. He glanced over his shoulder to see if Grendel could hear him. "It's going to be strange, Naming another dragon's young—especially one as controversial as Gariffred."

"You've come through worse," Grymric reassured him. "And whatever you think of Grynt, he supports you. These wearlings are special, Gabrial. The first true Erth dragons. And this is a fine, fine home for them. How do you like it up here?"

"It would be better without that." Gabrial nodded at the heart.

"Ah, yes." Grymric tightened his jaw. "A sad reminder of a loyal per. You're tasked with guarding it?"

"Orders from Gallen, to keep me quiet. I suppose you heard about Ren?"

Grymric glanced into the cave. "He's not with you?"

"No." Gabrial told him the story.

The healer huffed and puffed at every line. "It's hard on you and the boy, but I can understand Grynt's concerns. No species has ever crossed blood with us before. He had to report it. Any Prime would have done the same. But De:allus

Garodor is highly thought of. He'll treat Ren fairly, I'm sure. How's Gariffred taking it?"

"He doesn't know yet. I'm not sure what to tell him."

Grymric hurred in his throat. "Perhaps you could say that Ren needed to go back to the Hom for a while."

Gabrial shook his head. "He'll know it's a lie. They're close, Grymric. Ren is developing a strong telepathic bond with the drake."

"Here they are," said Grendel, approaching. She proudly presented the young ones to Grymric.

"Ah, excellent, excellent," Grymric said. "Such wonderful colors the Astrian bloodline produces." Gayl was a deep purple hue throughout, but it was already possible to see some subtle variations of that tone running right back to her emerging isoscele, where, unusually, there was a splash of white. Gariffred was equally striking. He was a typical, rangy drake. Blue was his dominant color, though he showed his sister's purple in his wings and at the very whip of his tail. Both wearlings did their best to bow politely to the senior dragon among them.

"Both looking so much happier," chirruped Grymric. "And that wing is completely healed, by the look of it."

Gabrial glanced at the place where, seven days ago, an arrow had ripped through Gariffred's wing, pinning him to a tree. The drake had recovered well from the wound. The wing was fully flexible again and he no longer dragged it when he walked.

Grymric turned the youngsters into the light. "Jaws wide open, please. Excellent. Excellent. And . . . roar for me."

What came out of the wearlings' mouths were two of the most incompetent roars Gabrial had ever heard, but he supposed he'd been no better at their age. A moment later, he had cause to demonstrate how a roar *ought* to sound when a crow settled on a spur of the cave mouth. One growl sent it squawking away.

"Crows again?" said Grendel.

"Just a scavenger looking for scraps, I suppose."

Grendel twisted her snout, making her golden braids twinkle from her nostrils to her ears. "Surely we're out of their range? I don't remember Givnay being troubled by crows?"

"Givnay would have curdled their brains and sucked the juice out through their nostrils. It's no surprise they avoided him. I'll kill the next one that comes and feed it to Gariffred. Which reminds me, I should hunt."

"Not now," she said. "They're going to be restless after the Naming. They'll sleep better tonight if we let them feed later. Bring them something tough they need to rake their claws through. Not too much fur."

"Yes, that's very . . . beguiling." Grymric's voice rose softly in the background.

Grendel turned to see. "Oh, look at that. Grymric's got them making i:mages."

Gabrial tightened his eye ridges a little. "Since when was making i:mages part of a fitness check?"

"Ask him yourself. All well, Grymric?"

"Oh, yes," he replied, coming over. "Good strong jaws. Keen eyes. Primary scales beginning to form. Gayl's even showing her first fang. Physically, they're perfect."

"But?" said Gabrial, sensing one coming.

Grymric dipped his head to whisper. "Well, it's Gariffred."

"What's wrong with him?" asked Grendel, immediately alarmed.

"Nothing," Grymric urged her. "Seriously, Grendel, there's no cause for alarm. He's just a little . . . unusual for his age."

"Unusual?" Gabrial repeated flatly.

Grymric nodded. "He's just made the most extraordinary i:mage. I think it was an attempt at the Erth moon."

Grendel glanced back at the drake. Gariffred had tired of making i:mages and had found a small pile of stones to play with. "There's nothing unusual about that," she said. "I used to i:mage Ki:meran moons. The Erth moon is dull in comparison, quite easy to produce."

"Not at his age," Gabrial said. "Isn't that what you're getting at, Grymric?"

"Partly, yes. A solid white circle isn't beyond a gifted young dragon. But this is what Gariffred constructed . . ."

In the space between them, Grymric reproduced a floating picture of what looked, roughly, like a quarter moon. The outer edges of the "moon" were very haphazard, almost jagged in places. And in the black cutaway part (that Gabrial assumed to be the night sky), there was a speck of yellow. "I'd say that was quite advanced," said Grymric. "I wasn't making shapes like that until I was old enough to hunt for myself."

The i:mage popped.

"I think it's just a messy blob," said Grendel, "the product of an untrained mind. Besides, he's never seen that phase of the moon. So how could he i:mage it?"

"Yes. Good point," Grymric said.

"What was the yellow speck?" asked Gabrial.

"I don't know. That puzzled me as well. I asked him to explain it, but he's still too young to form a comprehensible answer."

"What's he doing now?" Grendel muttered.

They all looked at Gariffred, who was selecting certain stones from his pile and arranging them in a line on the cave floor.

"Now, that's very curious as well," said Grymric. "I think he's putting them in order of size."

They watched Gariffred pick up a stone and plonk it down in a different position.

"Strange," said Grendel. "No wearling I know has ever been taught to do that." She barked a quick warning at the drake, who had just snapped at his sister for sweeping one of the stones out of line with her tail.

"Maybe there's De:allus in his bloodline," said Grymric.

"Or it's something he's learned from Ren," said Gabrial.

"That *would* be extraordinary," Grymric agreed. "A wearling adopting the behavioral patterns of another species. The new De:allus will certainly want to monitor that."

Or stamp it out completely, Gabrial thought.

"It's nearly time," said Grendel. She called the wearlings to her.

"I should leave you to prepare," Grymric said. "Good luck. Enjoy it. I'll see you all at Skytouch, shortly."

He nodded at Gabrial, opened his wings, and flew, almost colliding with the arriving guard that Gallen had remembered to post at the cave.

"Time for you two to join the Wearle," said Grendel as the youngsters reared up to touch her snout with theirs. She stroked Gayl gently and picked her up between her teeth.

"Rrren?" said Gariffred.

Gabrial looked over him at the guard. He had taken up position close to the heart and didn't look in any mood to communicate.

"Ren will be here soon," Gabrial said quietly. A lie, of course, but he could think of nothing better in the circumstances. And with a last puzzled look at the line of stones, he picked up the drake and flew him out of the eyrie.

14

Not since the death of Grystina and the inquest that followed had Gabrial seen so many of the Wearle together at once. The dragons were assembled like colored stars on the slopes that fed into the great ice lake, perched wherever they could find a hold. On the three stone pillars that rose like straight fangs out of the lake sat Gossana, Prime Grynt, and De:allus Garodor. Gallen was also in attendance, a bright glint of green off to Gabrial's right, the only member of the Veng present. In a strange imitation of the last time he'd been there, falsely accused then of treason, Gabrial stood on the pebbled shore opposite the pillars, this time with Grendel proudly by his side and the two restless wearlings in front of them.

As the sun shined down on Skytouch, Grynt bellowed, "Dragons, you are gathered here in the eyes of Godith to see two wearlings Named today. You all know of the tragic incidents that brought Gabrial and Grendel together. But let us not dwell on the events of the past. We are here to celebrate new life, new dragons, the growth of the Wearle!"

Hrrr!

A roar of approval boomed through the air, almost

bringing down a drop of rain. Gayl shied away from the blare and pawed at Grendel to hide her. Grendel soothed her with gentle whispers and nudged her around to face the Elders again. Gossana looked on disapprovingly at what she clearly saw as a show of weakness.

Gabrial, despite his various concerns, could not help but feel proud of this moment. He remembered the confusion he'd felt at his own Naming and how his father had extended a wing to him. He did the same now to Gariffred. The drake hurred in appreciation. Unlike Gayl, he seemed excited by the noise rather than overwhelmed by the occasion.

"In accordance with our traditions," Grynt cried, "I have instructed the mother of the young, in this case the fostering mother, Grendel, to share her names for the young with me. I now submit these names for the Wearle's approval. The wearmyss, a purple born of the Astrian line, shall be called GAYL. If any dragon has reason to contest this name, let them speak now."

A firm silence settled over the lake. Grynt let it hold for three heartbeats, then cried, "Accepted!"

Another huge roar tumbled down the slopes.

"And now we present the drake."

Gabrial felt his claws sinking into the pebbles. This was the crucial moment. There were dragons here whose ancestors had fought in lineage wars against Gariffred the Elder.

Anyone deeply connected to their history might not be willing to forgive the deaths of so many dueling dragons back then.

Grynt's voice boomed across the lake. "He, the drake, is also descended from the Astrian line. He shall be called GARIFFRED. If any dragon has reason to contest *this* name, let them speak now."

An uneasy silence settled. The wind jostled for position, tugging at Gabrial's bristling ear nodes. He had his aural sensors fully stretched and thought he could hear fire burning in the throats of some dragons. It would need only one to voice its disapproval, and others might follow. He noticed Gallen peering around, waiting to act on any possible trouble. The big yellow eyes of De:allus Garodor were also panning the slopes.

One beat slid past. Two. Three.

Nothing. Gabrial sighed with relief.

Grynt opened his jaws to make the announcement.

But no word came out. The whole ritual was suddenly interrupted by a piercing cry from a dragon in the air. A single Veng was approaching, shrieking an alarm that could not keep pace with the speed of its descent.

"What's happening?" said Grendel, as voices began to respond to the alarm. She gathered Gayl beneath her, all the while looking around for the Veng. "Is it attacking us? Gabrial?"

Gabrial was moving fast toward Gariffred. In the confusion, the drake had broken away from his parents and was flapping around a little farther down the shoreline, echoing the alarm call, as young dragons were inclined to do.

"Quiet that thing!" Gossana rapped.

A somewhat pointless demand; the whole Wearle was rumbling now.

The Veng made an untidy landing and began to give a hurried report to Gallen.

"Accept him," said Gabrial, trying to catch Grynt's gaze, but all the while twisting to watch the Veng. "Prime, accept Gariffred into the Wearle."

But Grynt's attention was all on Gallen. The Veng commander swooped toward the pillars, landing on a patch of ice that cracked beneath his weight. "Enemy," he growled. "Beyond the scorch line."

"What is it?" asked Grynt, rising up. The armored scales on his breast clattered into their battle positions.

"Dark vapor," Gallen said.

"Vapor?" Gabrial heard the second part. He stepped beyond Gariffred to better hear the rest . . . *Dead, in a cave,* he managed to pick up. *Hom . . .*

Without hesitation, Grynt barked the general command to fly. The colony rose as a flock, their shadows flickering over the ice.

"Gabrial, what's happening?" Grendel called anxiously.

He was still stepping away from her, creeping nearer to Grynt. He heard the Prime say, "Take whatever Veng you have and ten good roamers. Circle the area. Send a message back to me as soon as you know more."

With that, Gallen was in the air.

"I should go with them," De:allus Garodor said.

Grynt nodded. "I want to know how long it's been dead and by what means."

The De:allus spread his wings with a powerful *whup*. And he departed too.

"Fly to my eyrie," Grynt said to Gossana. "I will join you there shortly."

Gossana took off without hesitation, leaving a mystified Gabrial to ask, "What's happening? I heard Gallen say something about a vapor."

"Forget vapors," said Grynt. "Do your duty. Protect your young."

"If something is threatening us, I want to go with Gallen. I want to fight."

"Your orders are to go to your eyrie," snapped Grynt. "No, better still, gather the wearlings and follow me to mine."

"Why?"

The Prime dragon leaned closer. "So I know you won't disobey me."

With a sigh of frustration, Gabrial backed away. He explained the situation briefly to Grendel. Together they picked up Gayl and Gariffred and carried the wearlings on the short flight up to Grynt's eyrie.

Gossana voiced her objection the moment they landed. "What are they doing here?"

"I ordered it," said Grynt, touching down so smoothly he was barely out of breath.

Gossana gave a disgruntled huff. "I do not want to be tripping over wearlings if the goyles come again."

"Goyles?" Gabrial looked at Grendel and saw her shudder. "Gallen said vapor, not goyle. I don't understand."

"Neither do I," said Grynt. "So settle the wearlings and wait, like the rest of us."

"What about the Hom?"

Grynt sighed. "What about them?"

"Gallen said there were Hom involved."

"Not anymore."

"You mean some were killed?"

"If it were me, I'd burn them all," Gossana sniffed.

"Is that right? Hom were killed?" Gabrial pressed.

"I told you to settle your young," said Grynt, poking his isoscele in Gayl's direction. The young wearmyss was wailing in confusion. Gossana jumped back in disgust as the youngster nearly defecated on her foot.

"Bring Ren back," Gabrial said boldly. "If there's trouble with the Hom, let him talk to his tribe."

"Talk?" Grynt's fangs began to run with saliva. "There is a Veng lying dead in a cave beyond the scorch line—a dragon three roamers would struggle to subdue. Its eye has been pierced by a Hom weapon. What conclusion would you like me to draw from this, Gabrial? It's clear their aggression has not been tamed and their threat is growing. If this is the beginning of a Hom uprising, then Elder Gossana is right: We will respond—with ultimate force."

"And Ren? What happens to him?"

Grynt came closer, until they were almost snout to snout. "For the last time, protect your young. Do not speak to me about this again."

"Then let me speak about Gariffred instead. Is he accepted into the Wearle or not?"

Grynt glanced at the drake. The male wearling had settled in a bend of the cave. "The disruption will be seen as a sign that Godith did not bless his Naming."

"What? You can't believe that!"

Grynt closed on him again, fire licking around his nostrils. "You dare to stand here and tell me *you* know better than our Creator?"

"Gabrial." Grendel called to him softly. She'd been overhearing the conversation and was anxious to pull him back.

"The Naming will be reviewed," said Grynt. "That's all I can tell you. Now, rejoin your family, where you belong."

Gabrial snorted and turned away. "Come, Gabrial," Grendel said gently, using her tail to draw him past her. "Gariffred is anxious to show you his i:mages."

Gabrial settled in a sullen heap, allowing Gayl to snuggle into the space between his forelegs. "I feel so useless," he hissed. "Ren captured. More Hom dead. The Veng bringing back reports of vapors. Gariffred . . ." He didn't even want to go there. "What am I supposed to do, Grendel?"

"Nothing," she said, her eyes glowing kindly in the darkness. "Thankfully, the Wearle isn't yours to command." She licked Gariffred's head. "All we can do is wait as Grynt says. See what happens. Difficult, I know. Consider it a challenge." She yawned deeply. "I need to sleep. The wearlings are yours for now. Let them, not vapors, occupy your thoughts."

He watched her curl up and close her eyes. At rest, she was particularly beautiful, her face a flowing river of gold. By now, Gayl's head had also dropped, and small ripples of air were popping out of her nostrils with every slight rise and fall of her breast.

Gariffred, however, was wide awake and grizzling to himself.

Hrrr? Gabrial grunted. It was early days yet for any real

communication with the wearlings. A simple *hrrr* conveyed many useful meanings.

As could a "graark," which the drake replied with. His soft blue eye ridges came together in a gentle frown. Suddenly, a whole cluster of i:mages filled the air in front of him, lasting barely moments before they popped. They were fuzzy and half formed, with very little depth. The only shape Gabrial recognized was a tree, a tall one that Ren's kind called a spiker. Like the moon i:mage earlier in the day, this was also remarkably advanced for a dragon of Gariffred's age.

"Slower," said Gabrial, flicking a claw to set the tempo.

Raargh, went the drake, shaking his head as though it was important that the i:mages came at speed.

Out they came again.

This time, Gabrial set his optical triggers to record everything the drake was producing. A small organ at the back of a dragon's eye could store a set of i:mages far better than memory, and the sequence could then be replayed at will. To Gabrial's surprise, what he found in the i:mages was not one but a whole straggle of spiker trees, the sort of blur of greenery that a dragon might glimpse as it flew over woodland. But when had Gariffred ever done that? Of greater interest were two small bodies of water that showed up like glistening footsteps among a curving slew of hills. And finally an object

Gabrial recognized, an unmistakable outcrop of rocks that resembled the spread of a dragon's claws. It was just the sort of feature a dragon might use as a reference point if it was trying to map a location—or, more likely, remember a route . . .

Gabrial's second heart skipped a beat as a strange notion stirred in his head. He thought back to what De:allus Garodor had said about the Hom acquiring dragon powers. Dragons could communicate in thought if they needed to. Some, like Grystina, Gariffred's true mother, were also gifted in the art of *transference*. What if the bond between Ren and Gariffred was now so great that Ren was able to project pictures of his capture into the wearling's mind? What if that quarter moon i:mage, for instance, was not a moon at all, but a dragon's head partly blocking the entrance to a cave—or a pit?

"Can't you keep that thing quiet?"

Gabrial lifted his head to see Gossana glaring from across the cave. "He's hungry. I . . . need to go out and catch something for him—if the Prime has no objection?"

"Very well. Be swift," Grynt grunted.

Gabrial's heart thumped again. Being careful not to wake Grendel, he moved Gayl into her mother's warmth and rose to leave. Gariffred immediately protested, not wanting to be abandoned. Gabrial touched his snout to the drake and whispered, "Shush. Sleep. I'm going to look for Ren." This much

Gariffred did understand. He settled back, glancing warily at Grynt and Gossana.

And Gabrial was out of the cave and flying, not down into the lush green valleys where the rabbits and the goats were caught, but east of Mount Vargos, where lakes formed between the barren hills, and centuries of rain and ice and movement had combined to carve memorable shapes in the rocks. If the i:mages pouring out of Gariffred were true, this was where they had taken Ren, and this was where Gabrial was certain he would find him, in the place that had been the cause of so much tragedy: the abandoned fhosforent mines.

15

It was madness, of course; Gabrial realized that. A highly dangerous folly that could not only threaten his place within the Wearle but also the entire future of Grendel and the wearlings. The only excuse he could find to justify his actions was the grim reminder that if there were to be reprisals against the Hom, Ren would be the obvious target. Grynt was teetering on the brink of a difficult dilemma. The death of a Veng at the hands of the Kaal would give the Prime dragon all the reason he needed to wipe the boy out, along with others of his tribe. If Ren was not found and rescued, he was as good as dead.

But with the backbone of the mines still a distance away, time was very much a limiting factor. *Be swift*, Grynt had said. Any competent dragon could sweep the fields and bring back a small kill fit for a wearling before the heat had gotten into his wings. How long before Grynt grew suspicious and sent roamers out looking for his wayward blue? Gabrial might say he'd been distracted by the general rumpus and that he couldn't resist flying to one of the peaks to see if there was anything he might observe, but that would leave time for only one pass across the mines before he would be forced to turn and head back; a detailed search was out of the question.

And so he reeled in his initial impulse and set himself a more realistic ambition. He had visited the fhosforent mines before and knew the rough area Gariffred had i:maged. If he restricted himself to a controlled flyby, he could record better i:mages of the terrain and compare them to the patterns flowing out of the drake's head. Then, when a suitable opportunity arose or a critical commitment to rescue was called for, he would have a better idea of where to look for Ren.

But it didn't come to that.

As he approached the valley where the fhosforent had been mined, he saw a Veng positioned among the rocks just inside the quarry where Grogan had died. A guard. Of course. They had a guard on the spot. Gabrial didn't know whether to snort in triumph or grind his teeth in frustration. The sighting confirmed Ren was in this area, but if Gabrial flew too close and the guard reported his presence to Gallen, word would soon get back to the Prime. Then there would be difficult questions to answer.

So Gabrial recorded the guard's location and glided through an arc that would take him silently away from the quarry. At his present height, even if the Veng did see him, it would not be able to identify him. And as long as he kept a respectable distance, the Veng was not going to take off and challenge him.

He set a course for the smoking tip of Mount Vargos. In

forty wingbeats, he could be making the approach to Prime Grynt's eyrie (he reminded himself to catch a rabbit on the way). But something kept drawing his eye back to that Veng. From the moment he'd spotted it, it hadn't moved. Not even a grumpy twitch. No doubt it was a thankless task to have to sit alone watching the entrance to a hole (Gabrial thought he'd seen a dark depression at a relatively undisturbed section of the quarry), so it was reasonable to expect the Veng to be hunched. Yet something about its body shape was wrong. It appeared to be listing slightly. One wing was half spread over the rocks. It couldn't be warming itself because the sun was low in the sky and weak. And there appeared to be waste matter all around its tail. Was it sitting in a trail of its own *dung*? Even for a Veng that was lazy practice.

With a hurr of frustration, Gabrial switched his weight and circled the site once more. Every delay made his circumstances worse, but he had to know what was happening here. He dropped to a lower orbit, all the while sharpening his optical triggers. The Veng's green, studded eyelids were partially closed, and one of them appeared to be oozing fluid. The tail, normally so strong and ready, lay flaccid between two stones. Shards of broken claws were scattered all around. The nose-numbing stench confirmed it *was* dung pooling out among the stones. But this wasn't normal waste. This was the kind of slop wearlings ejected when they were terrified. Gabrial's primary heart began to quicken. Veng-class dragons had little need of rest; therefore, the guard was unlikely to be sleeping. To make sure, Gabrial let out a cry— no specific call or message, just a simple greeting from one dragon to another.

No response.

He landed two wingspans away, screeching at the Veng to "wake."

Nothing.

A nudge had no effect on it either. Was it dead or frozen? Gabrial simply couldn't tell. There were no visible signs of a fight. And no external wounds on an otherwise warm body.

Mystified, he scrambled toward the hole. "Ren?" he called quietly. "Ren, it's Gabrial. Are you down there?"

No reply.

"Ren?" Gabrial poked his head into the opening. A smell of damp rock and stale air filled his nostrils, but no scent of Hom.

Gabrial sat back, bewildered. It didn't seem possible that Ren's powers had developed to such an extent that he could climb out of a hole this deep and overcome the fiercest class of dragon in existence. That just couldn't happen.

Could it?

He had to report this. It was going to expose him and cause a lot of trouble, but the Elders had to know. He opened his wings. At the same time he heard a cry from the air and saw three, four . . . six dragons approaching, led by Gallen.

"Stay where you are!" the Veng commander roared.

Gabrial sighed. Perfect timing. He might as well confess his quest here and now.

He folded his wings and minimally disobeyed Gallen's order, moving slightly away from the body.

Gallen landed with a sturdy thump that made Gabrial's isoscele lift a fraction. The commander barked once at the stricken Veng, screwed his nostrils sideways at the smell, and squinted at the hole.

"You're too late," said Gabrial. "He's already gone." The other dragons landed; no more Veng, five good-size roamers. Not good odds if things turned nasty. "It was like this when I got here. I don't know what's happened."

Gallen ordered a roamer to investigate the hole. It dipped its head in and confirmed there was no prisoner.

"Where is he?" Gallen growled, his battle stigs zinging.

"I don't know," Gabrial repeated tetchily. "Something odd has happened here, Gallen. There's no point wasting time arguing about it. I need to speak to Grynt."

Gallen stepped across him before he could move. "Arrest him," he barked.

Arrest? Gabrial reeled back. "On what charge?"

"Killing a guard and aiding the prisoner to escape."

"No." Gabrial shook his head. A flush of red ran down his neck. His battle stigs began to rise. "I told you, everything was like this when I arrived. What are you even doing here, anyway? I thought you'd gone looking for a vap—?"

"We've taken a Hom prisoner," Gallen hissed, stealthily closing the gap between them. "We're here because the Prime wants to interrogate it. He planned to use the boy—but *you've* gone and set him free."

"No," said Gabrial. "I didn't. I— Agh!"

A sudden swipe of Gallen's tail ended Gabrial's protests. The blow went clean through a bone at the shoulder of the wing. A classic strike, intended to clip the wing and partially disable it. Flight would still be possible, but not escape.

"You'll come with us," said Gallen, "or die in flames here."

"I'm innocent," said Gabrial, wincing as he tried to pull the wing together.

"That's for the Elders to decide," snarled Gallen. "Take him!"

PART THREE

ESCAPE

16

The fhosforent mines, a short while earlier

From an early age, all Kaal children were taught to climb. For them, going upward against the sun was as natural a habit as feeling their bare feet walking the erth.

Like all the boys of his tribe, Ren's training had begun on simple gradients, where the holds were easy and grass grew thickly among the rocks to cushion the expected spills and falls. But it wasn't long before the son of Ned Whitehair was introduced to far greater challenges.

As early as his ninth winter, he was taken to the coarse gray rise at the foot of the sleeping mountain, below the meandering network of caves where many Kaal had lived before the skalers came to drive them out. There, one sunlit frosty morning, the men had pointed to a suitable ledge and sent him up.

Climbs like these could slice deep into a misplaced palm or graze any shin that disrespected the age-old stone. Ned himself had bluntly described it as the kind of drop that would knock some sense into a boy's dull head if his finger placements were weak or faulty. After two hard falls, one of which had all but snapped his ankle, Ren had managed it.

The men had rightly praised him—then sent him up again, this time with a clutch of dead hoppers on his back to remind him of the weight he would have to carry when his hunting days began.

And even when that was done, they dragged him away from his sleep one night and sent him out in the blustering rain to climb a slope ripped by wind and water. One foot was bound in cloth to mimic the burden of injury. Oleg Widefoot had loosed a few arrows wide of him, just to sharpen his resolve.

Harsh tests. Painful. Tough.

But Ren had managed them all.

Memories of this were going through his mind as he lay in the Veng prison close to the fhosforent mines. Even flat on his back with his head throbbing, he could spot the holds in the craggy walls above him. An easy climb for a boy of his talents, once his aching body had recovered.

But he hadn't reckoned on a guard being present. The first time he had tried to scale the pit, the Veng heard the movement and poked its savage head into the hole, shutting out a third of the light. The inner layers of its slanted eye expanded. It made a clicking sound in the back of its throat. Its jaws knifed open and out came fire. Not a blast intended to maim or kill—just a short lick hot enough to heat the rock and force Ren to release his grip. He jumped down, landing in a folded heap. A painful lesson, one his left knee begged him not to try again.

But he did try, when the light was fading and he could hear the Veng making what sounded like the hurr of a dragon asleep. He moved slower this time, keeping his breathing low and even as his fingers explored every small inflection in the sides of the pit. And he did get farther, but not far enough. Close to the opening, the rock smoothed out. To have any chance of completing the climb, he would have to swing over to the opposite wall, where the holds were better. The effort loosened up a fall of dirt. A patter of grains, no more, but enough to alert the guard. And so there came another flash like the first, followed by a plume of suffocating smoke. Ren rolled on the pit floor, choking. "What have I done?" he screamed in dragontongue, before the smoke had gotten too deep into his lungs and all he could do after that was cough.

It was while he was retching that he stretched out a hand and his wrist found a shallow fund of water. Desperate to clear the irritation from his mouth, he knelt and scooped his hand into the puddle. But as he brought the wetness to his lips, Grystina came into his mind and said, *Ren, beware.*

Ren paused. The water seeped through his fingers.

Look above you, she said.

Ren lifted his head.

Pink-colored cinders were glowing on the rock the Veng had just flamed.

"Fhosforent," Ren muttered.

The water runs with it, Grystina said. *I cannot foretell the consequence if you drink it.*

Ren thought on this a moment. "Will it change me, like the dragons that mined it?"

I do not know.

Ren pooled more water in the palm of his hand. "Givnay knew how to control it," he said, remembering the conversation he'd had with the disgraced Elder just before he died.

He thought he could, Grystina said. *It drove him to madness. Do not drink. I have a terrible sense of foreboding about this. Do you feel anything?*

"My bones are near broke and you ask me this?"

I do not mean pain. A powerful presence lurks here. Something unnatural, beyond the shadows.

Ren shook his head. He felt nought but fire in his throbbing joints, coupled with the burning urge for revenge. He staggered to his feet again. "I need to get out of here."

Not this way. Wait for Gabrial. He is sure to search for you.

Ren tongued the water. "Don't have time to wait for Gabrial."

No, Ren. The risk is too great. He felt her trying to constrict his throat. *You saw what the fhosforent did to the Wearle. Remember, you are part dragon now.*

"Part dragon; more parts Kaal," he said.

And he drank a good mouthful of the water, and more.

The result was not immediate, but it was not long coming. The world slowly began to spin, as if a dragon had pushed its tail into the pit, stirred the air, and turned the walls with it. Ren fell to his knees, a raft of broken i:mages flying through his mind. They were mostly of Gabrial, strutting back and forth, looking angry and confused. Some were of Grendel sheltering Gayl. Flashes of Gallen's green head appeared too. All of it from a huge, high cave that looked out across an endless mountain range.

"What's happenin'?" he murmured, panting hard. It felt as if a window had been opened in his mind. A fine layer of scales began to glow along his arm.

Gariffred, Grystina said excitedly. *You see everything but Gariffred. You are looking through the drake's eyes, Ren. Open yourself to it. Let your minds commingle. Then Gariffred will see what you have seen—the flight from the cave when the Veng took you. He may be able to i:mage your location for Gabrial.*

And she reached out, eager to contact her son. But as the memories of Ren's abduction poured forth, a more commanding presence began to press the borders of his newfound awareness.

Grystina quickly sensed the intrusion and immediately closed the link to Gariffred.

Ren, a dark spirit is upon us, she warned.

In the same breath, Ren felt his chest expanding as she instinctively tried to make him roar in his defense. But the incoming presence subdued it and almost split Ren's head in two. Something sinister tore into his auma. It flashed through his body like a rush of dark water, exploring every last part of him. He felt it most along his scaly arm, which snapped back hard against the wall of the pit as if possessed by a will of its own. Ren squealed in pain as the vessels near the surface of his skin erupted and blood, both green and red, trickled down his arm, leaving glowing burn marks. The force within him raged with what seemed like indignation as if a creature like Ren could have no claim to the auma of dragons.

Terrified, desperate, and knowing of nothing else to do, Ren closed his eyes and prayed to the Fathers for help. In an odd kind of way, the malevolent presence seemed to appreciate his right to do this. For half a heartbeat, the pressure eased. And in that single moment of time Ren's mind leapt to another place, a shadow realm where deities and vapors and spirits roamed freely, waiting to be called into being once more, waiting to answer any hopeful prayer . . .

It came first as a wind that howled around the pit, sucking up loose organic matter and spewing it into the open air. The dark force withdrew, though Ren had the feeling it was laughing still, as if Ren had drawn down a fate more deadly than the one the force had been planning for him.

Aboveground, the guard padded forward, ready to teach Ren another lesson. What it saw made it shrink back in horror. A ghostly form was emerging from the pit. A vapor with no light glinting in its eyes. A *thing* that had been much whispered about since a group of Veng, this one included, had destroyed the living dragon this phantom had once been. A dragon whose heart had turned to stone, a heart that sat on a pillar in an eyrie not far from these very mines. The spirit of Gabrial's friend and mentor.

Per Grogan.

17

What have you unleashed? Grystina said.

She came rushing back as the darkness left Ren. At first he had no idea what he'd done. But that was fear he detected in Grystina. Fear from a dragon who had no bodily concerns. If this phantom could raise that effect in her, what was it doing to the Veng on the surface?

Without hesitation, Ren began his third climb of the day. All the way up he had to close his eyes against the volley of grit falling back into the hole. On the surface, he could hear the Veng twisting and roaring in a terrible frenzy, scraping its spiked tail against the ground. It was still jerking left and right when Ren managed to poke his head clear of the hole. Straightway he was forced to duck as an outstretched wing scythed across the gap. In the flash of clear sky behind it, he saw the eerie figure of Grogan. The ghost was floating above the Veng, drawing its fire, tormenting it. The ground rumbled as the guard blew an arc of flame that colored the world bright orange for a moment. Blinded momentarily and curbed by the fumes, it was all Ren could do to maintain his grip. But as the haze began to clear, he could see that Grogan was completely unharmed. He had simply faded into the sky and rematerialized in another place, calling on the Veng to flame again.

Run, said Grystina. *The vapor will kill you. I cannot protect you from it.*

Ren scrabbled from the hole and hid behind a rock. "Kill? How?" The apparition was a mess of blunted fangs and bloodied forelegs—a gruesome reminder of Grogan's horrific state when he'd died—but it clearly had neither substance nor fire. Physically, it was as useless as a twig against a sword. Ren could see no way it might injure the guard.

But Grystina's apprehension was still at a peak.

Do not look at it, she counseled.

But Ren did look. Until this point, Grogan had been a wraithlike shroud of common green. But now his lifeless eyes lit up and glowed a demonic shade of red. At the same time, he seemed to swell in size and swamp the space above the guard. So big did he become that his jaws looked capable of swallowing the Veng whole. Ren was certain he would see some ghostly fire burst forth. But instead of breathing out, Grogan breathed in. He seemed to be reaching into the Veng, as if he wanted to pull it inside out from the tip of the tail forward. The Veng emitted such a howl of terror that Ren winced and momentarily felt sorry for it. He heard its claws grind and snap against the rocks. A spurt of dung squeezed out of the hole at the base of its tail and painted the land beneath it brown. One of its slanted eyes burst open, sending a trickle of amber goo running down its quivering neck.

"GIVE ME MY HEART," the apparition cried. Its voice rocked the sky like thunder.

The Veng gurgled and slumped to one side.

Run, Grystina urged. *It has destroyed the Veng's auma. It will do the same to you.*

Ren looked all around him. There were many rocks he could hide behind, but he would still be badly exposed from the air. His only hope, he thought, was to drop back into the pit and pray that Grogan ignored him or . . .

"Can we phase?" he whispered. "Up there?"

He looked at the high walls of the quarry. If he could make it to the top without being seen, there was a chance he could escape, or at least find a better hiding place.

It is dangerous, Ren. This is not a game of seek. You have never tried to phase over such a height or distance. If you falter—

"I die," he said, ducking as Grogan peered around the quarry. "Which will be my fate anyway, if I don't try."

Then concentrate fully, Grystina said. *I:mage yourself to the top of the quarry. I will aid you all I can. But waver just once and Grogan will sense you.*

The vapor turned its head their way.

He senses me anyway, Ren thought. "Do it," he said, slipping closer to the ground. He huddled up and closed his eyes, picturing himself in the same position, behind a rock but outside the quarry.

With a jerk he was gone. When next he opened his eyes, the mountains were an endless ripple of peaks and the air was sharp against his face. He scrabbled to his feet and peeped down into the quarry. *Yes!* He punched the air in triumph. He had phased perfectly. In the distance lay the Veng, slumped beside the hole.

But where was Grogan?

A sudden rush of air answered that. Grogan appeared full size in front of him, wings outstretched, jaws bleeding with shadowy saliva.

Ren staggered back from the quarry edge, tripping and falling over loose shale. "I . . . I mean no harm on you," he babbled, raising a hand to protect himself.

"GIVE ME MY HEART," Grogan said, wailing like a wind from another world. And he tried to do to Ren what he had done to the Veng. But although Ren felt the pulse of energy, it seemed to disperse to either side of him as if it had hit an invisible wall.

He is trapped, said Grystina. *His spirit haunts the place where he died, but no farther. Unless he can cross that barrier, you are safe.*

Breathing hard, Ren got to his feet.

Leave, said Grystina. *Run while you can. Other Veng will come. They will hunt you, Ren.*

139

Ren calmly dusted himself down. He stepped closer to Grogan, being careful not to be swept into his auma. "My name is Ren," he said in dragontongue. "I would help you. I know where they hide your heart."

Grogan wailed again. The red eyes sharpened.

"They hold it in a cave," Ren said boldly. "A cave that was home to the traitor, Givnay. I know this because they took me there once."

That aggravated Grogan even more. He scratched and snapped at the edges of his realm, leaving misty streaks of blood in the air. "BRING ME GA . . . BRI . . . AL."

Ren shook his head. "Weren't Gabrial who put you here."

The vapor thrashed its tail, making it explode in a cloud of many parts. The whole body formed again, green. "WHAT—ARE—YOU?"

"I am Hom," said Ren, "but the auma of dragons runs deep in me." He held up his hand to show the star-shaped scar where Gariffred had bitten him. "Gabrial is sworn to me by blood, and I to him and his wearling kin. I will not see you set against them. But I mean to wound your spirit no further. I would wreak vengeance against those who harmed you. If I bring you your heart, will you join with me? Will you be at my call unto death? Against them?" He nodded at the stricken guard. "Your heart for the Veng. How say you, Grogan?"

The vapor swirled. It tilted its head, perhaps unable to believe the arrogance of the creature standing in front of it.

Growing ever more confident, Ren said, "I called you back to this world, spirit; I can send you to the other place again."

An idle boast, said Grystina. *I beg you, leave.*

Grogan accepted the terms all the same. "MORE VENG FOR MY HEART. BRING IT SOON, HOM."

Ren thumped his breast. "This is my oath. Injure no other dragon until I return."

And he turned his back and walked away, striking out for the distant straggle of smoke that always rose from the sleeping mountain.

Even before he had gone ten steps, Grystina was raising dire concerns. *This is a perilous bond*, she warned. *If you fail this oath and the vapor breaks free, it will kill you for pleasure or haunt you always.*

"I won't fail," said Ren. "Gabrial will come. Find me a hiding place. Somewhere the Veng can't sniff me out. One I can easily i:mage for Gariffred. The bond to the drake burns strong in me."

And when Gabrial is here, what then?

"We join together, with others, and take the battle to Grynt and Gallen."

Battle?

Ren smiled. He had thought long and hard about this. Lying in pain at the bottom of that pit had sharpened his base survival instincts. He was certain now that the dragon high command planned to kill him, or at least keep him prisoner until they were done trampling over this planet—but not if he could find a way to strike against them first.

He extended his arms and turned a full circle. "These mountains are my home, my land," he said. "I would share them in peace with any beast, including skalers—but not with those who would beat me or betray me. By the count of my fingers, there are three Veng left, including Gallen. We can defeat them with Grogan's help."

Defeat them . . . ? You would fight the Veng?

"Aye. Them, and Grynt too."

He felt Grystina rearing in his mind. *No, Ren. This is the fhosforent in you. I cannot let you form a dark wyng.*

"A what?" he said. He was moving quickly away from the quarry, searching for a heap of dragon dung. He was an exposed target on the open mountains, easily visible to the dragons' keen eyes. More so to their noses. But if he smeared his robe with their dung, it would hide his Hom scent. It had fooled them before; it would fool them again.

Meanwhile, Grystina issued her warning. *If dragons gather to fight the Prime, they are called a dark wyng. It is an unforgivable act of treachery. Grynt will kill you without hesitation if you rise up against him in that manner. Gabrial too, and any others you call.*

"Grynt wants me dead. What difference does it make?"

If he wanted you dead, we would not be having this conversation.

Ren raised his eyes to the sky. No sign of any roamers or changes of guard. He continued his search for dung. "Then what would you have me do?"

Surrender.

"Surrender? Nay."

Listen to me, Ren. It is the only way. Give yourself up. Tell them what happened when you drank the water. Tell them the fhosforent raised a dark spirit that made you bring Grogan back. Tell them what you saw him do to the Veng. They only have to commingle with your mind to know it's true.

"No. They imprisoned me when I had done no crime. I will not put myself in their claws again. We hide and call Gabrial."

Again I ask, what then?

Ren knelt down and surveyed the land. "Then there is a change of order," he said. "Then we take control of the Wearle."

18

"What do I have to do to make you understand that when I give an order I expect it to be OBEYED?"

Prime Grynt was so close to Gabrial's face that his words were almost indenting themselves across the blue's jaw. Gabrial tried to look up to find Grendel, but she was under guard at the back of the eyrie, accused of being complicit in his actions, too far away for him to see. The two distressed wearlings had been taken to healer Grymric's cave, there to be given sleeping herbs to calm them, if necessary. The only others present with Grynt were Elder Gossana; De:allus Garodor; Veng Commander Gallen; and, bizarrely, a terrified male Hom, cowering in a ragged heap off to one side.

"All I wanted to do—" Gabrial began.

"All you wanted to do, all you have EVER wanted to do," roared Grynt, "is disrupt the running of this Wearle. You were ordered to stay AWAY from the boy."

"And I have!" snapped Gabrial, wincing as his injured wing kinked. It had been a painful flight to the Prime dragon's settle, one that Gallen had made more torturous by taking a longer route around than was necessary. "I admit I went to look for him, but I didn't release him from that pit."

"Then what did?"

Gabrial ground his teeth. "I don't know. Maybe it wasn't the wisest of moves to put Ren in the quarry where Grogan died."

Grynt raised a claw to keep Gallen quiet. "You expect me to believe that the spirit of a dead dragon mysteriously rose up, murdered a Veng, and let the boy walk free?"

"The guard was *frightened* to death."

"And you know this how?"

Gabrial roiled his wings in exasperation. "Gallen has seen the body. The De:allus and Gossana have looked over it as well. There were no signs of physical combat—just . . ."

"The smell," said Gossana, wrinkling her snout.

"I didn't kill it," Gabrial insisted to Grynt. "I swear on the life of the wearlings. And I don't believe Ren did it, either."

Grynt walked around to the other side of him. "It doesn't matter what you *believe*. The facts are plain. Another Veng is dead, and the boy is our only suspect. He is now a dangerous fugitive. He will be hunted down and brought to justice. If he resists, he will be eradicated."

"No!" cried Grendel from the back of the cave.

Gallen stepped in front of Gabrial as he tried to move toward her. The resulting roar of conflict made the Hom man shrink back and cover his ears.

"Enough!" rapped Grynt. He turned again to Gabrial. "I am severely disappointed in you. After the battle with the goyles, I was prepared to believe that you had grown in stature and finally become worthy of your father's lineage. And now this."

"My father—"

"Be quiet. I haven't finished. Until I order you otherwise, you will be confined to your eyrie."

"What?"

"I said, be QUIET. Grendel and the wearlings will be allowed to stay with you. But you will not leave the eyrie, not even to hunt. Instead, you will suffer the indignation of others providing food for you and the orphans. Guards will be posted to make sure you comply. Disobey me again and you will *all* be returned to Ki:mera in shame. Do I make myself clear?"

Gabrial shook his head in frustration. "If you harm Ren, it will set Gariffred against you forever. He may be an orphan, but he has Astrian blood. Many dragons on Ki:mera would rally to an Astrian drake, whether he's a friend to the Hom or not."

"And you would fight for him?" Gallen hissed. He rolled back his lips to show all his fangs. "You dare to stand before us and threaten your Prime?"

"I dare to point out the truth," said Gabrial. He glanced at the terrified man. "We should settle our disagreements with the Hom. These clashes are dividing the Wearle and raising dark forces among us."

"Faah!" exclaimed Gossana.

"I mean it. I *feel* it," Gabrial growled. He pleaded with Grynt again. "Call off the hunt for Ren. Let me find him and bring him to you. He'll listen to me. He can talk to this Hom. That's what you wanted, isn't it?"

Grynt looked away. "It's too late for that. The boy's position has changed. He has set himself apart from us."

"Can you blame him? It was *you* who imprisoned him!"

"Two Veng dead!" the Prime dragon snapped. "Hom involved on both occasions. This is war, Gabrial. I've told you before, dragons don't negotiate with lesser species."

"Ren's different, you know that. He has our auma."

"He's a threat. That's all I need to know. If there is a dark force around us, maybe it resides in him."

Gabrial sighed deeply and looked at Garodor. The De:allus dragon had been silent throughout. Even now he seemed content to take the stand of an interested observer.

Grynt gestured at Gallen. "Get him out of my sight."

"Move," said Gallen, squaring up to Gabrial, "or I'll cut your other wing and make you crawl to your eyrie." He bundled Gabrial back toward the lip of the cave.

Over Gallen's shoulder the blue dragon cried, "How are we to know the truth about this vapor if we don't interrogate the Hom you've caught?"

"There was no vapor," Grynt said impatiently. "The Veng

that raised the alarm was mistaken. It destroyed a rain cloud, nothing more."

"A cloud in the shape of a black dragon?"

"I've heard enough." Grynt sighed. "Take him away."

"Clouds don't make such shapes," shouted Gabrial. "And why there? Why did it appear at a cave where one of Gallen's Veng lay dead?"

"Fly!" the Veng commander growled, poking his tail into Gabrial's chest.

Gabrial extended his wings, being careful to look after the injured one. Gallen had done a good job there. Even with a dragon's powers of recovery, the split was going to take days to heal. "Grendel," he said. "I won't leave without her."

"Oh, how touching," Gossana puffed.

Grynt tilted his head and gave a short command.

Grendel was brought to Gabrial's side. She stood up proudly, almost shadowing the blue. "When this is done," she said to the gathering, "you will know that Gabrial was right. I want Gayl and Gariffred brought to us immediately. Or it will be your names ringing around Ki:mera, telling how poorly you treat our young."

And with a hiss at Gallen that made him recoil, she launched, and called Gabrial away with her.

"Do I have your permission to punish her?" said Gallen. His claws were eager to draw some blood.

Gossana gave a cynical sniff. "Being with that idiot blue is punishment enough for any female."

For once, Grynt seemed to agree with her. "See to Grendel's demands," he said to Gallen. "Move the wearlings back to their eyrie—but do it gently. Use dragons Gabrial is familiar with. Find a roamer to do the hunting for them and to keep watch. A young dragon we can spare, no more Veng. Gabrial can't try anything while he's clipped. Go."

Gallen pulled in his claws and swooped away.

In the silence that followed, Grynt said to Garodor, "You've been quiet. How far did you get with this?" He turned and looked at the Hom prisoner.

Rolan was huddled against a dent in the wall as if he might draw some comfort from the rock.

De:allus Garodor blinked his eyes, lighting the cave with a pale yellow glow. "It's not been easy to commingle with. Its thoughts are muddled by the fear in its mind. But I did detect an interesting emotion. One that conflicts with Gallen's report that this Hom was involved in the slaying of the Veng we found in the cave."

"Emotion?" said Gossana. She didn't trust *emotions*.

"It feels betrayed," said Garodor. "It believes it was led into a trap."

Grynt's eye ridges narrowed. "By its companions?"

"No," said Garodor, "by this."

He i:maged a crow.

The man immediately kicked his legs and tried to press himself farther into the wall. Gossana, who was nearest to him, snarled in disgust and bared her fangs. "Why crows? They're nothing but noisy scavengers." She sucked in her saliva, arguably a sound more frightening than her growl.

Garodor let the i:mage fade. "Scavengers, perhaps, but they mean something to him. I noted some were present when we found the Veng."

"Doing what?" said Grynt.

"Watching. On whose behalf I can't be sure. I have a theory, though, that I think you should hear. This business with the goyles may not be over. When the dead Veng was pulled clear of the cave, I inspected the interior and found traces of unusual skin deposits. I analyzed them before coming to this meeting. They contain high levels of fhosforent. They were shed by a creature undeniably dragon in origin."

"Goyles?"

"Or a different strain of them."

Gossana shook out the tips of her wings. "I was assured that all the mutants were destroyed."

"From this Wearle, yes—but possibly not the first."

Grynt looked away uneasily.

Garodor went on, "I think they might be survivors from the first conflict that lay dormant for a while."

"Doing what?" Grynt hissed.

"Regenerating. Waiting for the optimum moment to emerge."

"As *crows?*" Gossana's eyes changed color.

"I don't know what they are—or, more important, where they are," said Garodor, "but I think this Hom does." He put his isoscele under the man's chin and tipped his head back against the cave wall. Rolan let out a frightened whine. A patch of warm fluid began to pool around his legs. "Gabrial's right. We need to find the boy. I believe Gabrial when he says he knows nothing about the slaying of the Veng in the quarry. He may be hotheaded, but he's not a killer. Even in my short time here I've come to see that he's smart and loyal. I suggest you start the search for Ren right away. And make sure Gallen uses some restraint. We want the boy alive and talking. We need to know everything this prisoner knows before it's too late."

"Too late—for what?" Gossana said.

"More deaths," De:allus Garodor said bluntly. And he pulled his isoscele away from Rolan and flamed the tip to be sure of removing any contamination.

19

"Gabrial, it's no use sitting here brooding."

Rain was spattering across the cave mouth, driven in on a sweeping crosswind. Gabrial was staring rigidly at the mountains, taking the brunt of the rain across his chest. Night was slowly closing in. Rumbles of thunder were shaking up the air. At the far right edge of the cave, standing guard, sat the lonely figure of Goodle. He turned his head when he heard Grendel speak, then looked away quickly as if he was embarrassed to be there.

"The wearlings are missing you," she said. "Come to the back of the cave. Please."

Gabrial shook his head. "I need to think."

She blew some air across his injured wing, letting the heat roll across the sensitive scales at the back of his neck. "Thinking's bad for you. You need to rest."

A funnel of smoke issued out of Gabrial's handsome snout and was quickly picked up by the next gust of wind. Out of Goodle's hearing, he whispered, "They're going to kill him, Grendel. Goodle says they have a wyng out looking for him. If I don't get to Ren before—"

"Shush," she said urgently. "We have a visitor."

She parted from Gabrial slightly as Garodor glided into the cave. The De:allus landed nearer to Goodle than to them and spoke quietly to that dragon before sending him away. Shaking off a light skim of rain, he folded down his green wings and crossed the cave mouth. Behind him, a faint flash of blue light briefly cracked the sullen night sky.

"Is the guard dismissed for good?" The sharp rise in Grendel's voice made clear the discontent she felt.

"No," said Garodor. "Goodle will be back."

"Kind of the Elders to give us a guard the wearlings are fond of, but are no longer allowed to play with."

"It was not my decision to make," said Garodor. "I hope the wearlings' confusion will be short-lived."

"What do you want, De:allus?" Gabrial asked bluntly.

"To speak with you," Garodor said.

"I said everything I have to say at Grynt's cave. Why has he sent you?"

"He hasn't. The Prime doesn't know I'm here. Grendel, would you leave us?" Garodor looked toward the rear of the cave. "I think I hear your drake calling."

She nodded, grim-faced, and backed away.

"Well?" said Gabrial, when she was gone.

De:allus Garodor settled lower, as if he intended to be present awhile. He was an elegant dragon and made no puff of sound as he relaxed. "I've been going over all the battle reports. You showed great bravery against the goyles. It must have been hard, losing so many dragons—especially my old colleague, De:allus Graymere. I understand you were at his side when he died."

"I could do nothing for him," Gabrial muttered, remembering the standoff he'd been forced to endure when Graymere had been wounded by a goyle, only then to suffer the further misfortune of crashing down among the bloodthirsty Hom.

"I taught Graymere everything he knew," said Garodor. "He had an excellent mind and would have taken my place one day. I was deeply saddened to hear of his death. Like me, he wasn't interested in matters of command; he just wanted to explore the truth. You and I share that conviction, Gabrial. It would be to every dragon's benefit if we could be friends."

Gabrial stared mournfully into the night. Vast storm clouds were blowing in from the sea. "How can we be friends? You're the one who's been brought here to take Ren apart."

"I can stop that if the boy cooperates with us. You're right, he could be a valuable asset, a key to our greater understanding of the planet. He needs to be brought back safely."

"Fine words," said Gabrial. He set his jaw straight. "But I hear Grynt's voice, De:allus, not yours."

Garodor shook his head. "On my honor, I come to you out of my own volition. But I will speak for Grynt. You judge him too harshly, Gabrial. He's impulsive, yes, and his decisions sometimes suffer for it. But this is a difficult time for him. It's not easy managing a Wearle of this size. A Prime dragon needs to be strong, and needs to be seen to be strong. But a good one will listen to reason, eventually. I've persuaded him not to have the boy killed. But if anything else happens, I can't protect Ren."

"Then let me go. Let *me* protect him."

"You know I can't do that. Besides, what use would you be with a damaged wing?"

"Then why are you here? What is it you want?"

"An answer to a question. One I wanted to ask you in Grynt's eyrie. I decided it would be in your interests if he didn't hear it."

"What question?"

"How did you know where to look for Ren?"

Gabrial felt his eye ridges twitch. He stared at a permanently snowcapped peak, which was just beginning to reflect the storm's light.

"For what it's worth," Garodor went on, "I believe your account of what happened at the quarry. I'm just . . . intrigued to know what drew you there."

Gabrial lifted his shoulders, sending scale dust running down the frame of his wings. "The mines are closed. It was the obvious place to take him."

Garodor flexed a foot. "I've been to the mines. They cover

a reasonably sized area. And there are numerous shafts and pits. You also had little free time in which to search. Yet you found the boy right away. That can only mean one of two things: Either the stars were shining on your quest—or you were guided to Ren's location. Someone—or something—helped you, didn't they? Tell me, Gabrial, does the boy command crows?"

"What?"

"I saw them in the mind of the Hom we captured. The man fears them greatly. I'd like to know why."

"Ren has never shown a liking for crows."

Garodor wrapped his tail across his back. "They were frequently around your old cave. Perhaps he learned to control them there?"

"Or perhaps the De:allus is thinking too cleverly for once."

Grendel stepped forward out of the shadows.

"You forget, there was a Veng on the ground," she said. "Gallen was lazy enough to post a vivid green dragon in open daylight. It would show up brighter than your unlidded eyes. That's what drew Gabrial to the right place: a mixture of fortune and Veng stupidity."

"Fanon Grendel—"

"*Matrial* Grendel," she corrected him, making him bow. "We thank you, De:allus, for your concern about Ren, but I would ask you to leave the eyrie now. My wearlings are a little frightened by the storm and I must attend to Gabrial's wing. And, look, here's Goodle returned with food. Our pleasant, trustworthy guard is attending to our needs as well as to yours."

Goodle landed quietly in the same place he'd left. He dropped a bloodstained goat on the floor of the cave and nosed it, with little enthusiasm, toward Grendel. He went back to his formal position, shuddering as he looked out into the night.

"Very well," said Garodor, rising up. "I will, of course, inform you of the outcome of the search. I'm sure it won't be long before we have some news. I hope, for everyone's sake, it will be good."

And he tipped his head to both of them and flew.

How much of that did you hear? asked Gabrial, placing the words, by thought, into Grendel's mind. He glanced at Goodle, who seemed more concerned about the growing storm than in overhearing any kind of conversation.

Most of it, said Grendel, beckoning him deeper into the shadows. *I had to get rid of him before Gariffred drew his attention.*

Is he well?

Oh, yes. He's more than well. Eager to show you something.

Gabrial caught her eye. Even in the darkness, their jeweled blue surfaces were softly glowing.

I know how you found Ren's prison, she said.

Gabrial drew closer. *He's i:maged something else? A new location?*

She nodded.

He glanced at Goodle, who was still peering at the clouds as though trying to predict which one would produce the first clap of thunder. "Show me," he whispered, far enough away from the cave mouth now.

To his surprise, Grendel dipped her head.

"Grendel? I have to—"

"No," she said firmly. "You don't leave the cave. One more breach of their trust and you'll be no livelier than that." She nodded at the motionless goat. "I couldn't bear it if they hurt you again—for good."

He stroked her back with his isoscele. "If I don't go, Gallen will succeed with his search. There are only so many places Ren could hide, and he won't be able to shield his scent for long. Gallen's no fool. He'll know to sharpen his sensors in case Ren tries smearing himself with our dung again."

"Yes, I've thought of all that," she said, nervously raking the ground. "I agree, we have to act quickly."

"Grendel, you're not going to tell them where he is? If you give Ren up—"

"You think I would? After everything we've been through?"

"No. So . . . ?"

She took a deep breath. "I have a plan. It's dangerous, but I think it will work. And it has to be now, while the storm is breaking. *I'm* going out to search for Ren."

"You? No!"

"Shush," she said. She glanced across the eyrie. A flash of lightning had just made Goodle jump.

"You are aware we're under guard here?" Gabrial hissed. "I know Goodle's about as fierce as a feather in the wind, but he still has eyes. How do you plan to get past him?"

"Because I know something about him you don't." She turned her head and stared at the skyline. "Goodle is terrified of lightning."

20

In general, dragons flew in all weathers. Some conditions they actively welcomed. Snow, for instance, cooled their wing joints and enabled them to take on water if they needed to, especially on longer journeys. And though extremes of temperature were never ideal, dragons could adapt to either state. During winter, their scales provided a thermal barrier against the cold, but were equally effective at deflecting the heat of the Ki:meran sun. When lifted by just a few degrees, the scales could be slid back minimally to ventilate softer tissues beneath. Rarely did a dragon look at the skies and decide it would be unwise to fly.

But lightning. That was a different issue. If a bolt were to hit, the charge could traverse the entire body network, disrupting navigational aids and weakening the seams along the framework of the wings. It was by all accounts an uncomfortable experience, one to be avoided wherever possible. But Gabrial had never heard tell of a dragon being *frightened* of a strike. Wearlings, maybe. But not a grown adult like Goodle.

Grendel explained how his fear had come about. "I'm two turns older than him," she said, "but our family settles were close. When we were young, we sometimes played together.

One day, we were flying through a deep-ridged valley, practicing rolls and other tricks, when we were caught in a storm and a bolt struck Goodle directly on a wing. He was a slow developer and his wings were weak. It burned a hole in the canopy and he lost control. He spiraled down and struck his head on a rock. He tumbled, unconscious, into a river. When I reached him, his head was underwater. He was too heavy to lift, but I was able to support him and keep his head up. I had to wait for the storm to blow out before any of our wyng could respond to my calls."

"You saved his life."

"I suppose so, yes. We never speak of it, of course, because no dragon, especially a male, wants to be reminded of a fall like that. But it left a scar in his mind. Look at him. See how anxious he is?"

Goodle was paddling his feet, quaking to the rhythm of the rolling thunder. He did look very uneasy.

"So what's the plan?"

"We bring him inside, away from the edge."

Gabrial looked bemused. "How's that going to help? Anyway, he can't leave his post. What if Gallen or one of the search team flies by?"

"They'll see you, a blue dragon, huddled up in the rain and assume that all is well. If you keep your head down and draw your chest in, you and Goodle are virtually identical. It's only a precaution anyway; they're not likely to fly in this. Even the Veng don't enjoy lightning."

"So we swap positions. Then what?"

"We let him sleep the storm out."

"Sleep? You want me to cuff him?"

"No, Gabrial. I don't want you to *cuff* him. What is it with males that they always want to hit things? I'm Fissian, remember. What are dragons born of my bloodline known for?"

Their ridiculous plans? Gabrial thought it best not to say. "You're going to sing to him?"

"Yes. He's emotionally fraught. That makes him more vulnerable to sleep—and to suggestion. I think it will work. The moment he's under, I'll go and find Ren. Then we'll wake Goodle up again and let him go back to 'guarding' us."

"Grendel, wait." Gabrial hooked his tail into hers and held her back. "Assuming this works and you do find Ren, what then?"

She wiggled her nostrils a little. "We hide him."

"Where?"

"Here, in the eyrie."

"Here?" Gabrial arrowed his isoscele at the cave floor.

"Yes." She glanced over her shoulder at Goodle. Thankfully, he hadn't heard. "There are lots of deep tunnels into the mountains. We could hide Ren and feed him for as long as we like. It's perfect. They won't think to look right under their snouts."

"They won't have to. As soon as Ren's back, Gariffred and Gayl will be all over him. How do you plan to shut them up?"

"That might need some work," she agreed. "But the only dragon likely to come close to them is Grymric, and he's on our side."

"I wouldn't be so sure. Not about this."

"Well, then, he gives us away!" she said tautly, blowing smoke sideways from the corners of her mouth—a typical show of frustration in a dragon. "What would you have me do, Gabrial? You said it yourself; if we don't act now, our chance is gone. You know you'll never forgive yourself if he falls into Gallen's claws again."

"But what if Garodor was telling the truth and Grynt is prepared to let Ren live?"

"What if he is? All they want Ren for is information. Once they know what's in the mind of this Hom they've captured, Ren is just as much a 'threat' as he ever was. Then he might as well be back in that pit."

"What if the information is important, though? What if the Wearle is under threat? You heard what Grynt said. Two Veng dead, the Hom probably involved. And now this peculiar business with the crows."

Grendel leaned close. "If we take Ren, we control what happens. We'll work out a way to get him to this Hom, and between us we'll find out what the man knows. By then, you'll be fit again and ready to act. Ren is bound to be more willing to cooperate with us than with Grynt or Gallen."

Gabrial tugged his upper lip back. "He also has his own way of doing things. If this goes wrong and he's captured again, or he dies while we're trying to—"

"Gabrial, it won't go wrong," she said quietly. "Listen, Ren's not far from here. If I've read Gariffred's i:mages correctly, one quick flight and it's done. Come on, while the storm is still growing." And she unhooked her tail from his and led the way to where Goodle was perched.

The guard sat up straight when he saw her coming, puffing his rain-soaked chest to its maximum. Water vapor was steaming off his neck. His appealing blue eyes were filled with alarm. "Grendel, you must stay back," he said, doing his best to muster an air of authority. His gaze shifted behind her to Gabrial, who had wisely sat down a short distance away.

Grendel stopped walking as a sheet of blue lit up the cloud base and flickered like Goodle's anxious hearts. "Dreadful night," she said, humming a melody under her words. One of the strange peculiarities of Fissian females was their ability to talk and hum at the same time. The most talented of them (and Grendel was one) could harmonize the sounds and create a vibration that was almost as unsettling as it was appealing. It was having an effect on Goodle already. The small frills around his ear holes were beginning to quiver. He tilted his head as she carried on speaking. "A storm like this is enough to make any dragon drop their scales. I expect Gallen and the others have settled somewhere safe. Not one of them would want to be where you are now."

"I have a duty to perform," the blue said proudly.

A loud rap of thunder boomed across the cave mouth, screeching as it split into three sharp echoes.

Goodle gave a start and leaned out of the wind.

"My father used to tell me that was the roar of Godith," said Grendel, blending a deeper tone into her song. "She wouldn't want to see you suffer like this."

Goodle gulped. His opened his wings a little and shook them. "Grendel, please go back," he begged.

She took a step closer instead, weaving her beautiful, beguiling head in a manner that encouraged him to follow the movement. "Goodle, we're old friends, you and I. I know better than any dragon what you're feeling. *Come inside, away from the storm.*"

Her eyes were glowing brightly now, their centers pulsing, seeking his. Somehow, he managed to break her stare and glance at Gabrial again. Grendel was swift to regain the initiative. "Gabrial wouldn't go out in this. Not with his wing the way it is. You remember what the storm can do to a wing, don't you?"

Goodle shuddered and dipped his head.

"Come inside," she said again, adding a chorusing echo to the words.

And as her song increased in volume, he finally slipped under her spell and began to move slowly out of the rain, deeper into the cave.

"You're not a guard," she said. *Come inside. Come inside.* "You were born to be a healer or a spiritual leader. Remember how we talked about it when we were young?" *Come inside.* "Remember how we would close our eyes and pray to Godith to let us become what we wanted to be? Do you remember that, Goodle?"

"Yes-ss," he muttered.

"Look at me," she sang.

He lifted his head. She brought her foreclaws together, and he did the same. *"Close your eyes now. Close your eyes and listen to the song of Godith."*

And she sang to him openly. A lullaby that could have soothed the wind. As the melody spiraled deep into Goodle's mind, he relaxed with his head in his chest.

"It's done," she said to Gabrial.

No response.

"Gabrial!" She poked him sharply with her isoscele.

"Um? Wazzat?" He sat up, losing his balance. He had all but nodded off as well.

"Wake up. Goodle's asleep. I have to leave."

Gabrial shook himself back to full alertness. "Right. Yes." He checked to see what the wearlings were up to. They had both moved into the spare chamber of the cave, away from the storm. "You're sure about this?"

"As sure as I'm ever going to be." She rose into launch position. A heavy sheet of rain lashed across the cave mouth. "Be ready," she said. "This won't take long."

And she propelled herself into the storm, her wings flashing as she found the wind, which took her in a rushed glide away from the mountain.

21

She found Ren hiding in a tall fissure that cracked the mountains like the slit at the center of a dragon's eye. He had i:maged it for Gariffred as best he could, though the storm and the darkness had made the drake's reproduction murky. The i:mage that better guided Grendel to the site was the outline Ren had provided of the mountains, seen when looking away from the fissure. He had managed to i:mage two graceful humps, one about half the height of the other, with a lopsided spread of snow in the bowl-shaped dip on the incline between them. Keeping that i:mage at the front of her mind, Grendel had circled the fhosforent mines, flying as low as she dared, recalculating distances, angles, and altitudes until her optical triggers locked on to a match. It was a technique mappers used all the time and, despite her lack of training, she trapped the location easily enough. Once she had that position fixed, it was a simple matter to land, look around, and find the fissure.

"Ren," she called through the driving rain, wary that her voice was drifting on the wind. It was unlikely that the search wyng would settle this low, but it did no harm to be cautious. "Ren, are you here?" The fissure was too small to take a dragon of her size, and instinct warned her not to poke her head into an uncharted gap. "It's me, Grendel. *Galan aug scieth.*" It was the first phrase of dragontongue Ren had learned. *We are one*, it meant. If anything would gain his trust, it would be that.

She scented him as soon as he moved. Rather than stay at a level where he might be spotted easily from the air, he had climbed down and entered the cleft at its natural opening by the foot of the mountains. He poked his head out and saw her perched on a trail of rocks that formed the bed of a shallow creek. A threadlike waterfall, one of many to be found around the mines, was pouring down between them.

"Where's Gabrial?" he whispered, shaking rain off his hair. He checked the skies for Veng. Nothing.

"Long story. He's hurt."

"How bad?"

"A wing clip. It will mend."

"How did it happen?"

"A brush with Gallen. Gabrial saw the i:mages you sent to Gariffred and went to the quarry to look for you. Gallen found him there and accused him of freeing you from the pit." She dropped a wing, inviting him to climb onto her back. "Quickly. We must leave. There's a search team sweeping the mountains. They'll take cover while the storm is bad, but that won't be for long." The rain was easing, Grendel noticed. Gaps were appearing in the body of cloud. Her primary heart pumped a fresh run of blood through her veins. If this went wrong, she could be taking her last ever flight.

Using the bones of her wing like stepping stones, Ren clambered into the gap between her shoulders and reached out to hold two stigs for support. "What of Gariffred?"

"He's fine. Concerned for you." She readied her wings.

"Where are we going?"

"To an eyrie Grynt gave us. We can hide you there while we decide what to do about you and your friend."

"Friend? What friend?"

Grendel chewed her tongue. She shouldn't have let that detail slip. "The Veng have taken another Hom captive."

"Where from? The settlement?"

"No. It was—"

"Why would they do that?"

"Ren, please—"

"Take me to Grynt! I'm going to—"

"REN!" She growled and flicked her ear stigs until he was quiet. "I know you're angry, but this must wait. If we linger, the search wyng will find us. We'll talk it through when I've got you safe. Hold tight. You're going to be exposed to the storm. It won't be pleasant, but the journey isn't long. Shout if you think you're losing your grip."

She beat down hard to gain height and momentum. Once up, she swung away from the mines and plotted a direct course for the eyrie. On the way she had seen no sign of Gallen and was confident his wyng was seeing the storm out. But her self-assurance swiftly evaporated when she spotted two silhouettes in the sky. They were flying some distance apart, but clearly searching in parallel.

"What's the matter?" yelled Ren. He had felt the subtle change of rhythm in her wings.

"Stay down, we've got company. Roamers, I think. They haven't seen me, but if they get too close they'll have my scent. Hold tight, I need to change course."

And she banked toward the western slopes of Mount Vargos, only to see another dragon flying solo near the rim at the mountain's peak. In the gloom, it was hard to pick out the coloring, but the shape suggested it could be Veng, possibly even Gallen. Her primary heart beat double. Her only hope now was that the cloak of anonymity extended both ways. At this distance, she could be any dragon. And if she tilted her body carefully enough, Ren would be hard to see. With that thought in mind, she went into a glide, pretending to search like the others. To panic now and flee would be a dangerous mistake. The best she could do was to hide in plain sight.

For a few moments it worked. Then the sky paled again

and Grendel was lit several times from above. She heard the solo dragon call and thought it had seen her. But when she glanced up, she saw it joined to the clouds by a jagged spike of lightning, dancing and crackling across its wingspan. It called again as the bolt released its grip. It was hurt and wanted assistance. Grendel looked toward the two in the distance. They had heard the call and were responding to it, already making a turn that would bring them directly across her flightpath. The squalling rain would blur her identity for a few moments more, but she had to move, and it had to be now.

"I need to phase," she said urgently to Ren, not knowing her words were blocked by the wind. Immediately her mind was filled with doubt. A short skip through time would get her out of there, but what would it do to Ren? There was no time to commingle and fix a common destination point. What if she disappeared and he was left floundering in midair?

Too late; it was a chance she had to take. She angled her sights on a suitable patch of ground, thinking land would be the safest option. In an instant she was scrabbling on the mountainside, spreading her purple-gray wings across the scree to camouflage herself. The oncoming dragons soared overhead. Grendel sighed with relief. She was safe, but lighter.

Ren was gone.

Gone, but not dead. In the instant that Grendel had phased, Ren *was* left floundering in the air. As the storm pressed in and he began to plummet, Grystina rushed into his mind and screamed at him to i:mage a safe place to land.

The i:mage that entered Ren's mind was a tree.

Once, during one of his climbing lessons, he had taken a chance on a slippery rock and had fallen into the branches of a tree that had seeded at an angle to the mountainside. It had left him with scars he could trace to this day, but had crucially not broken any bones or joints.

It was a tree that saved his life now. Not the tree that had caught him back then—his i:mage was far too vague for that—but one of the cluster of tall green spikers that formed the Whispering Forest. With a crash that scattered a hundred birds and broke more branches than the number of teeth he could count in his head, he came to a halt. His feet were caught up higher than his knees. His back was sorely twisted. Trails of blood were already racing along his arms. Spiker needles had taken root in every area of uncovered skin. His robe was torn, exposing one side. He was a mess, but he was alive.

You are clear of the mountains, Grystina said, with a slight element of wonder in her words. She was probably surprised that he'd managed to survive at all, more so that he'd managed to phase this far.

Ren was in no mood to offer any answers. His pain was

too great for that. He reached out and curled his fingers around a branch, wincing as the needles punctured his skin. It took a gargantuan effort to pull himself upright and the same again to free his robe from where it was caught. Finally he was stable, with room enough to move. He was glad of the rain filtering through the trees then. The damp spots tapping at his head and shoulders, combined with the continuous swaying of the trees, kept him awake and made him work. For what seemed like an age he toiled at his wounds, plucking out needles and cleansing any gashes with shreds of his robe. It was some way into this process that he realized he was being watched.

Ever since Gariffred had bitten his hand, Ren's capacity to pinpoint sounds and scents had improved beyond measure. The faint but deliberate rustle of a leaf confirmed that something was moving through the trees. He strongly suspected that one of the tribe that called themselves Treemen had heard his fall and come to investigate. But there was none of the mossy odor that usually accompanied a treeman's presence, just . . .

Twisting sharply to his left, he raised a fist to strike. Immediately, he wondered why he'd put his ribs through agony again. There was a bird half hidden among the branches. A dark bird. A caarker. What the blue dragon,

Goodle, had called a crow. Its shining black wings flicked up at the shoulders, settling again as Ren lowered his arm.

It watches you, Grystina said.

"Aye, let it," Ren said, with a shrug. Caarkers could look at whom they pleased, couldn't they?

The crow shifted sideways, making its eye fully visible. *Arrkk!* it called, and descended through the trees.

Ren thought no more of it.

Until a short while later, when he was startled to hear a man's voice drifting up through the branches. "You'd best come down, boy. Any skaler worth its weight could see the hole you've made in the trees. The storm is fast blowing out. This forest will be your friend if you want to stay hidden."

Who is this? Ren said to Grystina.

No one we have met before, she replied.

"And what are you? Friend or other?" Ren called.

Through the spikers he could just see the back of a figure, making his way through the forest on a whinney.

The man laughed. "I am what I am, Ren Whitehair."

Ren's heart thumped. "How do you know me?"

"The whole world knows you, boy. Your wild adventures are swift becoming legend. I have been most anxious to meet the child who journeyed beyond the skaler's scorch line, learned their tongue, and befriended their young."

Ren sought a better gap to spy through. What he saw made him jump so hard his head struck the branch above. "Pine?" he whispered.

She looked up from the back of a pure white whinney.

And she smiled, though it was not a smile that Ren had ever associated her with. It was Pine he was looking at, that was right enough—her unwashed hair, her small grubby face, those sly brown eyes so easy with the truth. All of that ticked a place in his memories. It was the mouth that perplexed him. There was the tooth that had earned her her name, growing in the center, big enough to plow a small field. But there, to either side of it, sat two more. Pine Threetooth. It had no ring to it. And what was she doing in the forest with a stranger?

There is only one way to find out, said Grystina.

She was right. Either he nested there or took his chances on the forest floor.

Stay alert, he said.

And he began to descend.

PART FOUR

CAPTURE

22

At the lowest branch, Ren paused to rest. He could see both whinneys clearly now. The leading one was brown and common and carried the stranger on its back. The other, Pine's white mount, had a horn twisting out from the center of its head.

What is this beast? Ren asked Grystina.

I have never seen its like before, she replied. *The horn resembles a dragon stig, but it has enchantments upon it that I cannot read.*

Ren focused on the stranger. "Say who you are."

"My name is Ty. I am a traveler," said he, a confident notch in his smooth, dark voice. He looked up and stared Ren full in the face. Ren thought he felt Grystina shrink back. "The girl I think you know."

Oh, yes, Ren knew her well enough. The last time he had met Pine, she had called the tribe down on him for bringing Gariffred the drake among them, an act that had led to the death of Ren's father. He had no love for Pine, no matter how many teeth she planned to grow or what strange beast she rode. "How is it you travel with her?"

Ty looked over his shoulder at the girl. He seemed to sense the tension between them, but made no comment about it. Pine smiled faintly, this time keeping her mouth fully closed.

"We are returning from a tragic quest," said Ty. "We and three others rode to a cave where we expected to recover the body of one of your tribesmen. We were disturbed by skalers. We two escaped. The others were burned."

"Burned?" Ren clamped an arm to stop it shaking.

Ty reined back his whinney before the beast could crunch into a spiker cone. "That is what skalers do, is it not? Burn all that stands in their way?"

He despises dragons, Grystina said. *Yet I feel he has an odd respect for us. There is something dangerous about this Hom. Be wary, Ren.*

Ren was paying no heed to her. "Which . . . ?" Which *ones*, he wanted to ask. Which dragons had killed yet more of his tribe?

Pine interpreted his question as "Who?" She rolled out the names. "Cob Wheeler, Oleg Widefoot, Rolan Woodknot. Their ashes fly on the wind."

Cob? Oleg? They were senior men in the tribe. And Rolan was scarcely five winters older than Ren. Ren's head swam with shock. "When did this happen?"

Ty stretched his fingers. "Barely one day hence."

While Ren had been imprisoned. Yet Grendel had said nothing of it. "Then . . . their captive was not one of you?"

"Captive?" Ty seemed surprised.

"I speak in the skaler tongue," Ren said, his eyes darting as he tried to make sense of all this. "One of them told me they had taken a man."

"Under what circumstance?" Ty now glanced harshly at Pine, as if she had done some wrong by him.

Ren thought he saw Pine lift her shoulders. She seemed changed somehow, not quite the wisp he'd left behind. It disturbed him faintly, but he could not say why. And all Grystina could offer was, *She too has a deep aversion to our kind.* There was nothing new in that. Most Kaal despised the dragons. Yet Ren was struggling to guess at a reason why a girl as slight as a flower stalk would go on a dangerous quest with the men. "I know not," he replied to Ty's question. "There was no time to ask why they took a captive." Was it his imagination, or had this slip of news angered the stranger?

Ty nodded slowly. "Then we must return to the settlement in haste and find out who has suffered this misfortune, and speak of what might be done about it." He clicked his fingers. A large crow descended from the trees. "Go to the mountains," he said to it. "Bring me news of any men you see." He stroked the bird's throat. "Send the chief watcher back to me. Do not give it a reason why." He thrust his arm high. The bird flew away fast through the forest.

"You command them?" asked Ren. "How so?" He had

once known a man who carried a one-eyed caarker on his shoulder and kept it there with scraps of food. But he had never seen the black birds do a man's bidding.

"But for their watchful eyes," Ty said, avoiding the question with an artful slant, "we might have missed your fall."

"And that?" Ren gestured at the white whinney, which had turned its head to look at him. There was a pleasing calmness in its pale pink eye, almost a longing to be recognized. He thought he felt an odd kind of kinship with it. But, mindful of Grystina's warnings, he did not look at the beast too long. "I have seen no whinney like it."

Pine stroked the mane as Ty gave another guarded reply. "Many wonders lie beyond the mountains, boy. Girl, step down."

"What?" said Pine, as if this was a huge impertinence.

Ty ignored her moody air. "The boy is hurt. He has more need of a ride than you." He turned back to Ren. "I say once more, the winds are changing; you had best come down from your perch, Ren Whitehair. You are fallen from the sky, ragged and scathed. Your mother, Mell, grieves daily for your absence. You will be a welcome sight to her. This burning you have learned of pains the breast, but do not let it hinder your escape. You *are* escaping, are you not?"

Ren tightened his lip. Despite Grystina's warnings, his desire was still to march back into the mountains and put a spear through Gallen's throat. He was certain the Veng were responsible for the deaths of Cob and the others. But the stranger was right. He was weary and hurt. It made sense to return to the settlement, recover, and think on what to do.

He looked at the ground. Spikers grew tall before they branched. The prospect of the drop was deeply unappealing. He could have phased to the ground with ease, but did not want to risk revealing his powers. So it was either the drop, or try to slide down and have his finger ends scraped off by the bark.

He dropped, landing in a ball of agony again, his left knee on fire, his back the same.

The brown whinney snorted. Ty pulled it around and started picking his way through the trees again. "Follow us when you are able. Shade will know the way."

"Urrr," groaned Ren, rolling into a kneeling position.

Pine dismounted and led the horse up. "Do not run, Whitehair. Shade will not allow it." She threw the reins at him, then started after Ty on foot.

"Pine, wait."

As she turned, he saw the new teeth again. She had fixed them in place with some kind of sap. They sat skewed in her mouth, like a broken fence. "Who is he, this stranger? Whence does he hail?"

"He is Ty," she said, as if that was all anyone needed to know.

"Why do you ride with him?"

"Because I choose to."

Again, she turned. Again, he called her back. "Your robe. Are you wounded?"

She looked at the stain, now dried to near black. A buzzer was jigging across it, trying to take what nourishment it could. In a flash Pine picked the creature off and put it inside her mouth. It was still buzzing as she swallowed. "No more than you," she replied. And she took a cloth off Shade's back and threw it at Ren, saying, "Clean yourself."

It was the kindest thing she'd ever done for him.

23

"My boy! My boy!"

Over and over Mell cried these words as she hugged Ren to her and kissed his wounds. Mutts turned circles, barking with excitement. Men and women abandoned their work. Children ceased to play. The whole Kaal settlement gathered in the clearing to look at the boy who had once been condemned to death for daring to consort with skalers. But gather was all they did. For with so many menfolk dead or injured, there were none rushing forward wielding their fists or spears to challenge Ren.

And so Mell showed him off proudly, a hero.

"See," she cried, standing behind him, her arms a protective brace across his chest. "See how my boy comes home to me, bleeding, torn in cloth and skin. Look at the color that flows from his wounds. Red. He is no skaler! He is Kaal!"

The crowd parted and one man did limp forward. Bryndle Woodknot was his name, father of Rolan. He limped because he had twisted his left foot, climbing, as a boy. The foot hung like a weight at the end of his leg, its best use a prop to keep him upright. Bryndle rarely involved himself in matters that fighting men decided, but his mind was sharper than most of their swords. He looked hard at Ty as the stranger dismounted, then back along the trail for Oleg and Cob. Longest of all he looked for Rolan, but saw nought but empty tracks in the erth. "Where is my boy?"

"And my husband?" said Merrilyn Widefoot. She drew a shawl around her as if she already knew to expect bad news.

"And Cob?" a few lone voices shouted, for Cob had no wife or kin to claim him.

"Have skalers been here since we traveled?" Ty asked.

"No," said Bryndle, his eyes as gray as a grinding stone. "Answer what you are asked: Where is Rolan, and Cob, and Oleg? Why are they not returned, but Mell's boy is?"

"Cob and Oleg are cruelly murdered; I fear your son is in the skalers' company."

Gasps of all kind accompanied this news. Merrilyn Widefoot fell to her knees, sobbing so loud it set the mutts howling. And though no one wailed for Cob, Ren could hear the Kaal muttering anxiously about who would lead them now. He looked around for faces of husbands and hunters he knew. His gut churned, for very few men looked back.

Bryndle raised a hand for silence. His fingers curled into a shaking fist. "Why? Why would they take my son?"

"I know not," said Ty.

Pine bent down and picked a small flower.

Bryndle came nearer, dragging his dead foot through the dirt. He wisely fell short of striking Ty, but his sorrow had boiled up quickly into anger. "You were with him! How did this seizing come about? What now of all your gallant talk? Your promises of how the beasts could be tamed?"

"Tamed?" said Ren. He wriggled clear of his mother.

"Aye," said Bryndle, sweeping around. "Your own ma it was who told us Pine had gone with the men because her songs would make the skalers *kneel*. What say you on that score, stranger? Did the girl forget her *lines*? Speak!"

So Ty explained how they had reached the cave and left Pine by the stream, tending the whinneys. He thought a moment longer, then said, "The skaler descended fast from the clouds, too quick for us to call on anything but prayers. We could not seek shelter in the cave, for the entrance was blocked by stones. The skaler saw us trying to break through. It must have believed we were violating the burial place of its companion. That was the only incitement we gave it."

There is some truth in this, said Grystina, flowing briefly into Ren's mind. *Yet I feel that Ty holds something back.*

"What color was the beast that attacked you?" asked Ren.

"Green, like the first grass of spring," said Ty. "In shape, less stout than most skalers you will see, but filled with double the spite."

Veng. Ren's thoughts went straight to them.

Widening his voice to the crowd, Ty said, "I witnessed Cob and Oleg burned. I saw no similar fate befall Rolan, for I was running to protect the girl. She was bravely riding up the hill on Shade and met me before the beast could turn its fire upon us. We used Shade's enchantment to disappear. After that, the beast let us be."

What enchantment? Ren asked Grystina. On the journey to the settlement, he'd been lulled into sleep by Shade's easy step. He had spent the entire trip lurched forward, his head against her neck, dreaming, oddly, of his father, Ned.

The beast can lose itself in a slip of light. It happened once on the journey through the forest, when it turned to look back at Pine. There is an auma around it like nothing I have ever encountered before. Yet it seems to be in some kind of torment.

Torment? Ren glanced worriedly at Shade. The whinney was calm, but staring around the camp as if looking for something that was no longer there. He turned his head as his mother spoke to Ty: "If you were with Pine and saw it not, why do you say that Rolan was taken?"

"For that, you would have to ask Ren," he answered.

And all eyes were back on Ned Whitehair's son.

"Well?" said Bryndle. The word could have skewered a snorter's throat.

"I . . . I too was captured," Ren said, nervous at having to speak so free. "But I have formed an alliance with some of the beasts—"

"Alliance?" Bryndle frothed with disbelief.

"Aye," said Ren, turning to face him. "Gabrial—the guardian of the young one I saved—is teaching me their words and has pledged himself to me. I learned from his companion that a man had been taken. That can only be Rolan."

"A *skaler* has pledged itself to you?"

"Aye," said Ren. He noted a light in Ty's dark eyes.

Those gathered muttered among themselves.

Pine looked on thoughtfully and plucked her flower.

"I know not why Rolan was taken," said Ren, raising his voice to the crowd. "But I say this to give you hope: The beasts are not dull of mind. They do not kill without reason."

This set alight a fire in Bryndle. Before Mell or Ty could stop him, he had gone up to Ren and struck him to the ground. "Nine men," he said, a deep quake in his voice. "Nine brave men, set alight at the edge of the forest as they journeyed to return your *pupp* to its kin. Where was the reason in that day's killing? Or would you have me *dull of mind*?"

"Fiend!" cried voices from the crowd. Women who had lost their husbands, sons, and brothers to the skalers. Children who would never see their fathers again.

"Targen the Old," Bryndle went on, drawing a fresh

lament from the tribe as he named another significant fatality. Targen had been the Kaal's spiritual leader, possibly the greatest casualty of all.

"Let him be!" snapped Mell, trying to draw Ren back. She clawed at Bryndle as if she would take an eye from him.

But Bryndle would not let it be. "Four women and a girl half the size of Pine, crushed or maimed when skalers and darkeyes warred above us. Nearly half our shelters flattened or burned. How can you come back and speak of an *alliance* when these beasts have brought nought but death upon us?"

Ren wiped his mouth. He rose unsteadily and stood before Bryndle. "The skalers are at war among themselves. But I cannot tell your ears what they do not want to hear. So I pledge these words instead: I will cross the line again and bring Rolan home."

"No," gasped Mell.

Ren held her away. "I have unfinished business in the mountains, Ma. I have enemies among the skalers, as well as friends."

Bryndle scorned him with a hollow laugh. "People of the Kaal! Listen well to this! The son of Ned Whitehair speaks bold to us again! He announces another reckless quest that will surely bring more fire upon us!"

"You would rather your son be abandoned?" said Ty. His interruption instantly quelled the crowd. He raised an arm. A large crow settled upon it. Ren noticed some squints of fear among the tribe.

"Speak," Ty said. To the bird, not Bryndle.

The crow shuffled nervously and spoke in low rasps.

Ty stroked its neck as though to thank it. "Bryndle Woodknot, your son is alive," he said. "He is held in a cave, high on the mountain the Kaal call Longfinger. He is hurt and cold, but not mistreated. The bird brings no clue as to why he is there." And quickly, before anyone could even murmur, Ty clamped the bird's neck in his free hand and crushed it. The throng gasped. Ren heard someone spilling their gut. Shade snorted and scraped a hoof. Ty held the crow aloft for all to see, then threw it to the nearest mutt. People turned their faces to the wind. Even Ren shuddered a little. But his mother, he noticed, though she looked upon Ty with fear and distaste, also showed a glint of admiration for him, perhaps because he had taken Ren's side. Whatever the reason, it troubled Ren more than the slaying of the crow.

"A punishment, for not informing me sooner," Ty said. And Ren thought he was speaking not to the Kaal, but to other watching crows. "I hear the boy's words and I say he speaks well. We must go back into the mountains and teach the beasts a lesson."

"How?" said Mell. She curled her hair behind her ear.

Now Ty looked upon her with the same admiration she

had shown to him. "I said a day would come when we might strike a blow against the skalers. That day is fast upon us. Boy, are you able to call this beast you say you befriended?"

Ren looked around. The faces were still in shock. "Aye, mebbe."

"Good. Then summon it."

"What?"

More gasps. Among them, Mell's. "Bring one here? Bring a *skaler* amid us?"

"Why not?" said Ty, looping his whinney to a post. "What better passage to those peaks can you think of, other than wings?"

24

They retired to Mell's shelter: Mell, Ty, and Ren. Pine lingered at the flap for a moment or two, but left in a cloud when Ty said gruffly, "The whinneys need water. And my rein was broken. See to it, girl. While I rest."

Ren was happy to watch her go.

He was less happy, however, seeing Ty on the hides his father had owned, as if they were Ty's to inherit now. "I would speak with the boy alone," Ty said. "There is a fury coming. You should be no part of it." He touched Mell's arm, letting his finger slide down her pale skin.

Not unkindly, she removed his hand. She took a cloth and soaked it in a pot of cold water. "Whatever plans you make will be mine to share. I will not part easily with Ren again." She held his hair aside and began to bathe the cuts on his forehead. "Is it true, Ren? Can you truly summon skalers?"

"Only one," said he. He looked stiffly at Ty, who had slid off his boots. "His name is Gabrial. But he will not come yet. He is injured, though dragon wounds quickly mend."

"Dragons?" said Mell, pronouncing it well.

"Their name," said Ren. "That is what skalers call themselves."

"A harsh word," said Mell. "I like it not." She dipped the cloth again.

"Injured how?" asked Ty. "Tell your story, boy. My ears grow ever keen to hear it."

With a nod from his mother, Ren told all he knew. He started with the Kaal being driven from the mountains when the dragons had burst through their fire star, and how he had crossed the scorch line in defiance and become involved with Grystina's young.

"You risked your life to save that little one?" Mell said. "I didn't know that."

Ren gave an unhappy shrug. For therein lay a terrible irony. His father had taught him all life was precious. But if his father and the tribe had listened to Ren's story when he had carried Gariffred back to the settlement, Ned Whitehair might be alive today. No spiker scratch nor dragon bite hurt as much as that harsh loss.

The talk then turned to the battle with the darkeyes and how those creatures had come to be.

"Goyles?" said Mell. "This word also means nothing to me." She dabbed at a gash by Ren's left ear. There were many broken spiker thorns still to be removed.

"If dragons eat too well of a rock they call fhosforent, they turn into goyles," Ren said, wincing away from his mother's attentions. She tapped his face and made him still. "They have closed their mines a'cause of it. Yet many dark rumors drift among them. Some say these goyles are the servants of a dragon whose name my tongue cannot twist enough to utter. A black beast, worse than a goyle. They fear this creature is about to rise and turn on their world. A place they call—"

"Do the dragons believe all the goyles are dead?"

Ty had been listening intently, picking slowly at the ends of his fingers. His sudden interruption slightly startled Ren.

"Aye. The goyles were all defeated. I faced the last on a high ledge on Longfinger."

"On Longfinger?" Mell put a hand to her breast. The horrors were stacking up.

"I saw it burned, Ma. A beast as ugly as you ever witnessed."

Mell wrung out her cloth. "So many dangers. It weakens me just to hear tell of them. And see how these ventures look on you. If you helped these . . . dragons in their quelling of the goyles, why do you return so beaten and scarred?"

Ren looked to one side, his eyes filling with resentment. "Seven moons after the fighting were done, they threw me into a pit."

Mell rested a comforting hand on his face. "Why, Ren? What wrong had you done?"

"Nought, Ma, I swear."

"He does not need to do wrong," said Ty, loosening his

robe at the neck. He picked up a piece of skewered hopper and ate without waiting for an invitation. "The answer is plain: The dragons fear him. Show your hand, boy."

Ren held up the hand that Gariffred had bitten. On the back was the star-shaped scar.

"That wound was made by their fangs," Ty said. "If Ren has their blood, they will worry that he may boast some of their gifts. They will not want their powers spread among the Hom."

"Is this true?" asked Mell, stroking the scar with a gentleness that might yet smooth it away. "Are you changed, Ren? Are you no longer the son I bore?"

Ren thought on this a moment and shook his head. "I have no wings on my back nor fire in my gut. I speak a little of their tongue, no more. I am still yours, Ma."

That pleased Mell greatly. She brought his fingers to her lips and kissed them. "You bear the weight of many odd whispers," she said. "They say you once brought fire from this hand and vanished like smoke on the day Ned died."

Ren glanced at Ty. The stranger's eyes had dipped toward his arm, where the faintest sheen of scales was showing. He drew his robe down and Ty averted his gaze. "Gifts or none," said Ty, "it is a wonder he looks into your pretty eyes now. Most captors would have killed him already."

"You speak as if you know their ways," said Ren, remembering Grystina's warnings about Ty. She had been decidedly quiet, as if she feared coming forward in his presence. She was there, all the same, prowling the distant borders of his mind, monitoring every word Ty uttered.

"I merely speak what I find to be clear," Ty said. "When providence dropped you into my path, you were fleeing from harm, were you not?"

"Bringing the forest with you," Mell muttered, moving her attentions to the scratches that covered Ren's legs. "How is it you have thorns where every hair grows?" She teased out another and threw it aside.

"I fell," said Ren, offering no more explanation than that. Fleetingly, he thought about Grendel and how she must be feeling. Deeply concerned, no doubt. As soon as possible, he must i:mage Gariffred. But not here, not in Ty's presence. He trusted this guileful stranger less than he trusted Veng Commander Gallen. "I would hear something of you," he blurted, cutting Ty off before he could raise another question. "Why should I call a dragon to your aid when I know nothing of your purpose?"

To his surprise, it was Mell who spoke up. Almost in jest, she said, "Ty has plans to steal a dragon heart."

"What?"

A pot fell over, caught by a sudden jerk of Ren's foot.

His mother sighed. "Not from a live beast." She righted the pot.

Ren's gaze drilled into Ty's. "What do you know of dragon hearts?"

"I know that one exists in those mountains. My feathered servants have seen it, held in a cave, guarded only by—"

"No." Ren pushed forward suddenly, as if he would tear out the stranger's throat. "No. You cannot take that."

"Ren!" Mell bore his weight against her hands. "Stay, boy. What vexes you so?"

"The heart he speaks of belonged to a spirit that helped me escape. I made a pledge to it . . . I . . ."

"Ah." Ty nodded slowly. A sly smile touched the corners of his mouth. He tore off another piece of meat. "Now I see your unfinished business—or some small part of it. You wish to reconnect this spirit with its heart. A dangerous errand, Ren. One that will find no favor with Bryndle or any Kaal who curses your name. They would wave you off and be glad to see you chewed by the first beast you meet, despite your talk of saving Rolan. And yet you yearn to have their regard. Despite their resentment, you would give them justice and see their lands restored. A fine hero you would be if you drove the beasts off. And there is a way. A way that I can help you with. Cob Wheeler and others fell wrong in their quests because they carried their resentment on the point of their swords. I offer you a different kind of counsel. You do not have to cut off a thousand scales to achieve your end. If the heart was returned to the spirit you raised, that spirit would promise an oath to you. Then you would have a powerful ally, a force that might be turned against those who imprisoned you. A spirit reborn is a thing to be reckoned with. Tell me, how did the dragon die?"

"Cruelly."

"Then it will have a loathing to bear." Ty slapped his knee. "There, Ren, we have our quest. For the good of these people, I offer you my service without condition. Summon your skaler and we will talk on this again."

Ren shook his head. "I have no need of your help. I command a fearsome dragon. What would sway me to join a mere band of *caarkers*?"

"An outcome neither you nor your dragon could accomplish. But one that is vital for your success. Now, I have journeyed long and my eyes are heavy. Woman, may I rest my head here awhile?"

Mell blushed a little and fussed with the cloth. Her head was spinning with a host of contrasting thoughts about Ty, but she had never been one to refuse a traveler rest. "Aye, if it pleases you to stay."

"It does not please me," Ren spat.

But his mother refused to hear his protest.

Defeated, he pushed her comforts aside and stood up to leave. "I say again, what lure do you offer me, stranger?"

Ty lay back and closed his eyes. "The heart has turned to stone around the fire inside it."

"I know this. What of it?"

"Neither you nor your dragon can break it—I can."

"How?"

A smile flickered across Ty's face.

"How?" Ren demanded.

"Ren, you have your answer," said Mell. "Ty's promise alone is your lure."

She nodded at the world outside.

And all Ren could do was storm from the shelter, bitterness chewing at his aching breast.

25

He went to the river to brood there awhile, for wherever he walked around the settlement, people went about their business and would not speak. Mothers drew their children away. Even the mutts took nothing from his hand. He had become that worst of all things: an outcast among his tribe.

"Where are you?" he said to his reflection in the water.

I am here, said Grystina. *Calm yourself, Ren.*

"I cannot." He rested his chin on his knees. "I am shunned worse than a stinking snorter. And Ty is making eyes at my ma. And she at him! Yet my father's spirit is barely loosed."

That may be the least of your troubles.

Ren picked up a stone. He threw it at his face, making ripples of his eyes. "Who *is* Ty? Whence did he come?"

What is Ty? *would be a better question.*

Ren shook his head in confusion. "I see nought but a man."

I sense more than a man. He shadows his auma and he does it well. But in moments of anger, a glint of darkness reveals itself. Think closely on the things he says. He rightly supposes that dragons would not want their power spread among the Hom.

"So?"

How does he know that dragons refer to men as Hom, when you are the only Hom who speaks our tongue?

Ren blinked and thought about this. "Does he read me the way some dragons can?"

Perhaps. More likely, Ty is like you. Somehow, he has gained some dragon auma.

"Then why is his manner so sly?"

I do not know.

There was a pause. Downriver, a honker called.

"What should I do?"

Join him. Form your alliance and go to the mountains.

"What? Previous you spoke against this."

Sometimes deceit must be met with the same. We must learn what Ty is about before we can turn the Wearle against him.

Ren thumped his hands flat on the riverbank. "But I don't go back to aid the Wearle. You know my quest! I would save Rolan's life, return Grogan's heart, and . . . and take my revenge on Gallen and Grynt!"

He almost felt her snort. *Ren, put away this folly. I read you better than you read yourself. Vengeance is not what you truly want. Justice, yes, Ty is right about that, but not war. You will die if you attack Grynt's eyrie. So will Gabrial. Grendel will be banished and my wearlings made savages. Grogan will be forever in torment. His spirit will haunt you all your days. For all your anger at Grynt and Gallen, they will sway in your favor if you unmask* this creature that walks like a Hom and says it can open a dragon heart. There is a threat about Ty that I cannot gauge. He *should be the one in their grasp, not you.*

Ren slapped his hands to his face in dismay.

You know I speak wisely, Grystina said. *Honor is something we treasure, Ren. It's true you have been badly treated, but do not turn against the dragons now. Trust me in this. Be guided by the love you have for Gariffred. Would you slay a dragon in front of the drake?*

"No," Ren said weakly, beginning to see her way. He could picture the horror in Gariffred's eyes if such a scene should ever come to pass. But the balance of power was rapidly changing. Gallen and Grynt must know by now that the simple Hom boy they'd thrown into a pit was more of a threat than they'd bargained for. And so Ren made a pact with himself: He would be peaceable if the dragons were. Let that be his one concession to "honor."

He cleared his hands from his face. "Then let it be so. I hear your counsel and will follow it—unless the Wearle should turn on me again. Shall I summon Gabrial as Ty demands?"

Not yet. There is more to learn. Take me to the horse.

"The what?"

The white whinney. We call them horses. They are gentle creatures, simple of mind. With my help, you might commingle with it.

I tried when we journeyed through the forest, but it was difficult while you slept. I wish to know more of the enchantments on it. The vanishing trick it performs can only be a clever act of phasing, which must have its origins in dragon auma. If we can learn how it—

A twig broke.

Ren turned to see Pine, standing behind him on the rise of the riverbank. The way she crept up like that unnerved him. His mind immediately flashed back to the night she had betrayed him to the oafish scoundrel Varl Rednose. An act that had led to so many deaths. He looked beyond her, worried that a mob might be coming. But it was just the two of them. And a flower, of course.

"What do you want?" he said, jumping up. He shuddered as he realized he'd rather have his back to the river than to Pine. Her strange new teeth made his flesh prickle. He was still uncertain where she stood in all this. Did she ride with Ty of her own free will, or had he dragged her under his spell?

"Bryndle Woodknot is bearing an ax," she said, her words floating like seeds on the wind.

Ren's heart missed a beat. He couldn't be sure what was more unsettling: the unspoken menace in Pine's short message or the calm with which she'd delivered it. Had he heard correctly? Bryndle, with an ax? What was that about?

She plucked a petal. "He says he will have your head afore this night."

Now Ren looked with some urgency at the shelters. They were a hundred paces off, behind a cluster of trees. There was no sign yet of any ax-wielding madman.

In one movement Pine sat down on the spot, her legs crossed, her feet tucked neatly beneath her. Almost playfully she said, "I come here to warn you. Bryndle makes haste to your shelter. He goes calling Ty's name, fully and loud. *Tywyll! Tywyll! Show yerself, rogue!*"

Tywyll. The name sat up at the front of Ren's mind. And Grystina was suddenly alive again. *Ren, do you know the weight this word carries? Do you understand the fear it raises in dragons?*

He didn't. Not fully. Though he thought he remembered Grynt speaking it once, banning its use throughout the Wearle. Tywyll. Was this not the root of an ancient legend that Gabrial and others feared so much? A word that warned of an evil black dragon? Tywyll. He rolled the word over his tongue. And suddenly, there was an answer. The crispness of "Ty" was softened when the name was spoken in full, but it was there all the same, plain as the blackest nose on a mutt. Ren gritted his teeth, cursing himself for not making the connection earlier.

We must escape, said Grystina. *Now we must summon Gabrial in haste.*

"No," Ren muttered, unaware that Pine was merrily

lapping up his confusion. He failed to see a faint smile flash across her lips. "Why does Bryndle come for me sudden?"

"He accuses we three of murder and magicks."

"We three?"

"Me, you, Ty. Your ma, Mell, also. I ran to the water, afeared of his wrath."

Ren tightened his fist. Magicks? He had done no *magicks*. He dashed a look through the trees. Somewhere in the distance, a man's brash voice was calling out a brutal challenge to another. "Girl, be done with your riddles. What gives Bryndle cause to rage at *any* of us?"

"The blight he found on Shade."

"What blight?"

Pine pointed to the back of her knee. "The scar that also showed on Wind."

What? Now Ren shook his head as if nought but fluff was pouring out of Pine's mouth. In all the years he had known the waif, she had barely spoken a jot. These two new teeth had made her chatter like a rattling pan. Here she sat, telling a tale about *Wind?* Wind was his father's pure white mare. She had died during Ned's ill-fated mission to the darkeye cave. Ren remembered his father telling him so.

He heard a woman scream. It could have been any woman. But it could, just as easily, have been his mother.

"I smell blood," said Pine. She picked the last petal.

Ren—

Grystina wanted to speak again. But Ren's energy was all in his feet. He pounded through the bracken, between the first shelters, and burst, panting, into the clearing.

Bryndle Woodknot was writhing on his back, his last breaths eking out of his mouth.

Buried deep in his chest was an ax.

A stain as big as a basket of berries had already spread the width of his robe.

All around him, scavenger crows were gathering.

Ren skidded up and knelt beside him. He tried to clasp Bryndle's hand, but Bryndle with his last act beat the hand away and clawed at Ren's throat as if he would tear Ren's soul right out of him. "Villain," he croaked. And, with a stuttering sigh, he passed into the world of spirits.

All around, the Kaal looked on in shock.

Ty was standing nearest to the body, waiting for it to twitch no more. His clothes above his waist were in some disarray, suggesting he and Bryndle had wrestled before a blow was struck.

Ren stood up and ran at him. "This was done by *your* foul hand!"

Mell dashed forward and placed herself between them, barely able to hold her son back. "No, Ren. Hold your wrath. Ty struck in our defense. A red fury had taken hold of Bryndle.

He came vowing death on all in this shelter. See the cut in the flap where his blade first struck. Ty wrested the ax from his grip, but Bryndle raised a knife and flew at him again. What was Ty to do?" Mell turned to the crowd. "All of you standing here witnessed this. I say again, what was Ty to do?"

A voice frail with fear called out, "Be gone, dark one!"

Ren thought he heard an old man mutter the word *demon*.

Despite this, Ren continued his argument. "He called me villain. Why? What had I done to anger him so?"

"Walk away," Ty hissed. He turned his back.

Ren pushed his mother aside. "Are you what they call you, demon? Speak, *Tywyll*. Is Shade my father's whinney enchanted?"

"What?" said Mell.

Ty stopped, mid-walk. "I told you to walk away, boy."

"Nay. I would hear about Wind," Ren said.

At the same time, a crow called out.

Ty whipped around and looked to the skies.

Someone screamed. Everywhere, eyes widened in fear. Fingers pointed at spaces in the clouds. Children started to howl and cry. Mutts whined and folded their ears. A harsh wind blew across the settlement, bowing every blade of grass in its path. Shadows as large as a shelter swept the erth. The air became less pleasant to breathe.

Ren, said Grystina. *The Wearle is coming.*

Feet stumbled before they ran. This way. That way. Crossing the paths of their own terror. Only Ren and Ty and Mell stood their ground. Mell shuffled closer to Ren, quaking as she gripped his arm for protection. *Boom! Boom!* The erth shuddered and cracked as one by one the skalers landed, creating a churning turbulence. One shelter was caught by an accidental wing that showered mud and thatch across the clearing. The crows dispersed like a flurry of embers. Six or more skalers formed a circle, bounding Ren and those who stood with him. Mell's hair whipped across her face as she spun and looked at each beast in turn. "R-Ren?" She was white with fear.

He too was turning, picking out the faces behind the fangs, wondering if he had any friends among them, wondering what it meant for him if he didn't.

He had his answer soon enough.

The flat of an isoscele came down with a bone-crunching *thwack!* on his shoulder. "Surrender, boy, or lose your head."

Gallen. Who else?

Ren's heart slumped.

He raised his hands slowly—a prisoner of the Veng once more.

26

"No!" screamed Mell.

Though she could not know what Gallen had said, she could see the sharp edge of his isoscele and no doubt feared the worst for Ren. She flung herself at Gallen's tail and foolishly tried to beat it away.

The commander's battle stigs immediately went back.

"Ma, no!"

Too late the cry. With a click, Gallen opened his tail spikes.

Mell gasped as a spike sliced into her hand, pinning it to the tail like a floating leaf.

Ren made to move, but the weight of the isoscele and the keenness of its edge held him steady.

It was left to Ty to go to Mell's aid.

"Mercy," he said to Gallen.

The Veng tilted his head as if his ears were deceiving him. Ren also blinked in surprise. He'd heard the word as clearly as the dragons had. Ty had called for mercy.

In dragontongue.

Ty gripped Mell's wrist and with a rocking motion pulled her clear of the spike. Her thin flesh ripped against the spike's serrations, spurting blood into the air. She screamed and fell into Ty's arms, weeping in agony. He supported her as she dropped to her knees. With a calm, strong hand, he tore a piece of cloth from Bryndle's robe and began to wrap it around Mell's injury.

Ren's mind was now in terrible conflict. For here was his mother, cruelly injured, yet tended by a man who spoke in dragontongue and called himself *Tywyll*. He found the word playing across his lips again as Gallen instructed a purple roamer to come forward and pick Ren up.

Louder, said Grystina. *Make them hear.*

"TYWYLL!" Ren shouted. He slanted his gaze and pointed at Ty.

The roamer gave a start.

Ty calmly continued to bandage Mell.

Ren began to fidget like an irritated buzzer. Had Ty not heard him? Did the man not see the danger he was in? Did he have no *fear*?

Gallen gave an irritated grunt and ordered the bewildered roamer to continue.

It was De:allus Garodor who said, "Wait."

The roamer paused again.

Gallen gave an irritated hiss. "My orders were to seize the boy if we found him here."

"And we will," said Garodor, "after we hear why he spoke as he did. Well, boy?"

Ren gulped and leaned away from the heavy isoscele. Sudden, angry movements made the scale rub dangerously close to a cut. "The girl," he panted, in reply to Garodor's question. His eyes flickered left and right for Pine. She was nowhere to be seen.

She is here, said Grystina. *I sense her, watching. She sits astride Shade, hidden from the dragons.*

"What girl?" the De:allus growled.

"A companion. She . . . rides with him." Why did Pine not show herself? "She identifies this Hom by the dark name 'Tywyll.'"

A light green dragon closest to Garodor made a noise like a startled whinney. It stood back a little and squirted some dung.

Gallen's snort of impatience smoked the whole area. "It's a Hom," he said, gesturing at Ty. "Kill it. In any way you choose. That's an order."

"Wait," the De:allus said once more.

The roamer rocked back, retracting its claws.

Garodor came forward and snorted at Ty. "You. Stand."

Ty stroked Mell's arm and rose to his full height. He looked scathingly at Gallen and wafted away the Veng's bitter smoke. He turned to face the De:allus.

"How do you know our tongue?"

Ty bowed his head. "I have traveled far."

So calm, thought Ren. *So certain of himself in front of a beast many times his size.* "Beware! He has enchantments upon him."

He was silenced by a flex of Gallen's tail.

"The boy mistrusts me," Ty continued, staring into Garodor's half-lidded eyes. "He believes he is the only Hom on this planet able to communicate with the heirs of Godith." He paused while Garodor took this in. "Unless your ears deceive you, the boy is mistaken."

Much to Gallen's muted pleasure, Garodor brought his tail around and put his isoscele under Ty's chin. "Traveled? Where?"

"About," Ty answered. "These mountains are a speck upon the rest of this world. You are not the first of your kind to visit."

Garodor's eyes shined a little keener, inviting Ty to keep on talking.

"I speak not of this Wearle or the one that came before it. I speak of dragons from centuries past."

"Don't listen to him!" cried Ren. "He's—"

But this time Garodor nodded at Gallen, who was only too pleased to turn his isoscele and strike the side of Ren's head, a blow so firm it brought Ren to his knees. Mell scrambled over and cradled him against her. She spat at Gallen, who paid her no heed.

"You are well informed—for a Hom," said Garodor,

instinctively revealing his fangs at Ty. "The name. How do you come to be called what you are? Answer me well or my angry companion will gladly flame you."

Ty reached up slowly and touched his black hair. "Among my kind, it describes my appearance. An uncommon name, yes. But a name, nothing more."

"He's lying," said Ren, coughing blood onto the erth. "He seeks to deceive you. He commands a wyng of crows and plans to steal Grogan's heart."

And to Grystina, he added: *My patience with Gallen wears thin.*

Be calm, she advised. *Do not distract the De:allus from Ty.*

Garodor looked into Ty's dark eyes, twisting the tip of his isoscele enough to lift the man's chin as far as it would stretch. "You stand accused, *Tywyll*. What answer do you give?"

"I say these words sound harsh," Ty gurgled, "coming from a boy who speaks ill of your Prime. He speaks low of me because he is threatened. I rode here on a noble quest. I planned to parley for the heart, not steal it."

"Why?"

"Such gems are prized. A dragon heart has healing properties."

"He makes bold that he can open it," said Ren. He pulled a loose tooth and looked again for Pine. Still the girl was nowhere to be seen.

"They're traitors. Both of them," Gallen growled. "I say we put an end to this here and be done."

But Garodor's thought-filled silence suggested killing was far from his mind. "Take them both to the mountains." He pulled his isoscele away.

"No!" cried Ren. "That's what he wants! Gallen's right. Kill him while you have the chance!"

"Take them," the De:allus repeated quietly.

The purple roamer stepped forward again and clamped Ty nervously in its claws.

"Get up," hissed Gallen, giving Ren a kick. "Our new De:allus sees fit to postpone your overdue departure from life. Get up, boy. Now. And don't even think about phasing or I'll feed this woman to your favorite wearlings."

"No!" screamed Mell, as Ren began to separate from her.

Ren held her off. "Ma, I must go. I will avenge the hurt they have caused you, I swear."

He glared harshly at Gallen. But reprisals, if they came at all, would not come that day.

With a grip that could squeeze the air from a stone, Gallen snatched Ren up in his claws. And the dragons left as they had first arrived, in a cloud of dust and air, sweeping their giant shadows over the fading Kaal settlement.

27

"You are *seriously* beginning to irritate me, boy." Prime Grynt was leaning over Ren's body, close enough to skewer a fang into his neck should Ren attempt to scrabble away. "I have a mind to slice you in half and feed a piece each to Grendel's wearlings."

"Then you'll learn nothing," Ren said angrily. He was on his knees in Grynt's eyrie, just the Prime and De:allus Garodor with him, plus a couple of guards at either side of the cave mouth. Gallen, having dropped him, had flown away to reassess his security network. "Where is Ty?"

"Under guard, with the other Hom," said Garodor.

"Rolan? Is he hurt?" Ren raised his head. He wiped a little snot away from his nose.

"No, but he will be," Grynt put in, "unless you answer Garodor's questions."

Ren slanted his gaze toward the De:allus. "If you're half as smart as Graymere was, you'll understand the danger you're in."

Grynt snarled again and pushed his snout so close to Ren's face that Ren could feel the heat drying up the spiker wounds. "Curb your tongue, boy. The De:allus, as I'm sure you're aware, is more lenient than myself or Veng Commander Gallen. He takes pleasure in understanding your scheming Hom mind. But mark me well, he'll slit your throat if I order him to, always assuming I don't cut you first. I hear the word *vengeance* in Gallen's reports and find myself wondering how long it would take the small animals of this planet to clean your scrawny carcass off the mountainside."

Ren turned his face away, fighting to keep his anger in check. "You're wasting time. Ty plots against you. He wants Grogan's heart, but I don't know why."

"Was it you who taught him dragontongue?" Garodor asked.

"No."

"Then how does he know it?"

"I don't know. Mebbe he told the truth. Mebbe there were other dragons here before you."

"Is that possible?" said Grynt.

Garodor cleared his spiracles. As usual, he gave a knowledgeable answer, though Ren thought he noted a measure of uncertainty in the De:allus. "There have always been rumors of unauthorized fire stars. It's not inconceivable that a rogue Wearle found this place and settled for a while. There was a lot of movement across the universe before the Higher established the voyaging laws."

"Then why have we seen no evidence of them?"

"It's possible we haven't encountered them yet; the recent battles with the goyles have depleted your numbers and stopped the mappers exploring widely. The planet is large, remember."

Ren shook his head and laughed at them. "Ty is sly. As dark as his name suggests. He enchants all he meets yet kills without feeling. I tell you he is plotting something. He stole the spirit of my father's whinney. How could you bring such a creature among you?"

"Whinney?" Grynt twisted a nostril.

"The Hom name for a horse," Garodor translated. "Explain yourself, boy. What do you mean, he stole the beast's spirit?"

Ren put his hands to his hair and found it matted with dirt and blood. For once in his life he ached to wash it. It was barely white anymore. "Pine, the girl I spoke of at the settlement, took two whinneys to Bryndle Woodknot, the man Ty murdered, for feed and care. Bryndle saw a mark on the leg of Ty's whinney that showed it to be my father's old ride. Yet my father told me Wind was dead. And now she returns—with a twisting horn full out of her head."

"You've seen this beast?" Grynt asked the De:allus.

"No," said Garodor, tightening his eye ridges. "A mistake on my part. I will seek out the girl when this is done and bring the beast here." He turned back to Ren and changed the subject. "Tell me about the cave."

Ren looked up. Each scaled head was twice the size of his puny chest. He had never felt quite so small in front of the dragons before. "Cave?"

"The place where your ill-fated friends slew a Veng."

"Speak," said Grynt, flashing a claw, just to remind Ren his life was on the line.

With a tingle of fear in his voice, Ren said, "My father and others were journeying there to raise two resting darkeyes against you. Their party was attacked and the dragon killed. That's all I know."

"Darkeyes?" Garodor tilted his head.

"Aye. This is how we called the goyles."

"And there were two? In the cave? You're sure of that?"

Ren nodded. "Two were spoke of, but none were found."

"Go on," said Garodor.

Ren lifted his shoulders. What more could he say? The dragons had seen the cave for themselves. "In the end, it were nought but a false quest. My father came home in sweat and torment saying there were no darkeyes there."

"That would confirm my findings," said Garodor, "about the skin deposits."

"Skin?" said Ren, glancing at his arm.

A growl gathered in the back of Grynt's throat. His anger came down on the boy once more. "Why have you said nothing of these goyles till now?"

Ren shied away from the heat of Grynt's breath and the sticky drool leaking off his fierce jaws. He shook his head at the irony of the question. "I tried," he snarled. "I chanced my way across the scorch line to warn you that my people were planning to turn these creatures against you. Then the battles began and there was no need. If the goyles are all dead, why does this vex you?"

Garodor flexed his tail. He extended his foreclaws and tapped them together. "The Hom you call Rolan was captured on the hill outside this cave. Why was he there?"

Ren sighed and scratched the back of his neck, where a nibbler was doing its best to burrow into one of his wounds. So many questions. So much time slipping away. Time that could be spent interrogating Ty. "Rolan had gone with Ty and others to take back the body of Waylen Treader, the man who slew the dragon. But they could not gain passage into the cave. The rest your murdering Veng must know."

Despite the rebuke embedded in these words, neither Garodor nor Grynt responded angrily. Grynt merely turned to Garodor and said, "There was no mention of a Hom body in your report."

"What?" Ren raised his head, almost twisting his ears like a dragon would. "That cannot be. Waylen were left for dead aside the dragon. I heard this too from my pa's own mouth."

"Could the goyle have eaten it?" Grynt asked.

Garodor's bright yellow eyes rolled inward, his gaze focused just beyond the tip of his snout. "There was no evidence of feasting. No Hom remains, but . . ."

"No, no," Ren insisted, as the wind blew around the sides of the eyrie and panic danced in his youthful heart. "I tell you true, there were no goyles."

But if that was so, where had the ugly creatures gone? And, more important, where was *Waylen*? "Let me speak with Rolan," Ren pleaded again. "If evil was done at that cave, he will know something of it."

At last, Garodor agreed. He nodded at Grynt, who barked, "Guard!"

The roamer on the far right snapped to attention.

"Find Veng Commander Gallen and tell him to bring the Hom prisoners to me. Quickly."

The roamer hurred in acknowledgment, spread its wings, and flew.

Ren stood up, finding balance difficult. After being slashed by spikers, knocked senseless by an isoscele, and then squeezed like a berry in Gallen's claws, his body was begging to lie level with the erth. But all the while his mind was buzzing, about Ty, the missing goyles, and not least his perilous promise to Grogan. "Where's the heart?" he asked. "You must protect Grogan's heart. If Ty steals it—"

"No power in this world could release that dragon's fire," said Grynt. "And I won't be distracted by your superstitious babble. The heart will be safe, wherever it's kept. Even your favorite blue could surely not fail me in that task."

"Gabrial is guarding it?"

"He'd better be."

"But I thought . . . ?"

"You thought what?"

"Nothing." Ren gulped, shrinking back, for once grateful of Grynt's intervening snarl. It had saved him from saying that he knew of the injury to Gabrial's wing, which would have implicated Grendel (and even Gariffred) in his escape from the fhosforent mines. And what *of* Grendel? Until this moment Ren had assumed she'd been captured on that stormy night and hauled away for interrogation; Grynt's reaction suggested the female dragon had gotten back to her eyrie undetected. "Are the wearlings with Gabrial?"

"Yes. Does that concern you?" Garodor asked.

"It concerns me that Grogan's heart is kept near them. That *Ty* might go near the pupps."

And Pine, for that matter. Ren was still deeply suspicious of her motives. If Grystina was right, Onetooth would have seen Ty taken from the settlement. So where was she now? What was she up to? She and the mysteriously reborn Wind. If Pine and Ty rode together, maybe they also plotted together.

The De:allus breathed in slowly. "You heard Prime Grynt; the heart cannot be opened."

"Yet Ty boasts that it can. What if he truly knows a way? Why would he put himself in this much danger just to trade words for a useless piece of rock?"

"I grow tired of this," said Grynt. "Have the heart brought here as well. Let's see how this arrogant Ty performs when he's under threat from my fire. I want Gallen, Grymric, and Elder Gossana in attendance. Go to her first. Call the blue as well, now he's fit enough to fly."

Garodor bowed in acknowledgment.

"And me?" asked Ren, when the dust of Garodor's departure had settled.

"You will stay where I can watch you," Grynt said. "I have still to learn how you fled that pit and killed one of my Veng in the process. If anyone is a threat to the Wearle, it's you."

"It was the spirit of Grogan," Ren said bluntly. "It rose against the Veng and stopped its hearts." And maybe it would stop his too, if he did not honor his promise to the wraith.

"Then we are challenged on all sides," Prime Grynt said.

"So let this be the day we reckon with spirits and dark enchantments and call upon Godith to settle all threats. You'd better pray that you are ready for it, boy. This may be the last time you look upon the light."

Or the last time you do, Ren said to himself.

And he sat, cross-legged, on the cave floor and stared thoughtfully into the pale blue sky.

PART FIVE

THE TYWYLL

❦ 28 ❦

Gabrial and Grendel's eyrie, that same morning
Graark!

Grendel raised her head and sighed.

The wearmyss, Gayl, was awake again and bleating.

Sometimes, being a mother was hard.

It was a curious fact that throughout Gabrial's enforced incarceration, the family slept whenever tiredness fell upon them. Often, that meant during the day. Even then Grendel was regularly woken by the timid wearmyss pawing at her neck and mewing for attention. It was usually the case that Gayl had been nudged beyond the curl of Grendel's tail by the awkward spread of her brother during sleep. A rearrangement of limbs and a hurr of comfort typically calmed her. This time it was different. The myss was hovering on the threshold of the sleeping chamber, calling Grendel toward the cave proper.

Mystified, Grendel rose up. Gabrial and Gariffred were fast asleep. The drake had his head tucked under his wing. Gabrial was snoring lightly and popping smoke with every exhalation. Grendel left them to it and padded over to stand by Gayl. She raked the wearling's back with her isoscele.

"Gayl, what is it?"

Graaar, the myss replied. Neither wearling had many words yet. When they needed to communicate, much emphasis was placed on the timbre of their growls and the physical gestures they made.

"The cave?" said Grendel, peering around. It all looked normal, if a little gloomy. Morning had struggled to make an impact. The semi-oval entrance to the cave was lit by a somewhat bland gray sky. To one side was the pillar bearing Grogan's heart. And at the corner of the cave mouth sat a bored-looking Goodle. He straightened his neck when he heard Grendel's voice.

"Is there a problem, Matrial?"

Like *he* would know. After Grendel's attempt to go to Ren's aid, Goodle had resumed his duties completely unaware he'd been glamored by her. Gabrial, whose wings were now at full strength, had muttered privately that Goodle was more of an ornament than a guard. But there was no animosity between the adults and the family had grown used to Goodle's presence. The situation was relaxed enough that Goodle tolerated the wearlings running around him during play. And he was always polite; Grendel liked that.

"Gayl is restless," she replied. She yawned widely, smoke curling in tiny balls in her throat. She puffed them out in a series of diminishing rings. "She's dragged me into the cave for some reason. Is something happening outside?"

"Not that I know of," Goodle answered. "A wyng of roamers flew over not long ago, led by Veng Commander Gallen. They were heading for Skytouch. De:allus Garodor might have been with them."

"A search wyng?" Grendel's primary heart was suddenly stoked with a flood of anxiety. Every time a dragon flew by, she thought about Ren and what might have become of the boy. She shook herself fully awake. "Did they have captives? Hom prisoners? Did they have Ren?"

"I don't know. I wasn't really concentrating." Goodle flicked his tail as if he was genuinely sorry he couldn't be of more help. He brought the subject back to Gayl. "She's been up for a while. I heard her shuffling around."

"Doing what?"

"I don't know. She was in the shadows. I heard her crying, but—"

"Crying?" A maternal snap crept into Grendel's voice.

"I assumed you would go to her," Goodle said. He broadened his shoulders. "As you know, I'm not allowed to leave my post."

Gaa-raar.

Gayl was mewing again. While the adults had been

talking, she had moved into the light and picked up a small rock. It was a little bigger than she was comfortably capable of lifting, but not only did she lift it, she threw it almost vertically upward. The clatter when it landed made Goodle start.

"Now, why has she done that?"

Grendel looked around the cave again, her locatory stigs beginning to bristle. Was it her imagination, or could she smell the sweat of a warm-blooded animal being faintly tossed around whenever the wind eddied? She took in a deeper swatch of air and looked over her shoulder toward the tunnels. "Goodle, has anything entered the cave?"

"Of course not."

"Are you sure? A bird? Anything?"

"I'm fully alert," he said, bristling a little. "Nothing has come past me." Rarely, for him, he showed his fangs.

Grendel moved into the open. She picked up the rock that Gayl had thrown. "Like this?" she said, lifting it.

The wearmyss nodded.

"Then down?" Grendel dropped the rock in front of her.

Gayl looked at it, then swept it out of sight with her tail.

Now Goodle was even more confused. "Is she playing a game?"

"No," said Grendel, quietly drumming her claws. "Gayl is sensitive. More observant than several Elders I can think of.

She's trying to tell us something." She picked up a similarly sized rock and dropped that in front of the wearmyss as well. The youngster swept it into the open sky. Then she raised her tail and used the budding blob that would soon become an isoscele to point nervously across the cave.

Grendel's gaze came to rest upon the pillar that supported Grogan's heart.

A beat passed.

Goodle blinked.

Somewhere in the distance, a crow screeched.

Then . . .

"GABRIAL!" Grendel roared so loudly that grit showered down from cracks in the ceiling. In two pounding steps, she was by the pillar.

"What? What is it?" Goodle fussed. "Grendel, what's the matter?"

"A dark force has visited the cave," she muttered.

"That's impossible. I was—"

"GABRIAL!" Grendel roared again. "Look!" she said to Goodle, a growl in her voice. "What do you see on the pillar?"

Goodle flustered his wings. "Well, it's Grogan's heart, of cour—"

But it wasn't Grogan's heart. He could see that now. It was nothing but an ordinary rock, about the same size and shape as the heart but with none of its hardened veins and walls.

"Gayl saw it," muttered Grendel, looking out at the sky. "She saw it lifted and she saw it disappear. This stone has been put in its place to fool us."

"Saw what disappear?" said Gabrial, approaching.

"Raise the Wearle," Grendel said urgently to him. "We're under attack by an invisible spirit."

He followed her gaze and looked at the bogus heart on the pillar.

"Grogan's heart has been stolen," she said.

29

Barely moments later, De:allus Garodor arrived at the cave. "Gabrial, I am to escort you to Prime Grynt's eyrie."

"You'll want to hear about this first," Grendel said.

She pointed to the stone and told the De:allus all she knew.

"This is not a false strategy to free us," she added, noting Garodor's glint of suspicion. She had to concede that in his position it was easier to believe that one of the dragons inside the cave had arranged the swap, rather than accept that an unseen force had snuck past Goodle. She looked twice at Gariffred in that regard, for the drake was unusually fond of collecting stones and had lately found some odd-shaped ones in the tunnels. But after commingling briefly with Gayl, Garodor confirmed that something had indeed stolen the heart. He said, "Gabrial, come with me. Goodle, stay here and be on your guard. Look after Grendel and the wearlings."

"Look after us?" Grendel snorted, making Gayl cower. "Is that the best you can offer?"

Garodor said, "You're in no danger. If this force had meant to harm you, you'd be dead already."

"He's right, Grendel," Gabrial agreed. He stroked her neck, though for once she took little comfort from it.

At that moment, Gariffred came forward and spilled three rocks in front of his guardian.

"Thank you," said Gabrial, touching the drake's snout. "We'll play with those later. You stay with Mama now."

"No, wait," said Garodor, as Gabrial prepared for flight. He looked down at the rocks and studied them carefully. "Where did you find those?"

Graark? said Gariffred. He dipped low to the ground, afraid he'd done wrong.

"He picks them up in the tunnels," said Grendel. "An odd quirk, nothing more. Healer Grymric is aware of it. Please don't frighten him. He's not used to the glare of your eyes."

Garodor shuttered his eyelids a little. Pointing at the rocks, he said to Gariffred, "May I show you something, little one?"

Gariffred wiggled his snout—and nodded.

The De:allus picked up all three rocks and turned them deftly in his claws, until . . .

Gaaaaar! exclaimed the drake, his eyes as round as the pale Erth moon.

His exclamation was echoed by Goodle, who said, "Is that . . . ?"

"A memory stone, yes." Garodor held it up for all to see. Gariffred's pieces had fused together and transformed themselves into a glowing orb. The structure appeared opaque at first, but when Gabrial peered closely, he could see threads of movement at its turbulent center, like plant strands twisting in water.

"Can you read it?" he asked.

"I'm not sure," said Garodor. "It's been encrypted with the mark of an Elder."

"Givnay," said Grendel, pulling back. She shuddered at the thought of what evils the stone might reveal.

Garodor turned the orb left and right. "Givnay may have kept the pieces hidden, but I don't believe he created this stone. It looks too old."

"Could he have found it here?" asked Gabrial. "Perhaps a dragon from the first Wearle created it?"

"Perhaps," the De:allus muttered, studying the moving memory threads. He focused his extraordinary eyes on the stone. For several moments, waves of yellow and purple light flickered back and forth as he scanned the contents.

Gariffred, seeing this, became excited. He sat up and reached for the orb.

"No!" said Grendel, with a mild growl, concerned he might break Garodor's concentration.

The drake grizzled and sat back on his tail. But by then the pretty lights had ended anyway.

"I'm sorry, I must keep this," the De:allus said to Grendel, holding the stone out of Gariffred's reach. "If he finds any more, notify me."

Grendel nodded. She drew Gariffred under her wing.

"He's clever," Garodor said, admiring the drake. He glanced at Gayl. "They both are. I'll send you extra protection. Oh, and I have news. We found Ren."

Rrren, the drake echoed, widening his jaws.

"Alive?" asked Gabrial. He put his tail across Grendel to stop her saying anything out of turn.

"Yes," said Garodor, noting Gariffred's agitation. "He's covered in flesh wounds, but he's lively enough. He's with Prime Grynt. We need him to help us interrogate a new Hom prisoner."

"Where was he? Where did you find him?" asked Grendel.

Garodor turned and looked at her. "The Hom settlement. We had a roamer sweeping the area from the time Ren went missing. You seem surprised. Where did you think the boy might be?"

Grendel tried not to let her neck scales flush. It was a well-known fact that all De:allus dragons had a keen eye for detecting guilt. "I want him brought back to us," she said, proudly strengthening her hold on Gariffred.

"You know that's not possible," Garodor replied. "But if the boy helps us, Grynt may be persuaded to look kindly upon him. That's all I can promise you. Gabrial, come with me."

Rrren! Gariffred cried a second time.

I'll protect him, Gabrial said in his thoughts to Grendel.

He looked at Goodle, who sat up smartly. "Defend the eyrie with your life," he said, and departed at Garodor's side.

At Grynt's cave, Gabrial's ears were lashed again. "Stolen? You were supposed to be guarding the heart!"

"I can't fight what I cannot see," snapped the blue.

"You wouldn't see your own tail if it poked you in the eye," said Gossana.

Not for the first time, she and Gabrial exchanged a venomous glance.

"It was Pine," said Ren, bravely coming between the dragons. He put a hand on Gabrial's neck to calm him.

Are you well? Gabrial asked, hoping Ren would receive the message. Although they had dabbled with the transfer of thoughts, Ren was no expert.

But Ren heard it and replied, *Been better.*

Gabrial nodded to say he understood. *Who is Pine?*

A Hom girl. An enemy, perhaps. Ren turned to Grynt and Garodor again. "There is an enchantment on Wind that veils her. Pine must have used it to get into the cave."

"How?" said Grynt. "The cliff is too steep. No horse could scale those heights."

"Unless it phased," said Garodor.

"Phased?" Gossana twisted her snout as if something unsavory had landed upon it.

"The gift of concealment may not be its only trick."

Gabrial was the first to respond. "But . . . how could a simple-minded creature like that gain such powers?" he asked. He had clearly missed a great deal during his confinement.

"I fear this is the work of the goyles," said Garodor, blowing a solemn wisp of smoke. Turning directly to Grynt, he said, "I stand by my earlier theory. We know from Ren that two goyles were in the cave. I believe their bodies have gone through a critical metamorphosis, one that involves the shedding of the dragon-goyle form. If I'm right, their auma might be able to travel between hosts. If one of them entered the horse, for instance, it could alter the horse's physical—and mental—composition. It would explore the material capabilities of the creature and attempt to make improvements. Some means of flight would be a natural progression. It's one of the superior attributes that separate us from beings like the Hom, after all."

Ren jutted his chin as if to remind them he was not "inferior." But before he could comment, Grynt was speaking again. "Why? What does it benefit these creatures to move into other, weaker, life-forms?"

"It makes them harder to detect," said Gabrial.

"Precisely," said Garodor. "We would flame a goyle without hesitation; horses or men we would not perceive as threats."

"But what is their *purpose*?" Gossana thundered. Her impressive ruffle of sawfin scales billowed behind her ears. "Why would anyone want a hardened *heart*?"

"For the prize inside it," Garodor replied. "The untamed spark of life."

"But you swore the heart could not be opened," said Ren.

"Perhaps I was wrong," Garodor replied.

None of this found much favor with Gossana. "This is ridiculous. We're going around in circles!"

"Could the memory stone give you an answer?" asked Gabrial, believing he was helping Garodor's cause. The look on Garodor's face suggested he would rather have kept that knowledge quiet.

"Memory stone? What memory stone?" said Grynt.

Garodor held it up to the light. "This was found in Givnay's eyrie. We know that the Elder took a great deal of interest in the fhosforent mine and what effects the ore could have on our auma. This may turn out to be a record of his findings. I'm . . . close to unlocking the code that binds it."

"Givnay . . ." Gossana growled, in a manner that suggested she'd chew that dragon's head off, were he still alive.

"I never asked," Grynt said, his voice a low rumble. "What did you find when you went to the mines?"

Garodor shuttered his eyes a little. "Nothing I feel able to comment on yet. It will take time to establish the mechanism of the mutation. For now, we should concentrate our efforts on what's in front of us."

"I have a question," said Gabrial, in the silence that followed. "The De:allus said there were two goyles. If one is in the horse, where has the second one gone?"

Garodor took a measured breath. "I believe it's in the man we seized at Ren's settlement."

"Ty!" gasped Ren, beginning to understand. He remembered Grystina's thoughts when she'd met him: *I sense more than a man. He shadows his auma and he does it well.* "That's why you didn't find Waylen's body! Ty is Waylen, changed by a goyle."

"I want that Hom here now," said Grynt, thumping his tail down hard. The reverberation almost pushed Ren's stomach through his ribs.

Garodor looked out at the sky, a puzzled expression challenging his normally composed features. "Didn't you send word that Gallen should bring him? Shouldn't the commander be here already?"

"Something must have happened," said Gabrial. "We

should investigate." He exchanged an urgent glance with Garodor. Both dragons set themselves for flight.

"Take me with you!" begged Ren, his senses still rocking with the horror of Garodor's revelation.

"Be quiet," said Grynt. "You're going nowhere."

"Unless it's off the cliff, with my help," Gossana muttered.

"He could be useful," said Gabrial.

Garodor agreed. "The blue's right. We still need to hear what the other Hom knows. And it will work to our advantage if Ty continues to believe that Ren is our prisoner."

"He *is* our prisoner," Grynt rumbled.

"You cannot hold me!" Ren snapped back. "I can phase and—"

His rant quickly ended as a glistening claw pressed under his chin. "You've seen enough of us, boy, to know how deep this claw could penetrate. I could scratch out your soft Hom brain before you could even *think* of phasing."

"Prime—?"

"Be quiet," Grynt snarled, without looking at Gabrial. Drilling his gaze into Ren, he said, "I'm going to take the advice of my De:allus and give you one last chance to save yourself. You will learn everything this prisoner knows and give the information up to Garodor. Betray us and I'll come for you myself. Is that clear?"

Ren gulped and gave the slightest of nods. A greater movement would have lanced his throat.

Grynt pulled his claw away. "He's your responsibility," he said to Gabrial. "Keep *that* in your impulsive mind."

"I will," said Gabrial. "Ren . . . ?"

Ren clambered onto Gabrial's back.

"Godith help us," Gossana said. She looked scathingly at Grynt. "What kind of leader sends a Hom boy in search of a Veng commander? I'm going to my eyrie. I need to rest."

With barely a lift of her wings, she dived into the open and was gone.

As Gabrial and Garodor prepared to do likewise, Ren looked starkly at Grynt and said, "Know this: I never wanted to war with you."

And without giving Grynt a chance to respond, he slapped Gabrial's shoulder.

And they flew.

30

Since the day of his capture, Rolan Woodknot had been held on a steep, stark crag that projected skyward from a singular outcrop high on Mount Vargos. The crag was open to everything the skies could throw at it. An arch-shaped indent close to its base offered meager shelter from the storms that continually battered the crag, but nothing could keep out the biting cold.

Rolan's guard, a stout green roamer called Gus, who blended neatly with the dark gray rocks and the withering patches of lichen that grew on them, had kept him fed—or at least had tried to. Throughout the first day, Rolan had shivered with his head against his knees, refusing to look at the long-eared hopper Gus had killed for him. But on the second day, with the threat of malnourishment clawing at his gut, Rolan had turned in desperation to the offering. He had picked up the hopper and held it straddled across his palms. "Can't eat this!" he'd wailed, spreading his thumb across fang holes stinking of congealing blood. He made biting movements, showing that he wanted to eat, but the kill was too wet, too raw. He opened his hands and dropped the hopper with a splat, gesturing at Gus to say it was useless, even putting out his tongue and making a face the way a moody child might. He let Gus see the blood dripping from his fingers. The dragon tilted its head and made rumbling noises. *Hopeless*, thought Rolan, and buried his head in his knees again.

But, amazingly, his captor seemed to understand. Gus had heard from other roamers that the Hom liked to eat their meat *hot*. So he picked up the hopper and moved it to a flat rock, then roasted it in flame, cooking it in seconds. With a look that suggested his actions were a waste of a perfectly good kill, he tossed the charred hopper back to Rolan. Rolan scrabbled after it. He picked it up at the third attempt, the blood on his fingertips fizzing and bubbling against the heat. He tore away the blackened fur and bit into the sweet, hot muscle underneath, nodding gratefully at Gus as he ripped and chewed. The dragon sniffed and settled back to his duties. Rolan ate on, and learned that day that skalers were not the pitiless brutes he'd always been led to believe. It was a lesson that would come to have serious consequences on the fourth day of his captivity.

That was the day that another roamer brought Ty to the crag. Rolan leapt up as soon as he saw him. Even before the dragon could drop its cargo, Rolan had picked up a stone and hurled it at the rogue. The stone missed by some way and clattered down the mountain. Gus responded with force, pinning Rolan back against the rocks.

"Kill him!" Rolan cried, making claw shapes with his hands. "He walks with evil! Kill him! I command you!"

Raar! Gus bellowed, spraying specks of hot saliva.

Rolan shrank back in terror, protecting his ears.

The approaching dragon put Ty down, less than five paces away. It exchanged a few sounds with Gus, then took off, leaving Gus to guard both men.

Ty, none the worse for being clamped, adjusted his clothing and smiled darkly. Without looking at his fellow prisoner, he said, "We meet again, Rolan Woodknot. I took you for a dead man. Clearly, I was wrong." He hunched down as comfortably as the space would allow, shaking his dark hair off his shoulders. "A fine view," he said, panning his gaze across the silent hills.

"How can you talk of such things?" spat Rolan. He took a threatening step forward, only to be warned away by a low rumble from Gus. The dragon had settled on the peak of the crag, but was ready to intervene at the first sign of trouble. "I saw what you did to Pine. If this beast were not present—"

"You would throw yourself at me and find yourself dying at the foot of the mountains." Ty turned his head and looked at him harshly. "Tell me, Rolan. Speak it true: How badly do you want these beasts defeated? How much do you want these mountains returned to the Kaal?"

"I would pick up these mountains and walk with them

before bending my ear to any foul oath of yours. Before my eyes, you slew an innocent child. I will avenge Pine's spirit if I have to hunt you down in this life or the next."

Ty flicked a grain of rock off his knee. "You speak bravely, boy, but your threat has no substance. What you saw by the cave was a change in Pine. She is not dead. Her memories and more still float within her. I opened the vessel that contains her spirit and gave her strength beyond her means. I did the same for Waylen Treader. Look upon me now. Is this not the man you once called friend?"

And right before Rolan's astonished eyes, Ty's dark hair faded to the color of wheat and he changed his features to resemble Waylen's.

Rolan was immediately sick to his stomach. He bent forward and retched, coating the crag in a foul yellow slick. Gus snorted impatiently and stretched his neck to see what was happening. Ty, who had transformed for only an instant, pointed the blame at the latest batch of hopper remains, then stared at the sky as if nothing had happened.

Gus grunted and settled back on his perch.

"What are you?" growled Rolan, when the bile had ceased to burn his throat.

"I told you," said Ty, his gaze drifting to the far horizon. "I was dragon once, noble, kind of spirit. I was sent from my world to explore this place. We were ordered by our Prime to seek out and mine an ore called fhosforent. Working with the fhosforent changed our nature, mutating us into the form you call 'darkeye.' The mutation was harsh, impossible to control. One of our hearts was destroyed in the change, cutting our sacred bond to Godith."

"Godith?"

"The Creator," Ty answered, growling as his thoughts pored over the word. "She who made dragons in Her i:mage. The mutation turned us against Godith and everything that looked to Her light for guidance. So we fought the i:mage we had once been proud of. We defeated the dragons, leaving two of us surviving."

"The two that were tracked to the cave."

Ty nodded. "By then we were changing again. Our bodies were shrinking, no longer of use. By the time Ned Whitehair found us, our transformation was almost complete."

"The pink mist," said Rolan, knuckling his freezing hands together.

Ty nodded. "Aye. That was our auma. You saw it reawaken Pine."

Rolan tightened his fists. He well remembered the horror of that moment. "And what of Oleg and Cob? You called a skaler down upon them. What hope did they have of waking again?"

His angry tone made Gus stretch forward. The dragon

smoked both men and let them see his primary fangs. Rolan lifted his hands in surrender. Gus snorted and again pulled back.

"I needed a passage into the cave," said Ty. "Only a dragon could move those rocks. I had not planned to kill Oleg and Cob. But they were nothing to me. And they were dead men as soon as Cob became trapped."

"And *me*? What was I to you?"

"You were the companion I wanted, Rolan."

Rolan shook his head in disbelief. "You would have cut me the way you cut Pine?"

"In preference to the girl, aye. She was nought but a whimsy; an easy vessel if you were lost—though it would have amused me to see her try to sing herself clear of a dragon's flame."

Rolan fired a gobbet of spittle at him. "Have that for your 'amusement' and your 'preference.' I would rather die in a skaler's flames than make a friend of you."

"Then you are a fool." Ty wiped his face. "In this form, you would have many powers. The whole history of your birth line would be known to you. Imagine that. Knowing all that your Fathers have seen. Knowing the true history of men and skalers . . ."

"You mock me, villain. I care nought for your riddles."

"Then pray. For that is all you have left. Darkness is about to descend on this world. I serve a new master, and so does Pine. His blood is in the mountains, his heart is in the *air*. A legend is ready to rise again, Rolan. Graven, son of Godith, is here. The black dragon is coming."

A sudden scraping of feet above them announced the fact that Gus was moving. He appeared to have spotted something in the sky, though it was too far distant for Rolan to see. Ty was as calm as he had been from the start. But as the object drew closer, furrows of surprise appeared around his eyes.

Rolan, likewise, was equally stunned. "Is that . . . Shade?" he muttered.

A white whinney, with wings, was flying toward them, traveling as smoothly as any bird. As it drew nearer, Rolan could see that it was indeed Shade. On her back sat Pine, one hand on Shade's mane to guide her, the other hand clutching what looked to Rolan like a large stone.

"What breed of magick is this," Ty muttered, in a manner that suggested he did not approve of this new development in the horse. "At least she has the dragon heart."

Gus rose to his full height and roared a warning.

Shade flew on, lowering her head so the horn was pointing firmly at the dragon.

Gus roared again. The crag shook as his giant wings extended.

"Choose now, Rolan Woodknot," Ty said calmly. Despite the narrowness of the ledge, he jumped to his feet. "Your skaler guard is about to fall. If you would be victorious, join me."

Shade swept overhead.

Gus turned clumsily to watch, sending a shower of gravel down the crag face. His tail thumped the rocks, scattering some of the hopper remains.

"Why does she wait?" growled Ty. He shouted at the sky, "Why do you wait, girl? Kill it and be done."

"Ty."

Ty turned to see Rolan on his feet. Rolan was holding a sharp-ended hopper bone.

"I choose them," said Rolan. "I choose the skalers."

And without hesitation, he drove the bone toward Ty's neck.

31

Ty saw the strike coming and immediately transformed into the shape of a crow. The bird was bigger than Rolan remembered, but that would be part of Ty's undoing. For Rolan, despite his disaffection for violence, had always been quick with a blade.

And so it happened that the point of the bone made a vital contact with the body of the crow, tearing enough of a hole in its breast to rip out feathers and cause a leakage of the "auma" Ty had spoken of. The mist puffed out in a haze of pink. But as it began to swirl and regather, it was blown some distance away from the wound in the downdraft of air as Gus took off. The crow screamed, more in annoyance than pain, and flew at Rolan's face. It went straight for his eyes, claws out, raging. But Rolan, remembering the attack on Oleg, was ready for it. In a flash, his hands went up and he caught the bird in a muddling fury of wings and claws. Yet try as he might to murder the thing, he did not have strength enough to snap the shoulder bones or crush the belly cradle inward. And all the time the beak was jabbing, jabbing and snapping, forcing him to turn his face away. This was how he came to lose an ear. For the thing he had least expected was that Ty, in this form, would be able to issue the same kind of venom usually seen from the mouths of darkeyes.

Fzzzt!

Out came a vicious jet of it. It burned with savage intensity, melting the shell of Rolan's ear and hissing along the walls of the canal that fed into his throat. Rolan screamed for all creation to hear, for it seemed like the center of his head was ablaze. He backed away, shaking his head. In doing so, he lost his balance—and fell. Even then he had the presence of mind to cling tighter to Ty, hoping, perhaps, that whatever impact awaited him would also crush the evil in his hands. But the crag, though steep, had many swellings and spurs. One of those spurs stopped Rolan's fall, catching him like a piece of blown rag in the pincers of a narrow rift in the rocks. It was enough to force him to let go of Ty. The bird fluttered away, leaving Rolan for dead. Rolan, his chest stoved in at one side and his head half eaten, knew his part in the fighting was done. Before he passed out of consciousness, the last thing he saw was Gus turning, about to bear down. "Burn it," Rolan whispered. "Burn this evil." And all went black for him.

❧

Gus's principal orders were very plain: guard both Hom; punish them if they try to escape; above all, keep them alive. The last thing Gus had expected to see was the two men fighting. And then one become a crow! He immediately wanted to confront the crow. There was a growing rumor among the Wearle that the birds were plotting against the dragons, absurd as that might seem. It was the sight of the flying horse, however, that propelled him into the sky. Ever since the goyle attacks, any sizable creature with wings had to be considered a serious threat. So as the horse flashed over and veered away, Gus took off in pursuit, challenging the beast to identify itself. Within a wingbeat or two he was in its slipstream, gaining with every flap. He locked his battle stigs into position and sucked in air to ignite his fire sacs. Pine looked over her shoulder for him. She smiled and slapped the whinney's neck. Shade flashed her tail and performed a roll, fading out of sight as she twisted. In confusion and panic, Gus flamed the broad area in front of him. The flames died in a pretty array of whorls.

Nothing squealed or dropped out of the sky.

Meanwhile, with Rolan helpless and beaten, Ty was trying to stabilize his auma. The stiff flow of air around the crag had strung the pink mist into a cloud. A simple act of concentration was all it required to collate the wisps into a tidy trail, ready to be drawn into the wound site on the crow's belly again. But as Ty was about to complete the act, Pine brought Shade to appear in front of him.

"*Ark!* Stay back! You'll draw the dragon!"

Ty was right to be concerned. Every segment of Gus's brightly jeweled eyes was sweeping the sky, looking for the horse.

Shade hovered in front of the crag, the hustling beat of her wings disrupting the auma trail even more. Pine stroked the pure white mane and said, "But I can outfly any skaler, *Master*. See plain my endeavor. Now we *both* have wings."

There was a caustic charge in the way she spoke these words, for she was in control of things now. "Look, I found the heart," she said brightly. "It was in the cave, where the crows showed it to be. I stole it with ease."

"The dragon!" Ty rapped out another reminder. He flew to a less-exposed part of the crag.

Without another word, Pine stretched her fingers over Shade's horn. A bolt of energy surged from its tip. It lit up the auma trail and blew it apart, creating even more strands than before.

"What are you doing?" caarked Ty, the crow voice weak.

"Winning," said Pine. "You were right: The horse has many gifts. When Graven awakes, he will glorify me, and me alone."

Shade pricked her ears and gave a warning snort.

"Aye, I hear it," Pine said calmly. "Good-bye, *Ty*." She clicked her tongue and the horse flashed away.

A heartbeat later, Gus appeared in the space she'd deserted. He had detected the activity and phased to mount a blistering attack. An impossible roar of heat and fury swept toward the crag. The fires lashed around the rocks, vaporizing water pools, cremating plant life, catching Ty's auma, setting every strand of pink alight. Like fuse trails, they closed at speed on their goal. Ty screeched in alarm, but there was no escape. The wisps burned down and exploded where they met at the body of the crow. Ty was gone in a spreading star of gray-and-white smoke, not even a feather to mark his end.

High in the sky, Pine reappeared and smiled.

She held up the heart and caressed its folds. "Time to call our dark wyng together," she whispered. "Take us to the trees now."

And Shade flashed her wings again, setting a course for the body of trees the Kaal called the Whispering Forest.

32

Even for a dragon of Gus's size, it required some effort to recover Rolan. By wedging himself between a side of the rock where Rolan lay trapped and the sturdy backbone of the crag, the dragon was able to use his weight to snap the rock apart and pull Rolan clear. The Hom was silent, limp but alive. Gus laid him down as gently as he could. His primary orders had not gone well.

While he was bending over the body, concerned about the spreading pool of blood, Gallen unexpectedly turned up.

Gus shuffled to attention.

"What's going on?" the Veng commander snapped. "I smell fire. Where's the other prisoner?"

Gus hardly knew where to begin. He blurted out his report.

"Fighting? You were supposed to be GUARDING them!"

"I was. I . . . I did," Gus spluttered. He looked down at Rolan. "This one lives. Just."

Gallen made a grating noise deep in his throat. "You're certain the other one is dead?"

Gus nodded, relieved that a question, not a fireball, had

entered his ears. He pointed at a blackened area of stone, the backdrop to Ty's explosive end.

"Which way did this girl and her flying beast go?"

"West. Toward the forest. Commander, she was carrying—" Gus had forgotten to mention the heart. But Gallen was already in the air. In a single wingbeat, he was away toward the distant trees.

"What shall I do with the Hom?" Gus cried.

Gallen roared something terse in reply. But by then he was a dot among the clouds and his words were just as puffy. The order sounded like "Don't let him die," though it might just as easily have been, "Squash him and fly."

Gus drooped his wings and settled back again.

Not for the first time, the wind began to sling icy spots of rain across the crag. Gus turned down his scales and checked the horizons. Grainy clouds, fully laden with moisture, were ghosting across the mountain peaks. Yet another storm was coming. He shuddered and put a wing over Rolan to shelter him. In a strange way, he wished he could do more for the Hom. The man had shown bravery against the crow, which was clearly some form of malevolent spirit. It irked Gus that Commander Gallen hadn't paid more attention to that. Surely this clash between the men was important? Shouldn't the Elders at least be advised that one of the prisoners had turned into a *bird*? At that moment, Rolan swam back into consciousness. He groaned in pain, his fingers clawing the bleak, cold rock as he clung to the frail precipice of life. Gus shuffled uncomfortably. What had appeared to be an easy assignment was turning into a difficult test. If his orders *were* to keep the Hom alive, what was he to do? He could fly the man to healer Grymric's cave, but that would mean deserting his post and taking the prisoner back into the inner domayne. But if he stood here tapping his claws doing nothing, the Hom was going to die.

Leaning down, he gave Rolan a nudge with his snout. Gus had never understood why the Hom didn't try to heal themselves. They covered their wounds well enough, but never seemed to lick them or bathe them in healing auma. Dragons had learned many centuries ago that healing stemmed from the fire within. Not every blow could be repaired, of course. A strike to the eye was often fatal, as was a thrust to the primary heart. But common cuts, no matter how deep, were easy to mend, especially if herbs were taken to aid the recovery. Rolan groaned again. There was a gash in his shoulder the size of a claw's width. A trail of small creatures with hardened shells and feelers that looked like minuscule stigs were starting to explore it. Gus snorted and blew them away. The flow of air made Rolan open his eyes. He saw Gus arched over him and groaned as if he'd stepped out of one bad dream and straight into another.

"Kill me," he grated, his chest whistling from more than one hole. "For the sake of mercy, let me suffer no more." He looked at the dragon's powerful isoscele restlessly making patterns in the sky. One blow from that would take him to the Fathers and end this misery for good. But his hand had no strength to demonstrate the motion. So he closed his eyes and tried to roll, thinking he might throw himself off the mountain.

Gus immediately prevented the fall.

"No," croaked Rolan, coughing up blood. "Let me die, skaler. Let . . . me . . . die . . ."

But Gus would not allow it. With one claw, he hooked up Rolan's robe and dragged his prisoner to a position of greater safety.

The movement caused Rolan to howl in agony.

That was it. Gus could stand it no longer. He studied the shoulder wound from two directions, then put out his tongue and licked the groove clean of dirt. Rolan yelped like a new-born wearling. Gus licked on and ignored the cries. Discomfort during healing was to be expected; the man would thank him when this was done. He seared the cut as he would any wound, stemming the steady ooze of blood and pouring saliva over the quivering flesh. Lastly, he spread the end of his tongue, using its array of flexible barbs to catch the wound and draw the walls together, fusing them with more heat as they joined. Rolan arched his back. His high-pitched scream seemed to split the air and had birds responding with similar cries. His body was gripped by such a wave of tremors that his head fell sideways and knocked against the rock. His eyes rolled. His legs thrashed out a disjointed rhythm. Bubbles of red froth popped from his nose. Gus leaned back, unsure of what he'd done or what now to do for the best. The Hom should be feeling better, not worse. But the convulsions raged on, and were still active when De:allus Garodor and the blue roamer, Gabrial, suddenly descended on the crag. They landed, spraying water off their wings, steam rising from every pore. Both had a frantic look in their eyes.

Gus sighed through his spiracles.

This duty was going from bad to worse.

33

To add to Gus's wave of confusion, the Hom boy, Ren, immediately leapt off Gabrial's back and knelt by the prisoner, urgently speaking Rolan's name.

Gus had a mind to swat the boy aside, but did not wish to anger the De:allus. Garodor was the senior dragon here now and a show of respect never went amiss.

It was Gabrial who opened the dialogue. "Where is Ty, who calls himself Tywyll?" He was panting lightly, his hot breath flying away on the wind.

Gus aimed a puzzled look at both dragons. The flush of color in their necks suggested they had flown here at battle speed. Maybe the rush of air through the nostrils had fuddled the blue's brain. Why would he ask a question about the Tywyll?

"The dark Hom, the second prisoner," Garodor explained. He noted the flame marks on the crag.

"Dead," said Gus. "By my own flame. *Tywyll?*"

"Gabrial, why is Rolan shaking like this?"

Ren had his hands on Rolan's shoulders, trying to steady his fit. Rolan's eyes had swollen to the size of pebbles and were staring into the mournful sky.

Gus explained: "The men were fighting. The dark Hom

changed into the form of a crow. He attacked this prisoner and cast him from the cliff. I was chasing another beast, a strange flying horse."

"A horse—with wings?" Garodor queried. He and Gabrial exchanged a glance.

"Now we know how it reached my eyrie," Gabrial muttered.

Gus nodded. "It disappeared as I phased. The crow was in my line of fire . . . I couldn't help it, De:allus. I—"

"He's talking," said Ren. Leaning close to Rolan, he whispered, "Rolan, it's me, Ren Whitehair, son of Ned. I pledge you my help, but I need yours also. Ty is dead. But there is evil around us still. If you can speak, friend, say what happened at the cave." He put his ear to Rolan's lips.

"De:allus—?"

Garodor raised a claw to quiet Gus. "Wait. I want to hear this Hom's words."

"Ty took a knife to Pine," Ren reported. "Rolan thought she was slain, but . . . a mist came out of the cave and entered her through the wound Ty made. She woke anew. He says Pine was weaker than Ty. She called him Master, but lately turned against him. They argued, a'cause some of the mist went into Wind . . ."

"Then the auma of the second goyle was split," said Gabrial, "between the girl *and* the horse?"

"It would appear so," Garodor muttered. "It may even be stronger for it. This beast," he said to Gus, "which way did it fly?"

"In the direction of the forest," Gus said. "Veng Commander Gallen was here before you. He is in pursuit of the creature. De:allus, the girl had a dragon heart with her."

"We need to go," said Gabrial, grinding his claws. "Gallen may be in danger." He flicked his wings and looked toward the forest.

"Wait," said Garodor, "the man has more."

Rolan had gripped Ren's robe and pulled the boy to him. He spoke in fragile whispers, twice prompting Ren to say, *"What?"*

"Well?" said Garodor. "Quickly, Ren."

Ren sat back on his knees. "This makes no sense to my ears. He says Ty spoke of raising a creature whose blood is in the mountains . . . "

Gabrial stilled his wings. "What creature?"

"Go on," said Garodor. "What else, Ren?"

"He speaks also of a heart, but it can only be babble."

"He must mean the heart the girl stole," said Gabrial.

"Where?" said Garodor, leaning forward. "Where, Ren? Where is this heart?"

Ren shook his head.

"Where?" pressed Garodor.

"The air." Ren lifted his shoulders. "He says the creature's heart is in the *air*." He looked up as a band of crows flew over.

At that moment, Rolan convulsed again and spewed bile from the side of his mouth.

"Garodor, we should fly," said Gabrial.

"No," said Ren, hugging Rolan to him. "Gabrial, don't leave. My friend is dying. You have to help him. Please. He may yet know more."

"Ren, his wounds are too great. And you said yourself, he is speaking nonsense. I must pursue this enemy. My duty—"

"He's not dying," Garodor intervened. He turned sharply to Gus. "Guard, as we arrived, I saw you hunched over the prisoner. Did Gallen order you to kill him?"

"No!" cried Ren, thinking they might.

Gus rattled his scales. "My orders were to keep the Hom alive, De:allus."

"You were trying to heal him, then?"

Gus swallowed, sending a ripple along his neck. "I seared a wound. Was that wrong?"

Gabrial glanced at the exposed shoulder and the hot red seam that Gus had created. Was it his imagination, or was the repair beginning to show the soft shine seen on emerging dragon scales?

"The Hom are not like us," Garodor said. "Your intentions, though noble, may have caused him greater harm."

Gabrial immediately turned his head. "But Ren survived Gariffred's bi—"

The De:allus raised a claw to silence the blue. Looking at Gus again, he said, "Take this man to healer Grymric. Explain to Grymric exactly what you've done. This command supersedes anything from the Veng. When you're finished with Grymric, fly to the Prime and give him your report. Tell him that Gabrial and I are following Gallen in pursuit of this girl. Do not speak of your attempts at healing. Prime Grynt will not be pleased about that. Take Ren with you to Grymric's cave."

"Me? No!" Ren protested.

"Ren, the De:allus is right," said Gabrial. "The situation has changed. You know your own kind better than Grymric. You can help him save this man. You've done what you can for the Wearle and we're grateful. But there are unknown dangers ahead. I can't have you on my back in a fight. How would I protect you?"

Ren stood up, beating his chest. "I made a pledge to Grogan to return his heart. And I know Pine better than any. Mebbe I can protect *you*."

But Gabrial would not be persuaded. He aimed the slightest of nods at Gus.

Ren screamed another fierce protest. But even as the words were leaving his lips, Gus picked up him and Rolan and flew them away.

"Brave to part with him," Garodor said. "He will not forgive you easily."

Gabrial spread his wings, tilting them to minimize the buffeting of the wind. "Is he right—about the girl? Could he have helped? Is she still Hom, or just a cloak for the goyle?"

The rain began to fall in sudden earnest, poking glimmers of brightness in the gloom. Garodor slid back his eyelids to light the way. "If I'm right, the goyle will adapt itself to her neurological systems and look for ways to enhance her, physically, much as it has with the horse. But it will use the Hom senses in the same way she would. In that respect, she is still the girl she was, and will act like it. So, yes, Ren has a point. But this is not his battle. We must destroy this goyle and recover Grogan's heart. You must have no qualms about attacking the girl should it come to that. Likely she will die if the goyle leaves her anyway. Now, follow me to the forest."

"De:allus—one last question. If she—it—plans to challenge us, why would she fly to the forest, not the mountains?"

"There are trees there," Garodor said. "And trees offer shelter to the creatures who serve her."

Gabrial threw him a searching look.

"Birds," said Garodor, pointing at moving specks in the sky. "She's calling the crows. The forest is where her dark wyng will gather—and where the true evil will rise. Fly."

34

Although speaking while airborne was never ideal, especially in the sort of slanting rain that Gabrial and Garodor found themselves flying through, dragons could still rely on the telepathic exchange of thoughts to hold a dialogue. And that was exactly what they did. Gabrial dropped back alongside the De:allus, opened his mind, and said, *I don't understand. What evil? And why would she call a wyng of crows? They have no strength or power.*

A strange answer came back, one that sent a shudder running all the way to the blue dragon's wing tips.

How much do you know about the black dragon?

A gush of rain swept across Gabrial's face. He vaporized the water in his nostrils and said, *Only what my father told me as a wearling.*

And what did he tell you?

That when the world began, there was a dragon named Graven, who so angered Godith that She tore his third heart out of his chest. Godith turned the heart to stone and broke it into a thousand fragments. She hid it from Graven so he could not rise again. Why are you asking me this?

The yellow eyes glinted in the rain. *I have a small confession* to make—about the stone Gariffred found in your eyrie. I was able to unlock it quite quickly and transfer its memory core into my mind. I've been working through the contents ever since.

I thought I noted your displeasure when I mentioned it to Grynt.

Yes. I didn't want to give Grynt any details until I was clear in my mind about what I'd found.

Gabrial looped his wings against the upward flow of air, making the downdraft powerful enough that he could glide and catch a moment to think. *Does it say . . . about the fhosforent?*

Yes, but in a way you'll find hard to believe. Givnay didn't create the stone. I suspect he stole it from the Kashic Archive before he was posted here.

Stole it? Why? What does it reveal? And why are you telling me, not the Elders?

Because you're brave, like your father. Trustworthy. Strong. Clever—when you give yourself time to think. Most of all because you tried to save Graymere. He wasn't just my pupil; he was my son.

Your—?

Stay close, Gabrial, we don't have much time. We'll reach the forest soon, and there is no telling what perils await us there. Listen to me now and listen well. Protect this knowledge and let it guide you; it may have a bearing on your wearlings' future. The stone contains a record of Erth's history. *The Higher have known about this planet for centuries, as far back as you or I could imagine.*

Gabrial tightened his eye ridges, causing runnels of water to trickle down his snout. *You mean . . . we've been here before? Before the first Wearle?*

Long before the first Wearle. If you had been present when the dark Hom, Ty, was captured, you would have seen evidence of it. He knew words of dragontongue and spoke about a history of dragons on Erth. The words he used are easily explained by the presence of the goyle controlling him, but the goyle should not have known about the colonizations. Even senior dragons like Grynt and Gossana have no knowledge of Erth's true place in our history. This suggests to me that the goyle was accessing memories in the man, memories so faint that time had almost wiped them out or made fables of them. Ty used them cleverly to save his life.

Memories?

Stories of our visits, passed down through generations of Hom.

Is this a threat to us?

The stories? No. It's what else the goyle might have found that concerns me.

With a swoosh, the De:allus banked to his left to avoid the turbulence rippling his wings. The large sails of tissue on a dragon's wings were as tough and sturdy as a row of scales, but a sudden head-on gust could set up a wave of undulations that would make the most experienced of fliers giddy.

Gabrial swept alongside again. *Is this to do with the black dragon?*

Garodor changed his beat, found a new current, and peered ahead. Despite the poor visibility, he could see they were still some way from the forest. He had already calculated that they could have phased closer, in stages. But without a specific location to aim at, there was little point wasting energy that might be required later for battle. And there was still a good deal to tell.

To answer your question, we must go back to the first time Erth was colonized. The memory stone's archive chronicles the work of a young De:allus. His name was Grendisar. He had powerful transference skills and was considered to be what older dragons call a Sensaur.

He saw spirits?

Something like that. Grendisar detected a presence here. A dark force he could not identify or trace, though he was sure it was carried in the minds of the Hom. The Hom in his time were different from the men you and I have encountered. They were hairier, less upright, far simpler of mind. But their use of tools, and traps to catch prey, marked them out as potentially intelligent. Grendisar captured a Hom and commingled with it. He found no hint of the force he was looking for, but there was an unusual admiration for a prominent species of dark bird: crows.

Gabrial felt his mouth turn dry.

The stone tells how Grendisar caught some crows and commingled with them. Individually, though mildly intelligent, they showed little potential. But if he commingled with several at once, he noted a deeply disturbing development: The communing of the birds seemed to generate a speck of auma that was closely related to, if not the same as, ours. This prompted him to form a bold theory. He bravely suggested to the Higher that he'd found Godith's hiding place, that here was Graven's shattered heart, spread among a sinister genus of birds.

What? Gabrial snorted a shower of raindrops.

Garodor slackened his jaw—a movement as close as a dragon ever came to a wry smile. *I suspect your response would not be dissimilar to the reaction of the Elders to whom Grendisar reported. Initially, the De:allus was ridiculed. The story of Graven's downfall had long passed into the realms of myth. But that link to the crows must have worried the Higher, for they ordered Grendisar to continue his research. The planet was isolated and the Hom monitored for signs of conspiracy with the birds, but no threat ever materialized. And though Grendisar's work was passed on to other De:allus after his death, his theory gradually lost its import. Wearles like yours were still sent to Erth, but at longer and longer intervals, and only the Prime and some trusted Elders knew the real reason the colonies were there. Everything changed the day your father's Wearle disappeared. You know that story—the fhosforent, the goyles. This flight is the ongoing legacy of it.*

Then you believe it? You think Grendisar was right?

271

Garodor twisted through the air again, gathering up his feet as he banked toward the northern end of the forest. *I don't want to believe the black dragon exists, any more than you do. But the signs are there and I am bound by my breeding to investigate them. When Ty boasted that Graven's heart was in the air, I believe he was talking about crows in flight.*

What about the blood in the mountains?

Fhosforent. I analyzed a sample when I first arrived. It appears to be crystallized blood.

Graven's blood?

I fear so, yes.

But . . .

For a moment, Gabrial was lost for words. He had to open every spiracle along his neck to relieve the plug of air trying to gag his throat. The blood of the Tywyll? Here? On Erth? The thought left him hollow inside, fearful for the lives of Grendel and the wearlings. He tilted his body against the rain and beat his wings to keep up with Garodor. *Why has this only been discovered now? Why not in Grendisar's time?*

Garodor banked again, his powerful eyes scanning the first cluster of trees. *I haven't had a chance to check the mapping sites yet, but I would say those early colonies simply settled in a different location. Like I said to Prime Grynt: It's a large planet.*

So my father's Wearle was just . . . unlucky?

Desperately so.

But these mountains are huge. Perfect for dragons. I find it hard to believe that Grendisar's mappers didn't locate them.

I agree that is odd, said Garodor. *But at the moment, I can't think of a better explanation than the one I've just given you.*

And neither could Gabrial. *So all this time, Graven's auma has been . . . surrounding us—in the fhosforent and the crows?*

Yes. It's hard to detect because it's widely scattered, though Grendisar was sensitive enough to feel it. Over the years, it must have been further diluted as the crows died off, though it would still be carried within their descendants. Godith did Her job well. Her fallen son was effectively stranded with very little chance of being found or recovered. The situation changed when dragons arrived in these mountains and began to ingest large quantities of fhosforent. Those who did mutated quickly. I'm certain that was Graven, fighting to take control of their auma, forcing them to regenerate in his i:mage, all the while clutching at the fire within them, but never quite being able to claim it: the "dark eye" Ren speaks of is proof of that.

Gabrial nodded. He had seen the goyle eye. Dull. Lifeless. Yet radiating bitterness. Graven's bitterness. Even in flight, it made him shudder.

And now they have changed again, said Garodor, *into a much more dangerous form.*

The mist?

The De:allus nodded. *How or why that happened I cannot*

say, *but the Hom are the perfect host for it. We know how cunning men are. With Graven's assistance, doubly so. He awakened himself in Ty and Pine, enough to make them do his bidding.*

And steal Grogan's heart?

Yes. He wants fire in its purest form, Gabrial. Even cast in stone, a dragon's spark is a powerful source of life. Perhaps Ren was right and there is a way to free it. If so, we must assume that the goyle we're tracking can use the spark to draw the remaining fragments of Graven from the crows. Restoring his heart would be the first step to raising him.

On that note, Garodor turned his head sharply. His nostrils flared. *Do you smell that?*

The scent of dampened, burning wood, clinging to the sweeping rain. Gabrial had it now too. He looked down, adjusting his optical triggers. They were crossing a stretch of open land, a variegated mash of greens and browns, dotted with streaks of crude gray rock. But in the near distance, only a matter of wingbeats away, was the staggered edge of the forest. Deep within it was a winding trail of smoke. *That's dragon fire. It must be Gallen.*

Garodor pointed his battle stigs. *I'll go to it; you circle and cover me.*

You're not a fighting dragon. I'll go. You cover.

The De:allus flattened his chest scales. The hardened layers that terraced his eyelids slid into their protective

274

positions. *This is my chance to avenge my son. I want that goyle. Now, do as I command and—*

A sudden screech made both dragons look up. In the region of trees from where the smoke was rising, a dark creature had appeared above the forest. Gabrial raced ahead, roaring into full attack mode. Behind him, Garodor was urging caution. But here was an alien creature, dragon-shaped, black, struggling violently into the sky, limbs kicking, claws slashing, tail whipping, hissing nonstop battle tones. Gabrial rolled and immediately engaged it, for surely this was the true Tywyll, the source of so many wearling nightmares.

Whoosh! From the blue's jaws came a funnel of flame, so hot it made his airways squeal. Fire ripped along one side of the creature, fully igniting a wing. Flesh blistered, popped, and flared, the devastating scent of it plugging the gaps between the bulbous raindrops. The creature wailed, writhed, and fell back, scattering flakes of black in its wake. As Gabrial blasted a pathway through them, he realized the flakes were incinerated feathers, turning to dust as they landed on his scales. Puzzled, he banked around and looked again at the falling creature. To his horror, he saw green beneath its black exterior, the unmistakable gloss of Veng-class scales. Only then did he realize what he'd done. He'd brought down a dragon obscured by crows.

He'd killed the Veng commander, Gallen.

❧ 35 ❧

No time for guilt, inquiry, or reason. As Gallen's body dropped, a catch of wind took him onto his back and he plummeted fast toward the trees. What remained of his wings flapped open—to one side a full sheet repeatedly holed; a blackened skeletal frame on the other. The surviving crows broke clear of the body as the forest loomed up. Gallen hit the trees with a mighty crack, sending ripples far across the bright green canopy. Scales flew in all directions. Spots of green blood mingled with the rain. The body sank, sprang back, and then came to rest as the trees buoyed its spreading weight. Only the tail slid out of sight. The claws clutched at empty space. The slanted eye was a dead slit, closed.

For a few windswept seconds it seemed as if Gallen would remain like this, swaying on the treetops in the rain, pinned through the throat and twice through the chest by what the Hom called spiker branches. Then the crows descended once more, to tear at the bleeding lacerations.

Deeply distressed, and driven by a fury he hardly recognized, Gabrial turned and swooped on them, crunching several in his monstrous jaws while he frantically rekindled his fire sacs. By then, they were on him too. More birds, it seemed, than the trees could hold. They rose like leaves that had forgotten which way they were supposed to fall. The air shuddered to their calls, a din so loud that Gabrial had to fold his ears into his head to prevent them bursting. He slashed and whipped and sprayed arcs of fire. Every flying thing in his onward path was immediately reduced to ash. On he flew, dipping through a cloud of cinders and rage. But there were just too many crows to kill. And soon they had him surrounded. They were everywhere, pecking at his tail, his stigs, his wing tips. He even felt them poking in the horny dips at the backs of his knees. So many talons, all over his body. They came for his eyes, of course, initially to block his optical triggers and disorient him, then to dig at the supple joints between the glinting facets that together made up the jewel of the eye. Never had he suffered a feeling so disturbing as the relentless tapping of a beak in those spots.

Phase!

Suddenly, Garodor was back in his mind, the one place the sharp beaks couldn't reach.

Phase! Now! the De:allus called. *Go high, Gabrial! As high as you can i:mage!*

Burn them!

I can't! They're on me also. Phase, Gabrial. It's your only hope!

And so the blue dragon tensed his muscles and i:maged himself among the clouds. In a flash he was high, high, high above the forest. Those crows with talons hooked under his scales were taken up with him. For a moment it seemed to be a pointless maneuver; the birds pecked on as if nothing had happened. But it wasn't long before their ireful chirrs turned to suffocating squawks. And now Gabrial saw the wisdom in the move. There was no air for the crows up here—certainly not enough to sustain their lungs and prevent their tiny brains from dizzying. And while it was a fact that dragons were susceptible to blacking out at altitude, they had the advantage of a built-in reservoir of air, which took the form of a flexible sac that sat just under the bronchial web. It inflated at takeoff and deflated at landing, unless the lungs drew from it during flight.

One by one the crows fell away, until Gabrial was easily shaking them off. He immediately prepared to attack them again, only to be steered off course by Garodor, who had phased to a similar height.

Don't waste your fire! Look at them. They're dead.

The De:allus was right. The crows were dropping like large black hailstones.

The smoke; we must go to its source, said Gabrial. *The girl has to be there. She's commanding the birds. If we fly together—*

No, we must withdraw, said Garodor.

Gabrial swept underneath him. *That was Gallen I brought down!*

I know that. And I know what you must be feeling now. But he was almost certainly beyond our help at the point you flamed him. We need to regather. We must go to Grynt and organize the Wearle.

You go to Grynt.

Gabrial—

I'm not leaving, Garodor. I KILLED a Veng commander. I have to avenge him.

And you will. But not like this. Go to the trees and the birds will simply come for you again. You can't phase forever. Eventually, they'll bring you down. Think about this.

I could phase into the forest and surprise the girl.

There isn't space enough. You'll just be trapped. And the forest is huge. We don't know where she is.

Then we should burn it. Burn the whole thing down.

No. Destroying the trees is not the answer. The girl would just vanish, and so would our chances of defeating her.

Then what should we do?

I don't know. But we need to get to Grynt and warn the whole Wearle—starting with them. He gestured toward a patch of sky. In the distance, three dragons were approaching, flying side by side. Gus will have given his report by now. Grynt will have sent them to aid us. Go to them. Turn them back to Skytouch. That's an order.

Gabrial circled again, his frustration as evident as the air rushing out of his spiracles. What if she does it? What if she opens the heart while we're gone?

That's a chance we'll have to take. Now fly. I'm going to make one more sweep of the forest for any detail that might help us.

But—?

Don't worry, I'll fly high. My eyesight is better than yours. Go. I won't be far behind you.

Reluctantly, Gabrial swept away.

Garodor was right about the three dragons. They were two roamers, led by Gus, who'd been sent back to the forest as a punishment for being inept. Gus was even more reluctant than Gabrial to go back and face the Prime again, but was easily persuaded when he learned that Gallen had perished (though Gabrial didn't speak of his part in it).

And so they turned and Gabrial fell in behind them, glumly bringing up the rear. Before long they were closing on the mountains again, skirting the snaking cluster of peaks that would bring them to Skytouch and the great ice lake.

It was as they turned to make their final approach that Gabrial looked down and realized they were passing Grymric's cave. He saw Ren near to the cave mouth. The boy looked up when he heard the sound of wings.

Gus and the roamers sailed past, but Gabrial let the wind slow him. He glided through one full circle, looked at Ren again, and had an idea.

Moments later, he landed at the cave mouth.

"Get on," he said to the boy.

Ren looked puzzled, but only took the time to glance over his shoulder before clambering onto Gabrial's back. "Where are we going?"

"Gabrial, is that you?" Grymric's voice floated out of the darkness deep within the cave.

Gabrial didn't reply. He took off and immediately, powerfully, gained height.

"Where are we *going*?" Ren asked again. He had to shout to make himself heard.

"The forest," said the blue, leveling out.

Ren looked down. "You're going the wrong way." Gabrial had just banked south, toward the ocean.

"I'm taking a long way around. Garodor mustn't see me. He won't like what I'm planning, but I don't have time to persuade him. I need you to do something, Ren. Something no dragon can. It will be dangerous. And it may be too late, anyway."

"What do you want me to do?"

"Go into the forest and find the girl."

"You want me to kill her?"

"If you have to. Whatever it takes to fulfill your promise."

"Promise?"

"You made a bond with Grogan. Steal back the heart and return it to his spirit. That's what I want you to do."

36

Gabrial set Ren down on a grassy rise where the forest thinned out, as close to the trees as he dared to land. The storm had been short and had blown itself out, leaving the ground sodden but the landscape clear. From where they stood, they could see the entire span of woodland, stretching its weave of greens and browns over the interlocking hills. No crows had challenged them on the approach, but Gabrial had been clever and flown through a patch of light hill fog, almost skimming the ground in places, a tactic that wasn't lost on Ren. "You flew low. Do you fear that Pine will see you?"

The blue folded his wings and studied the nearest cluster of trees. "Not Pine."

He told Ren about the crows and the battle with them.

The boy's jaw dropped. "Gallen is dead?"

The dragon's neck stigs bristled uncomfortably. "I was to blame. No matter what Garodor says in my support, Grynt will condemn me for the death of his commander."

"You think this plan will settle his ire?"

"No. It will infuriate him. But I need to act, to avenge Gallen's spirit. I would enter the forest if my size permitted and seek out Pine myself. Instead, I call on your pledge by the crag. You said you knew the girl better than any Hom. You can track her."

Ren squinted at the trees. Trying to measure their number was a daunting task. "My pa used to say the forest is as big as the sky, this close. My teeth might rot before I find her."

"Not if you let Grystina help you. You've felt the auma of Grogan's heart. Grystina can use that energy to phase you somewhere close to it. Do you see that twist of smoke in the distance?"

Ren cupped his eyes. He could just make out a gray trail rising where the tree mass hollowed.

"That's where Gallen came down. Let that be your physical mark."

"If I find the heart, what then?"

"Bring it here. I'll be waiting. Phasing back to a start point is easy; Grystina will guide you."

"Then we fly to the quarry and raise Grogan's spirit?"

Gabrial nodded. "If the heart is returned, the danger will hopefully pass."

"Hopefully?"

The blue dragon took a long breath. "There's more you need to know."

He told Ren, in brief, the story of Graven, making sure Ren understood why dragons sometimes called him "Tywyll."

Ren crouched down and brushed his hand over the wet

blades of grass. "If this beast were to rise, what will it mean—for you, for the Wearle?"

Gabrial shook his head. "I don't know. But I don't want to risk the lives of Grendel and the wearlings finding out. Act now, Ren—or leave in peace. I won't stop you. I cannot make you do this."

Ren stood up slowly, drying his hand on the sleeve of his robe. "Can Pine be saved? Can the goyle be driven out and the girl brought back?"

Gabrial blinked, remembering what Garodor had said. "It may be too late for that. Do you care for the girl? Do you forgive her allegiance to Ty?"

Ren sniffed. "I care for her as much as you care for Gossana—but she is Kaal. I say she was bewitched by Ty."

"Then save her if you can. And I will help—if I can."

"Crows," Ren said suddenly. He stepped back and slapped the blue's side.

Gabrial took off in an instant and was away before the crows could think to chase him. With a *caark* of annoyance, their leader changed course and called them onto Ren. Six of them, all squealing their threats.

Grystina, are you with me? Ren said.

She rose in his mind. *You know I am.*

Is it possible to phase as Gabrial says?

Yes. But you must be sure and swift. Do not look at the crows. Remember Grogan. Let his angry spirit fire you. Concentrate. Fill your mind with your quest.

Ren closed his eyes, remembering the quarry. "For Grogan!" he yelled.

Caarak! Caraark! the crows spat back.

Ren felt the air flowing off their wings. The first crow was almost upon him.

The smoke, said Grystina. *Picture it. Now.*

Claws slashed.

But all they hit was empty space.

Ren was gone like a blink of sunlight.

Into the depths of the forest.

37

One thing Ren had yet to master was the technique of holding himself together during phasing. As well as i:maging their endpoint, dragons were taught to visualize themselves in the correct position once their leap through time was accomplished. Mentors of young dragons would deliberately let their charges land upside down, often with their snouts half buried in dirt, to teach them the importance of self-awareness. Ren learned it himself that day when he materialized in the forest.

Landing on sloping ground on his shoulder, he was immediately catapulted head over heels into a downward roll. The forest floor was mossy and soft, but there were rocks a-plenty poking through the bracken, enough to register a bruise at every flip. *Ohh! Urgh! Owww . . .* The knocks came hard and fast. And, once again, his body was reminded that spiker branches, even dead brown ones, were quick to pierce exposed Hom flesh. An old tree stump eventually broke his tumble, bouncing him sideways into a slide. With a final groan, he reached out for something to anchor him. His hand grasped what felt like a moss-lined branch. But as his fingers explored it he realized it wasn't a branch at all. He rolled his head to see a face staring back.

A grim, dead face.

It had no eyes.

"Agh!"

He broke away and scrabbled to his feet, kicking at the body as if, even in its lifeless state, it would rise and attack him. It was a treeman, one of the strange tribe of people who inhabited the forest. Like all his kind, the man was clothed only at the waist. What could be seen of his milky-white skin was covered in the foliage that grew unhindered in the forest erth. He looked particularly old. His feet were wrapped in a twining weed that had latched to his ankles and sent suckers up around his knees. Graycaps were sprouting from the pits of his arms. Shallow roots of crusted lichen shined where he'd rubbed their tops off his belly. Although he was slight of build, he had hair enough for three grown men, most of it gathered in a knotted red beard that had broken eggshells among its strands. Something white and disturbingly frothy was germinating in his knobbly ears. Three of his fingers had turned to wood.

But the eyes, or the lack of them, were so very wrong. Treemen rarely blinked, and this one was never going to blink again. The crows, Ren suspected, had killed the man and torn out the eyes, probably to eat or keep as trophies. A host of black nibblers was already laying claim to the sockets, writing their patterns in the sticky red blood on the treeman's cheeks.

I see you, Ren Whitehair.

Suddenly, out of the mouth came a voice. Pine's voice. How it had happened, Ren could not tell. But he jumped back again with a yelp of fear, snatching up a spear that had fallen from the dead man's hand. Three or four times he stabbed the body, but the poking brought no more response from it.

Here, Whitehair. Here I am.

The voice came again, this time from behind. Ren whipped around, gripping the spear shaft underhand and double, like he would if he were facing a charging snorter. The forest trees stood like bare-legged giants, light fanning eerily between them. Many had been blackened by Gallen's fire. The scent of charred wood doused by rain overwhelmed every other smell in the forest.

Here!

Ren jumped like a frightened hopper.

More trees.

More gaps.

A twist of shadows.

A crackle of bracken.

A breeze.

No Pine.

"I would see you now, Onetooth! Show yerself!"

High above, the treetops began to bristle.

From somewhere among them a crow called down.

Ren jabbed his spear upward.

It's coming, Whitehair.

What? What was coming? The trees had begun to sway as if they'd been brushed by the wings of many dragons.

Look here.

Now the voice was at his left, farther down the slope. Ren crept toward it and briefly saw the shape of a straggle-haired girl. A vapor, flashing between the trees.

Is it her? he asked Grystina.

I cannot be sure.

What's wrong with the crows?

He turned on the spot, looking upward again. It was impossible to see the birds, but their calls were beginning to multiply.

Why don't they attack?

The goyle commands them. It must want you alive.

Ren gritted his teeth. *Then we must see what it wants*, he thought.

He pushed on again, to the bottom of the ridge where the light was full and strong. Through the trees he saw a clearing.

The bracken was thinly layered with ash, still warm from Gallen's fire, but all plant life was scarred or extinguished. At the center of the clearing, by a dead gray stump, stood Pine.

She was plucking petals off a blackened flower.

On the stump lay the dragon heart. It had shrunk to half its size but was glittering like a young dragon eye, shedding sparks of purple light.

"Have you come to kill me, Whitehair?"

Her voice drew Ren into the clearing. He glanced around him. They seemed to be alone. "Many times I have wished it so," he muttered.

Where's Wind? he asked Grystina.

"Not here," Pine replied. A flower petal dropped. She shook back her hair. "I read you, Whitehair. Your auma is strong. The dragon inside you would growl if it could."

She smiled, showing off her crooked teeth. She wiped a hand down her bloodstained robe. Ren saw the rip where Ty had cut her.

"Then you will know why I stand here, *goyle.*"

"Aye, I do."

"Give up the heart."

Pine shook her head. "Nay."

"Then kill you I must."

"Not yet," she said calmly. "First, you must listen."

Ren turned the spear in his sweating hand. *Listen? To what?*

The thump of my heart? The gathering wind? The clouds were slowly coming together, stirred like a whirlpool in a river. The crows cleared off in a sudden clatter, flying in all directions.

"They are fleeing," said Pine.

From the Wearle, Grystina? Does Grynt come?

No, she replied, *they are fleeing from . . .*

"Grogan," said Pine.

The last petal dropped.

She has summoned the vapor, Grystina said.

Ren shook his head. His eyes darted skyward. "No. Grogan's spirit haunts his death place. It cannot leave there."

"It can, Whitehair. Shade has freed him. Her magicks have torn down the veil." She cradled the heart. "It is Graven's command."

Ren, we must leave. Phase back, said Grystina.

"Your dragon fears him," Pine said quietly. "But you are right to stay. Kneel before Graven, as I will kneel, and he will accept us both as his servants."

Ren lifted the spear. "What have you done? How did you open the heart?"

"I have not."

"Then why is it changed?" Every vein was glowing. And the purple sparks continued to fly.

"It has taken what it needs from the birds," said Pine. "Two things more shall make it crack . . ."

RAAAARRR!

A roar so loud it blew ash from the ground came funneling down from the sky.

The spirit of Grogan was descending on the clearing, a huge and terrifying apparition. Just to look upon those wraithlike jaws was reason enough for a boy to pass water. Ren stumbled backward, dropping the spear. Here was the vapor that would haunt him all his days or suck out his soul, whichever appealed to it more. The horrifying sight of it rendered him speechless. Not even a gasp could escape his mouth. But Pine was showing no fear at all, and had still to complete her statement. Two things more would make the heart crack, she had said. And Ren was about to learn what they were. "The spirit of the body whence the heart came . . . and the blood of a wearling—a drake," she said.

Grogan's spirit. Gariffred's blood.

Bring them together and Graven would live.

❧ 38 ❧

Phase! Grystina urged Ren again.

And phase he did. But it was a short skip. A minor blink. He had not come here to flee from danger. Instead, he i:maged himself in front of Pine with his hand clasped firmly to the heart. He was thinking of his promise to Grogan and saw it as a means of appeasing the spirit, which was floating now, above the clearing, like a bag of malevolent air.

The move worked—but for one thing. Pine was quicker than Ren had expected. He found himself in front of her all right, but with his hand on her hand, which covered the heart.

Their gazes locked. Ren saw the goyle swirling pink in her eyes, but there was still an inkling of the girl he remembered, the one-toothed waif who would waft around the settlement, plucking flowers and knowing everyone's business. Would she go back to that life if she could? How much of the orphan child still existed? Only by defeating the goyle would he know.

His hand trembled on hers.

"Kneel," she said. The goyle speaking through her.

Ren did not reply. But that opening of her mouth had given him an idea.

He raised his free hand. With the smallest finger he scraped his own teeth, as if to indicate she had something stuck between hers.

Her eyes narrowed—in confusion or disgust, it didn't matter. Ren's act had created enough of a pause for the auma of the girl to momentarily surface. He pinched her wrist, yanked away her hand, and snatched up the heart.

The goyle immediately regained control. It forced a burst of spittle out of Pine. The venom hit Ren in the uncovered hollow at the front of his neck and began to eat away at his tender flesh. But spitting was the worst thing the goyle could have done. It had now exposed itself to Grogan. The spirit of the dragon turned on Pine with the same degree of virulence it had shown to the guard in the quarry. Ren watched in horror as Pine was stretched to the tips of her toes by the sucking force of the vapor's breath. As Grogan drew the goyle out, Pine's teeth, those falsely acquired, shattered like falling shards of ice. Only the center tooth remained. She shook like a blade of grass and fell to the ground in a feeble heap. As she did, the mist came free of her body and wriggled into Grogan. For several beguiling moments it fought to control the spirit. A strange, unnatural tussle took place, a clash of mist and claws and color. But this would be the undoing of both. Ren saw the mist shrink to a spot and implode. Black streaks flared all through the vapor, puncturing its form a thousand times. The main body of the dragon was first to disappear; last of all, the snarling head. Such a chilling sight that was: a transparent skaler head fading into nothing on a swag of eerie, wretched moans. One final snap of jaws and it was gone.

Ren was on his knees at that point, trying to counteract the torture in his neck. He could find no water to quench the burning and no thick leaves to cover the wound. Nothing. Just the dragon heart, shrinking in his hand. It was now no bigger than a spiker cone, but just as alive with light.

You must destroy it, Grystina said.

Ren brought it closer to his face. It was an extraordinary thing, horrific and beautiful in equal measure. It compelled the eye to gaze upon it. He could feel its pulse through his hand and arm, resonating closely with the beat in his chest. The pain in his throat began to lessen. *It seeks to heal me*, he said.

No, Ren, it seeks to control you in the way the goyles used Pine and Ty. Be rid of it. It is a thing of evil. You heard what Pine said. It has taken what it needs from the crows. Graven's auma must be inside it.

It's fading. Like the goyle. It grows smaller.

No. It grows stronger. It senses the blood of Gariffred in you.

Gariffred. Yes. The heart was in the hand the drake had bitten.

Ren came to his senses and realized the danger. Grogan

295

might be gone, but what if the heart could still be opened by a body infused with a wearling's auma?

He tried to throw it aside.

Too late.

It did not so much open as dissolve into fire. Ren cried out—in shock, not pain. But the flare was finished as soon as it had started. A trail of ash dispersed into the breeze. Ren turned his hand this way and that. Front and back were unburned, normal. But the bite wound glowed like the blink of a star. Ren touched his neck. The skin was fast regrowing, but now had a hint of roughness to it. The heart *had* healed him—with the kind of repair a dragon might make to itself.

What's happened? he asked Grystina.

She did not reply.

Grystina, where are you?

"Ohhhh . . ."

Across the clearing, Pine's fingers twitched.

Ren hurried over. He dropped to his knees and cradled her head. She was alive, just, but as weak as water.

Behind him, he heard a beat of wings and looked back to see Shade landing softly in the clearing. Until then, he had given no thought to the whinney and feared for an instant it might attack. If he remembered correctly, part of the auma of the goyle was inside it. But that recognition only seemed to strengthen his daring. He stood up calmly, Pine draped across his arms.

As fast as the light that moved between them, Ren commingled with the whinney's mind. He recognized the innocent auma of Wind, still pining loyally for his father, and he saw the goyle that had given the whinney wings and a twisting horn capable of magicks. To his amazement, the goyle tried to shrink from the contact. But Ren was too strong and held it fixed. Out of his mouth came a voice that could have made the mountains shudder. "You are mine now. You will obey me. Come."

The horse snorted. It lifted one foot as if it would rake the ground before charging. And then it bowed its head and did its best to kneel.

"Come," Ren repeated.

The horse padded over.

Ren put Pine across its neck and climbed on behind her. "Fold in your wings. Draw back the horn. You are Wind again, until I speak otherwise."

The horse did as Ren commanded. *Where should I take you . . . Master?*

"Nowhere," Ren said. He raised his confident gaze to the sky. Two dragons crossed over in the space above the clearing. "The Wearle is coming to me."

39

De:allus Garodor had done exactly what he'd said. After sending Gabrial to turn Gus and the other dragons back to Skytouch, he had scouted the forest looking for clues to Pine's whereabouts. Though he yearned to avenge his son and was ready to launch a solo attack if necessary, he'd been wise enough to keep his distance from the crows. As it happened, the birds had settled and the forest had shown him nothing, though he had mapped the entire clearing. It was empty on both his flypasts, causing him to make the (incorrect) assumption that Pine had moved deeper into the forest. In frustration, he had then flown back to the mountains. At Prime Grynt's eyrie he had arrived just in time to see Gus having his ears chewed for his incompetence and to hear Grynt blaring, "Since when did you take orders from a BLUE?"

"Where *is* Gabrial?" That had been Garodor's immediate concern. The blue was nowhere to be seen.

Gus meekly replied, "I . . . I don't know, De:allus. He was just behind us when we reached the mountains. He must have dropped away. To his cave? I don't know."

Grynt put his snout close to Gus's head. Despite the roamer's bulky size, Gus shied away like a frightened wearling.

"Get him," Grynt hissed. "Bring him to me now. Do you think you can find his cave without *bumbling*?"

"Y . . . yes," Gus said. He left quicker than the dust motes could dance.

In his absence, Garodor gave his report.

"Gallen, dead?" The Prime was visibly shaken.

Garodor opened his wings to express his condolences. "Gabrial tried to . . . drive the crows off, but the commander was clearly failing by then."

"FAILING?"

"Forgive me. A poor choice of word, perhaps, but . . ."

"The Veng do not *fail*." Grynt thumped the wall hard. The thinly plated rock sang a note of distress. He swung again at a hanging spike of ice, shattering it all over the cave. "Call the Wearle. These birds are going to feel my fire. And I will have the head of this girl who commands them."

"That may not be easy. The trees offer them natural cover."

"Then what do you suggest? That I sit here and brood while my colony of dragons is slowly picked off?"

"No. We should surround the forest and watch for developments. In the meantime, let me run through my i:mages and think about the best tactical approach."

Grynt blew a draft of hot, reddened smoke. "I'm done with thinking. I want to burn something. I— Yes, what do *you* want?"

Gus had returned, slightly out of breath. "Prime, the blue, Gabrial, is not at his cave."

"He'll be with Grymric," Garodor said. "I sent Ren to the healer along with the surviving prisoner. Gabrial will be—"

"No," Gus cut him off. "I thought of that. I went to Grymric's cave as well." He paused for a moment, perhaps hoping the Prime would look upon him kindly for using his initiative. But the look in Grynt's eyes suggested he'd be kicked off the cliff in a wingbeat if he didn't continue his report. "Grymric says that Gabrial flew away with the boy on his back."

"They must have gone back to the forest," said Garodor. "I did not counsel this." He turned again to Gus. "Fly to the peak. Call the Wearle together. Now."

Gus gave a hesitant bow.

"Well, don't stand there scraping your claws!" Grynt thundered. "You heard the De:allus. Get to it, you lump!"

Gus backed up, shuffling his tail. "Prime, I have another important message."

"Then I suggest you speak it—quickly," said Garodor. Grynt was beginning to visibly seethe.

"The prisoner I took to the healer's cave . . . he has dragon scales along his shoulder."

"What?" A trail of hot saliva wriggled down one of the twisty stigs that grew beneath Grynt's studded chin. It dripped onto the cave floor and fizzed among the dust and rock chips there.

"Grymric asks what he should do?"

"Do?" Grynt raised a cynical growl. "Tell him to burn his ridiculous herbs and place his foot across the Hom's throat."

"That would be ill-advised," said Garodor.

"Did I *ask* for your opinion?"

"No, but I'm giving it. This is the prisoner who fought against Ty. He doesn't deserve to die. It will simply create more tension with the Hom."

"You think I care about that? How did *this* one get our auma?"

Garodor took a breath. "Gus tried to heal him."

"*WHAT?*"

"His saliva was enough to cause a reaction."

"Prime, I—"

"Be QUIET!" Grynt thundered at Gus. "So now we have two of them?"

"I condoned it," said Garodor. "That's why I sent the man to Grymric. I take full responsibility and will present my reasons to the Higher if necessary. My opinions on this commingling of species have altered since I arrived on Erth. My role—"

"Your *role* is to follow my orders," snarled Grynt. "Has every dragon in this colony forgotten that? You," he snapped at Gus. "Do as you're commanded."

"The Wearle. Call them," Garodor said quietly.

With Gus departed, Grynt moved to the front of the cave, grinding his teeth so tightly that the sound would have made a vapor wince. "I should never have called upon the Higher for advice. If I'd flamed the boy when I first saw that bite mark, none of this would be happening."

"Perhaps not," said Garodor, "but Ren has shown his worth more than once. He doesn't know it, but he's helped me to solve the mystery of this planet. You need to listen to me carefully. The enemy on Erth is not the Hom."

"Get ready to fly, we're leaving," Grynt muttered.

"I read the memory stone," Garodor pressed. "I know what's behind the goyle mutations. What I have to tell you is going to send ripples of fear through the universe, never mind the Wearle."

"Do you hear that, De:allus?"

Gus's voice was ringing out loud across the mountains.

Garodor sighed and lifted his head. "I do."

Grynt stared long and hard at the sky. "That is a call to battle. If your blood still runs green like mine, then fly with me—or stay here and chew on your theories. Either way, I'm going to the forest to finish this."

And with a whump of his wings, the Prime dragon launched, calling the dragons circling Skytouch into their formations, ready to follow.

40

And so they came to the clearing, where Ren was waiting, seated astride Wind.

Gabrial, who had seen the crows departing, now looked west from his standpoint by the forest to see the Wearle approaching. After a moment of indecision, he went up to meet them, tagging on to the rearmost wyng, wisely keeping out of Grynt's sight. When the Prime gave the order to disperse and cover every area of the forest, the blue glided alongside Garodor and said, *The crows have gone. I sent Ren into the trees to find the girl.*

What?

Garodor, it was the only way.

It wasn't. You should have consulted me. Grynt is furious. If he turns on Ren now, I can't protect him.

There he is, said Gabrial as they circled the clearing. *He has the girl and the horse! He must have defeated the goyle.*

Garodor opened his eyes a little wider. *We can't be certain of anything yet. Follow me down—and be on your guard. And no matter what happens, don't argue with Grynt.*

And so they swept down, Grynt and Garodor, with Gabrial slotting in behind the De:allus.

Grynt locked his gaze onto Ren. Thumping two paces forward, he said, "I will give you breath enough to tell me where the goyle is, and then—"

"It's dead," Ren said. He wiped a bloodstained fingernail on his robe.

"How?" said Garodor. He gestured at Pine, who was as limp as a rag. She still lay across Wind's neck.

Ren looked up. "She drew the spirit of Grogan to the clearing, believing it would crack the heart open. Grogan called the goyle out of her and did battle. They destroyed each other. What you see is the result. Me, the girl, the whinney." He stroked Wind's mane. "The girl lives— barely."

"This is a trick," snarled Grynt, emitting small bursts of flame from his mouth.

"Where's the heart?" asked Garodor.

"Inside me," said Ren.

"What?" gasped Gabrial.

Ren lifted the hand that Gariffred had bitten. Before the dragons' eyes, it began to scale. "My companion is dying— and I have a will to save her. I waited so I might offer you peace. These are my terms. From this day forth, you will allow the Kaal to roam freely across the scorch line or you will answer to me. If you choose to fight, any dragons that declare their allegiance to me will be spared and looked upon as friends." He glanced at Gabrial, who didn't know whether to gulp or blow a smoke ring.

This was all too much for Grynt. Without another word, he unlatched his jaw and released a great flame against Ren. The fire burned long and scorched the erth for a full thirty paces. Spiker needles crackled. Small ground fires ignited like flowers behind Wind. Yet amazingly, Ren and his companions were completely untouched.

"So be it," the boy said calmly. "We will meet again, Prime Grynt."

He clicked his tongue and Wind turned away.

And she, and those who rode her, vanished.

They reappeared, in flight, outside Gabrial's cave. Grendel heard the clatter of hooves as they landed and came to the cave mouth to investigate.

"Ren!" she gasped. Joy filled her to see him. The last time they had been together, she had feared him dead on a mountain slope.

"Matrial," he acknowledged her.

She blew a soft haze of smoke. "Where's Gabrial? What's happening? The Wearle was called to battle. They even took Goodle. So it must be serious."

Ren dismounted from Wind, pulling Pine into his arms again. "There will be battles, Grendel. But not today. And not between us."

Grendel looked at the strange winged horse and its cargo. Was this not the creature Gabrial had talked about? And the girl rider they suspected of stealing the heart? "Ren, what brings you here like this? You seem changed somehow. You no longer speak entirely like . . . a Hom." She felt herself wanting to back away from him.

"I'm not entirely Hom. I have an extra heart. It once belonged to the per you called Grogan."

Grendel's own hearts thumped in unison. She reared back slowly. "Gariffred. Gayl. Go to the tunn—"

"Grendel, look at me."

The words were so mesmerizing she could not resist them. Ren's eyes, which had always been a minor source of discomfort to her because they were so soft and vulnerable, were now as radiant as any dragon's. And just for a moment, a hideous image danced at their centers. A terrifying beast with a black dragon body and a face like a snarling wolf. Its piercing eyes were neither slanted nor round. And though it displayed no obvious fangs, Grendel was in no doubt that it could tear through any beast it chose. But the features she would most remember were the rigid plates of scaly flesh that rose like sails at either side of the creature's head, almost carving its face in two. She was looking at the fiend that dwelled in shadows. The *thing* that haunted every dragon's nightmares. The monster that lurked in the eyrie of the mind.

"Sleep," said Ren. "You need not fear me."

And Grendel collapsed where she stood, as easy as a cloud setting down.

Gariffred, far from running for the tunnels, had come into the light and seen his mother fall. *Graaark? Mama?* He wandered up and nudged her chin with his snout.

Ren knelt beside him and laid Pine down. "Don't be frightened, Pupp. It's just a game. Mama will wake very soon." He stroked the drake's head. "Gayl, come to me."

The wearmyss emerged from the shadows, anxiously swishing her tail. Ren put out a hand for her to nuzzle. "My friend is dying. I need your help to save her."

Graaark?

Ren laid Pine's hand on his. Her limp white fingers fell across his palm like willow branches. He ran his thumb across them and smiled. "Bite her," he whispered softly to the wearmyss. "Bite her and she will rise again."

Graaark?

Ren snapped his teeth together. "Like this, as Gariffred once bit me. Then her auma and yours will be one." He offered the hand to Gayl's mouth. "Bite."

And the wearmyss, knowing no better and seeing no harm, sank her teeth into Pine's weak flesh.

The hand broke in several places behind the knuckles. No part of Pine moved, bar the flicker of an eyelid. Shaking her tail end, Gayl backed up and ripped as she'd been taught to eat prey. Skin and muscle were torn from Pine's bones as easily as a man might pull off a sock. Blood poured like water from the wound.

Gariffred's tiny eye ridges twitched.

His nostrils flared at the scent of Pine's blood.

He dipped his tongue into the pool around her hand.

A cold breeze ran through the cave, blowing strands of Pine's hair across her face.

Ren stood up and climbed back onto Wind.

"Welcome to the New Age," he said.

And as Grendel began to wake, he turned Wind to the open sky and disappeared.

GLOSSARY

Auma—the life force or spirit of a dragon, derived from an ancient word for "fire." When a dragon dies and sheds its fire tear, its auma is believed to return to the Creator, Godith.

Buzzer—Hom name for a fly.

Caarker—Hom name for a crow. Crows are deeply revered by the Hom, who will often wear their claws and feathers to bring good fortune.

Commingle—a "coming together," usually of minds. All dragons develop the ability to communicate telepathically, i.e., using thought alone. A deeper extension of telepathy is *commingling*, in which a dragon focuses its awareness to such an extent that it is able to meld with another dragon's consciousness and read or know *all* of that dragon's thoughts.

De:allus—a highly intellectual class of dragon whose lives are devoted to understanding the wonders of Godith's universe. De:allus are scientists or problem solvers, characterized by their bright yellow eyes. It is not known how their eye color developed, though it's often said (somewhat disparagingly) that their optical triggers have become impaired because the De:allus like to look too long at *small* things.

Domayne—any parcel of land claimed by a dragon; their home territory. The term can also describe a large region of land mapped out during colonization.

Drake—a young male dragon (sometimes also called a weardrake). A dragon will usually lose this tag around its second turn.

Elder—a senior dragon (usually male) whose role is to steer and advise the colony.

Erth—home planet of the Hom.

Eyrie—an ancient word of dragontongue meaning "high nest." Now more commonly used to describe a superior cave or settle, such as that of a queen or the Prime dragon.

Faah!—a shocking or vulgar exclamation.

Fanon—a word from the old dragontongue meaning "a female yet to have young."

Fhosforent—pink crystalline mineral found in Erth's volcanic rock. Ingesting large quantities of fhosforent is known to cause devastating mutational effects in dragons, though some still believe the ore can be used to a dragon's advantage.

Fire star—a portal in time and space, called a "star" because of the flash of light emitted when something passes through it.

Goyle—a word used to describe anything ugly or grotesque, particularly the mutant form of a dragon (known to the Hom as a "darkeye").

Heart(s)—dragons have three hearts, closely linked. The largest, the primary heart, drives the body and is concerned with power and strength; the second, about three-fifths the size of the primary heart, controls love and emotional reactions; the third, which is small and just hidden by the second heart, gives a dragon its spirituality.

Higher, the—a name for the collective minds of the most advanced beings on Ki:mera. These creatures (their exact number is uncertain) have evolved beyond their physical form to exist in a floating, neural web (sometimes called a "wisdom cloud"). It is not known if the Higher evolved purely from dragons, but they guide dragons in everything they do.

Hom—an early form of the human race.

Honker—Hom name for a goose.

Hopper—Hom name for a rabbit.

I:mage—the ability to create external structures from mental i:mages. There are two types of i:maging: *natural* and *physical* (see also **phasing**). A natural i:mage is a floating three-dimensional picture (a kind of hologram) that fades as soon as it outlives its usefulness. Physical i:maging is used to create more permanent structures or to alter the parameters of existing matter.

Isoscele—the triangular scale at the end of a dragon's tail. Primarily for balance during flight, it is also a valuable tool in battle and is commonly used to point or gesture.

Kaal—a tribe of humans. The origin of the name is thought to derive from "cave" and refers to the Kaal's preferred choice of habitat: any mountainous region near water.

Kashic Archive—a history of dragonkind, protected by the Higher, held in thousands of memory stones.

Ki:mera—the homeworld of dragons, created for them by the breath of Godith. Literally meaning "place of fire and light."

Mapper—a dragon who maps out territories, especially beyond the boundaries of the domayne. A good mapper can "record" the layout of a landmass from a variety of heights or directional approaches and reproduce it accurately, in the form of an i:mage, for other dragons to see.

Matrial—an honorific title for a female dragon who has had wearlings.

Mutt—Hom name for a dog.

Myss—(or wearmyss) a young female dragon.

Naming—shortly after birth, young dragons are accepted into their Wearle in a formal act of "Naming." If a dragon should go unNamed, its family lineage will not be officially recorded or recognized. Such dragons are regarded as free-roaming savages who can have no place in dragon society.

Nibbler—Hom name for any kind of small bug.

Per—an honorific title given to a dragon who mentors a younger dragon, or one of lesser status.

Phasing—the ability to move through time—usually during flight. The technique is a sophisticated form of i:maging, in which the dragon must be able to "see" itself ahead of time and then "dissolve" into the dark energy of the universe as if it were no heavier than a breath of wind. Many dragons never master it. Some even die in the process.

Prime—an Elder who is also the supreme leader of a dragon colony.

Pupp—Hom name for a young mutt (dog), but can be used for any young creature.

Roamer—a young dragon who has reached sufficient maturity to be allowed to "roam" where he or she pleases, within reason. Nearly half of a colonizing Wearle will be made up of roamers.

Sawfin—fine scales in a ruff shape behind a female dragon's ears.

Scorch line—the line charred on the ground to separate the colony's domayne from the Hom, who must not cross it.

Scratcher—Hom name for a mouse.

Sensaur—a rare breed of dragon, thought to be able to see or sense spirits where others cannot.

Settle—a resting place. In mountain regions, a dragon will settle anywhere high. Barring caves (which are reserved for Elders or others of high importance), the most sought-after locations are rocky outcrops or ledges (where the dragon can proudly display its outline against the sky).

Skaler—Hom name for a dragon.

Slitherer—Hom name for a snake.

Snorter—Hom name for a pig.

Spiker—Hom word for a pine tree.

Spiracles—breathing holes in a dragon's body, most notably along the sides of the throat.

Tada—a word for "father," from the old dragontongue.

Transference—the ability to transfer huge amounts of information by mental power alone.

Turn—a Ki:meran year.

Tywyll—in the old tongue, Tywyll means "the darkness." The word is commonly used when dragons are fearful of some threatening force they can't see or understand. (See the character GRAVEN.)

Vapor—a floating dragon spirit, a "ghost."

Veng—a particularly fearsome class of fighting dragon, used as security for a colony.

Wearle—a large community of dragons. A Wearle would number more than a wyng, but anything more than a hundred dragons would be considered a fixed colony. There were twenty-four dragons in the first Wearle to visit Erth, sixty in the second.

Wearling—a young dragon of either gender.

Whinney—Hom name for a horse.

Wyng—a small group of dragons with a common purpose (e.g., a search wyng). A "dark wyng" is the name given to any group of dragons that turn against their Prime. Over time, the term has been used more loosely to describe any kind of recalcitrant group.

ACKNOWLEDGMENTS

A big thank-you to everyone at Scholastic US for continuing to make this such a fun series to work on. Between us, one of these days, we will get to the bottom of dragon mythology. *Hrrr!*

Turn the page for a sneak peek at the final book in The Erth Dragons series, *The New Age*!

It seemed to take an age for her body to disappear, as if the sky in its mercy wanted to cushion her against the drop. Gariffred skittered to the cliff edge, squealing, his wings extended, dragging the grass. The first of the Veng flashed by. The speed at which it cut across Gabrial's path blurred his eyes bright green for a moment and stopped him taking off in search of Pine. By the time his vision had cleared, the other Veng had landed close to Gariffred. It barked at the drake to make himself scarce. Gariffred put his foot into a hollow and tipped back on to his skinny haunches, hissing at the Veng for all he was worth. Allowing no margin for age or naivety, the Veng poured its flame over Gariffred's head, then sent a sharp burst in Gabrial's direction, a warning to the blue to stay back.

"Hurt him and I'll kill you," Gabrial roared, his claws plowing deep into the ground. Thankfully, the thrust of heat had done no more than scare the drake and bowl him aside. His body scales, not yet fully hardened, looked to have suffered some minor scorching: the Veng equivalent of a reprimand, a cuff. To Gabrial's relief the drake took to the air and faded out of range.

The Veng peered casually over the cliff, giving no hint of what it could see.

"The girl. Is she dead?" Gabrial pressed. In his mind, he pictured her floating, star-shaped, her tiny frame lapping with the shape of the waves, a better i:mage to carry back to Gayl than a body smashed against unforgiving rocks.

"I can't see her," the Veng said sourly. It graarked at its companion to check.

Gabrial twitched his nostrils. It couldn't *see* her? Maybe Pine had plummeted deep underwater? Though that was unlikely for the cliff was not sheer at this point. But if she'd hit the rocks, her body would be seen. Even if she'd slipped between the pointed crags that stood like guards against the foaming tides, her body would have bled. The scent of fresh blood would be easy for the Veng to trace. He watched the second one roll in midair, then dip out of sight beyond the cliff. A beat passed, yet no word came from it. Gabrial glanced at the sky and saw Gus circling. There was now no sight nor sound of Gariffred.

With his hopes for Pine dashed and his loyalties divided, Gabrial was now anxious to make a move. "I need to leave," he said, flicking out his wing tips. "The Prime is in danger. I must speak with him on a matter of great urgency."

"You're going nowhere till we find the girl," said the Veng.

"She's dead," snapped Gabrial. "You saw what happened. She took her life. Not even by my order. She couldn't survive a drop so deep. Now get out of my way. There's nothing for you here. Trust me, Veng, the longer I delay, the more you'll have to answer for later."

The Veng gargled. Not a good sign. They were known to possess a considerable range of intimidating noises, and this didn't sound like a yielding reaction. The moment Gabrial opened his wings, the Veng roared again. Its fire blazed so close this time it caused a heat mist to form in the blue dragon's eyes. As he blinked to cool them he noticed Gus had dropped lower in the sky. The roamer had his claws out, ready to attack.

The Veng that was searching for Pine reappeared. It flew over, giving a brief report. *Nothing. She must be hiding.*

The Veng confronting Gabrial growled suspiciously.

At that moment, Gariffred glided by, intent on doing his own search of the cliffs. The Veng in the sky closed in to shadow the drake's movements. In desperation, Gabrial said, "For the last time, hear me. I need to take Gariffred to Skytouch right away. He . . . he knows something about the boy."

Foolish. Even as the words were leaving his mouth, Gabrial wished he could bite through his tongue.

The Veng wound its slender neck forward. It opened its long, ferocious jaws. Strings of gluey drool wound down off its fangs, fangs that looked sharp enough to perforate rock. The shields came down on its slanted eyes. Veng shields were nothing more than a hard transparent membrane, a heat-resistant battle aid evolved over centuries of selective breeding. The membranes were clear at birth, but the Veng had learned to stain them a subtle shade of green by draining blood into them from nearby cells. The resulting "eyeless" appearance struck fear into their foes, which more than compensated for the slight impairment of vision. Even Gabrial, who had seen the effect many times, felt his primary heart skip a beat. The Veng lashed its tongue. A sign of its desire for answers— or conflict. "Where is the Hom boy? Speak or you die."

Gabrial closed his mouth. It would have been so easy to bow to the Veng and simply share Gariffred's i:mage with it. Had Grendel been beside him, she would have pressed this course for the sake of Gariffred's safety, if not his. But nothing in Gabrial's bloodline would make him back down from a head-on threat, even with an opponent as deadly as this. And so he raised his battle stigs and heard himself saying, "That's for me to know and you to find out, *sier pent.*"

The Veng reared back, offended by the slur (Gabrial had called it a "green fish"). But instead of launching an immediate attack, it snapped an order at its companion. Before Gabrial could work out what was happening, Gariffred was in the second Veng's clutches. It had pulled the drake clean out of the sky and now had him pinned to the ground by his neck.

"Tada!" Gariffred cried, squirming under the Veng's cruel claws.

Gabrial was helpless. And the facing Veng was quick to confirm it. It whipped its tail into the air and said, "One step, one puff of smoke, and his scrawny neck cracks. All I have to do is drop my tail. Now, *where is the boy?*"

"I knows where," said a voice.

If Ren himself had drifted by on a bed of cloud, Gabrial could not have been more astounded. Pine had suddenly reappeared. She must have climbed back on to the headland somehow, though Gabrial had seen no sign of it. For all he knew, she could have popped up out of the ground like a flower. Who knew what powers she'd inherited from Gayl? She was showing no cuts or other injuries. And her robe, though marked with some rips from previous adventures, was still intact. The thought crossed his mind that she could be a spirit returned from a very disagreeable death, though she didn't float over the ground like a vapor, and vapors—in his admittedly limited experience— didn't come bearing gifts. Pine was carrying an egg, carefully balanced on an upturned palm. A seabird egg. White. A little larger than usual. She offered it up to the bemused Veng, who seemed temporarily immobilized by this bizarre apparition.

Once again, Pine spoke in perfect dragontongue. "Look, Veng. See. Watch."

She wafted her fingers over the egg.

"It's coming," she whispered.

"What's coming?" snarled the Veng. Gabrial heard it suck in through its spiracles. It was filling its fire sacs, ready to incinerate her.

"Your death," she said.

And she closed her hand around the egg, and broke it.